*Praise for* HOTEL FOR THE LOST,
previously titled *Hotel Ruby*

"Prepare to be spooked and romanced as you
attempt to unravel the mysteries of Hotel Ruby!"
—Wendy Higgins, *New York Times* bestselling
author of the Sweet Evil series

"Haunting and hard to put down."
—*Booklist*

"Young accurately captures each resident's grief,
thus populating her novel with three-dimensional
characters whom readers will appreciate."
—*Kirkus Reviews*

"A fast and fun read. . . . A great purchase for libraries
where paranormal mysteries circulate well."
—*School Library Journal*

ALSO BY SUZANNE YOUNG

*The Program*
*The Treatment*
*The Recovery*
*The Remedy*
*The Epidemic*
*All in Pieces*

*Just Like Fate*
with Cat Patrick

COMING SOON
*The Adjustment*

# HOTEL
# FOR THE
# LOST

Previously titled *Hotel Ruby*

# SUZANNE
# YOUNG

SIMON PULSE

NEW YORK   LONDON   TORONTO   SYDNEY   NEW DELHI

SIMON PULSE

An imprint of Simon & Schuster Children's Publishing Division

1230 Avenue of the Americas, New York, NY 10020

First Simon Pulse paperback edition October 2016

Text copyright © 2015 by Suzanne Young

Previously titled *Hotel Ruby*

Cover photo-illustration copyright © 2016 by Neil Swaab

Cover photography copyright © Shutterstock

Also available in a Simon Pulse hardcover edition titled *Hotel Ruby*.

All rights reserved, including the right of reproduction in whole or in part in any form.

SIMON PULSE and colophon are registered trademarks of Simon & Schuster, Inc.

For information about special discounts for bulk purchases, please contact Simon & Schuster Special Sales at 1-866-506-1949 or business@simonandschuster.com.

The Simon & Schuster Speakers Bureau can bring authors to your live event. For more information or to book an event, contact the Simon & Schuster Speakers Bureau at 1-866-248-3049 or visit our website at www.simonspeakers.com.

Cover designed by Russell Gordon

The text of this book was set in Cochin LT Std.

Manufactured in the United States of America

2 4 6 8 10 9 7 5 3 1

Library of Congress Control Number 2016939305

ISBN 978-1-4814-2300-7 (*Hotel Ruby* hc)

ISBN 978-1-4814-2301-4 (*Hotel for the Lost* pbk)

ISBN 978-1-4814-8439-8 (*Hotel for the Lost* eBook)

*For my grandfather*
*Walter "Shadow" Parzych*


*And, as always, in loving memory of*
*my grandmother Josephine Parzych*

STAY TONIGHT. STAY FOREVER.

# CHAPTER 1

The treetops curve above the road like an archway, blotting out the moon and stars. We've been driving through these woods for close to an hour, and our car headlights shine only a short distance in the thick fog. I glance into the backseat to check my older brother's current state of annoyance, but Daniel hasn't spoken to me since the rest stop near Vegas. He stiffens, aggressively ignoring me when he turns to face the dark outside the window.

"If we stay on this road," my father says, "I think there's a shortcut through the mountains. I remember taking it one time with your mother."

The air in the car hardens to cement and I still, the mention of my mother too taboo to slip into conversation. I hear Daniel shift in the backseat, and the tension tightens around me, a vise clamped on my heart. Just when I think I might choke on the grief, my father reaches to flip on the stereo, startling us from the quiet.

I stare out the windshield, my eyes stinging. I don't dare blink hard enough to let a tear fall. Normally, I'd turn to Daniel, but we've run out of comforting things to say.

Now the words feel false, hollow. So neither of us bothers to speak them anymore.

My brother knows this trip isn't entirely my fault. I've made mistakes since our mother died, but I'm not the only one. Daniel's coping mechanism is to deflect his grief, his resentment; and sometimes he hurls them at me. But our father, well, he's just lost altogether.

Now Dad is sending us to live with our grandmother, uprooting us from Arizona to Elko, some small town in northern Nevada. He claims it will be a "fresh start," but really, he's the one who plans to start fresh, leaving us behind with a DNA-matched stranger.

Truth is, Dad stopped seeing us. He looks through us like he can't bear our resemblance to our mother. Like we're invisible. Daniel and I have lost both of our parents, even though one is sitting next to me now.

"Can I change the station?" I ask. My voice is thick, and I realize I haven't spoken out loud since we left Vegas. How's that possible?

My dad glances over, seeming just as startled by my voice, and gives a quick nod. Daniel shifts in the backseat as I start pressing and then re-pressing the scan button, searching for a clear station. My iPod died nearly a hundred miles ago, and I haven't had a chance to charge it. I'm at the mercy of the DJ gods, and they have not been favorable toward me.

The radio search is met with static, save one channel

4

that's playing old jazz. I take a spin through the stations again.

"Hey, Aud," Daniel calls. My heart skips a beat, and I look back at him. He's our mother's reflection—platinum hair, blue eyes. It still startles me. "Can I have your Snickers bar?" he asks.

I choke on a laugh, covering my smile because this is Daniel's way of apologizing. I shouldn't give him the candy, not after he told me to shut up outside the dingy rest stop bathrooms. I'd made the mistake of mentioning our mother. I'm not sure why I did it, especially since I know Daniel hates when I do. I guess I just miss hearing the word "Mom" without the words "I'm so sorry" connected to it.

Once in the car, Daniel muttered from the backseat about my selfishness: "Ask Ryan," he said, thus beginning our silent war. But Daniel's my brother and he's the only person left in the world who cares about me. That deserves a candy bar. I grab the backpack at my feet and dig through the front pocket until I touch the softened chocolate. I toss it to him, and he nods his thanks, our temporary truce enacted.

The weight of tension has lifted, and I expect my father to be lightened by it. But his face is determined; he's focusing on his plan so the ache won't set in. He wasn't always like this. I can't pinpoint the exact moment he changed, but it was a swift progression. We were all too distracted to notice. I was busy self-medicating with all manner of troublesome behaviors; Daniel was retreating into avoidance and denial. We had no one to hold us together.

And after my father walked in on a spectacularly raucous party I was throwing, he seemed to calm, to steady himself when really he should have freaked out. Grounded me for twenty years. Instead he came up with a plan.

"It's just for the summer," he told me and Daniel over a bucket of KFC. "You know your grandmother would love to spend more time with you."

My mother's mother is nearly eighty, and I can't imagine she wants much to do with a rebellious seventeen-year-old girl or her selfish older brother. We've met Grandma Nell only a handful of times, none of which was particularly endearing. It didn't matter, though. Because that night, sitting in Daniel's dark bedroom, my brother and I figured she was the only person willing to take us in. Dad was giving us away. Giving up.

But now that Daniel's eighteen, he promises to bring me with him when he gets enough money to take off on his own. Although Dad puts on the ruse that he's coming back, we know he's not.

"Your grandmother told me they renovated the attic for you, Audrey," my father says from the driver's seat, not looking over as he talks. "They got a new bed, dresser—she asked your favorite color. I told her it was pink."

"It's blue," I respond, earning a quick glance. "I haven't liked pink since the seventh grade."

My father swallows hard, readjusting his grip on the steering wheel. "Well, I guess you can repaint. That'll be fun."

"And where am I staying?" Daniel asks. "Did they tidy up a haystack in the barn?"

Dad takes so long to answer, I'm about to repeat Daniel's question. But then our father cracks his neck and glances in the rearview mirror. "You'll be in your mother's old room."

I lower my head. At first I'm overwhelmed with betrayal at my grandmother's decision to give Daniel the connection to my mother's childhood instead of me. Locking me in an attic like a character from a V. C. Andrews novel. But when I can stand the pain, I turn and find Daniel watching me, his jaw clenched; the expression that tells me not to worry. We won't be there long. Even if it means running away.

I glance at the radio again, about to continue my rhythmic pursuit, when I notice a red light above the CD player. I can't recall a time when I listened to a CD in this car. Normally, I'd have my earbuds in, or nothing at all. Curious, I switch the mode and watch as the dash flashes PLAY.

I press it, but at first I'm met with silence. I'm about to skip to the next song when chords blast from the speakers, ten times louder than anything on the stations. I jump and then laugh, looking at my father. He doesn't react, though;

he's not paying attention. He's lost in his head again.

The song is an oldie, one I vaguely remember my mother enjoying. When I realize her connection to it, I reach to lower the music, unable to turn it off altogether. I don't mention the song, content to spend the remainder of the drive in emotional isolation, much like the last three months of my life. I close my eyes and recline the seat, opting for the escape of sleep.

The seconds tick slowly by, my inactive thoughts always haunted by my last moments with my mother, the way I took her for granted that morning before she left for school. She was a counselor at my high school, beloved. Respected. And I sent her away to her death without so much as a good-bye.

I clear my throat and turn in my seat, restricted by the seat belt. I unfasten it to get comfortable and then force down my sorrow. *Stop thinking.* I let the song lyrics flood my mind and wash away my mother. And in the absence of pain I finally drift off to sleep. It might have been only a moment or an hour, but when I hear the clicking of the blinker, I sit up, slightly disoriented.

"We're here," my father says in a tired voice. I'm stricken for a moment by the glistening of tears on his cheek. He wipes his sleeve over his face and then takes a hard turn that knocks my shoulder into the door.

There's a pathway into the trees, a road covered in debris of broken branches. I'm about to ask my father where the hell he's going when a set of open iron gates appears in front of us. They're ornate and oversize. Beautiful. Golden lights wrap their way up the tree trunks and illuminate the drive, now cleared. We pass the courtyard, a circle of stone benches and statues, low manicured shrubs with tiny lights brightening everything. But when the hotel itself comes into view, Daniel leans between the front seats.

"No way," he murmurs. "Are we stopping here?"

Here, in the middle of nowhere, is a grand building—lit up at 3 a.m. like it's New Year's Eve. A white stone front, huge archway with ivy crawling up the walls. I can't help but smile as we park at the entrance.

"I'm exhausted," my father says. "And when I saw the sign for the Hotel Ruby, I thought we could splurge for the night." I see a shadow of my father, of who he used to be. "Think of this as our family vacation," he adds.

"Well, in that case I want my own room," Daniel says from the backseat.

Our father sniffs a laugh, and agrees. He turns off the engine just as a guy in a burgundy uniform approaches the car. Daniel disappears into the back of the SUV to grab his suitcase, and I tug my pack onto my lap when the driver's door opens.

"Welcome to the Ruby," the guy in red says. I can't quite place his accent, but he's handsome—dark hair and dark eyes. He glances inside and notices me. "Can I help with your bags, miss?" His lips curve with a smile, and I'm not imagining that he's flirting with me. But I'm disoriented from the drive, from my father's behavior. I shake my head no.

"I've got it," I tell the valet. "But thanks."

He comes around to open my door, and I'm aware of how close he's standing when I have to dip under his arm to get out. The guy helps to load bags onto a gold rolling cart, and my father tips him a fold of money before opening the massive wooden doors. I glance back and find the valet waiting. He smiles again, his chin lowered as he watches me. I quickly turn away, an uneasy feeling crawling up my arms.

The lobby is an explosion of grandeur: rich wood furniture, fringed velvet fabrics, and an impossibly large chandelier hanging above it all. Paintings and tapestries decorate the walls, which must be at least three stories high. I turn to Daniel and he smiles—an actual smile.

"Guess I should have worn my clean hoodie," he mutters.

"You don't own anything clean," I say. "I haven't done your laundry all week."

Daniel puts his arm around my shoulders and pulls me into a sideways hug. "When we get to Nana's, I'll start washing all of my own clothes. I'll even wash yours."

I laugh, because Daniel would certainly destroy anything he put into a washing machine. But secondly, he's taken to calling our strict old grandmother Nana. I can't wait to see her face when he lays that one on her.

Dad stops at the front desk, Daniel and I behind him.

There's a haggard desk attendant in the corner, tapping the computer keys while he surfs the Internet. He doesn't even lift his head to acknowledge us. I clear my throat to get his attention, but when he still doesn't respond, I sigh and lean my elbow on the counter and glance around the lobby. I'm on sensory overload, unable to take it all in. I feel completely out of place here, especially in regular clothes. I should be wearing a cocktail dress, a ball gown maybe. Suddenly a door the same color as the wall opens from behind the desk, and a bald man with a small, pleasant face walks out. He glances in the direction of the other attendant, but the guy is gone. I didn't even see him leave.

"Welcome to the Hotel Ruby," the man says joyfully. "It's a beautiful night."

"Morning," I correct. The man turns to me, giving me a quick once-over, as if he's not exactly sure he wants to answer. I read his name tag: KENNETH—CONCIERGE.

"So it is," he responds with a chuckle. Before he can ask, my father places his license and credit card on the counter.

"Three rooms," Dad says. "Just for the night."

Kenneth nods politely, reading the name. He takes a moment to study me and Daniel, and then leans over the counter toward my father. "I apologize in advance, Mr. Casella," he says. "It seems we are overbooked tonight." He pauses, as if waiting for me to interject that it's morning.

11

My father's posture sags. "Is there another hotel close by? A motel maybe?"

"Oh, dear Lord," Kenneth says quickly, waving his hand. "We wouldn't dream of inconveniencing you like that. The problem is clearly on our end. Let's see." He taps a few keys. "I have two rooms on the sixth floor, and if your daughter won't mind, we have a room available for her on the thirteenth floor. There are some renovations under way, but I assure you"—he turns to me—"you won't be disturbed."

I can't imagine what they would want to change about a place this beautiful, but I'm grateful that we won't have to spend the night in some sleazy motel along the interstate.

"The rooms on the sixth floor," Kenneth continues, "have wonderful views of the Ruby Mountains. And, of course, you all have complimentary late checkout. I hope that's acceptable?"

Kenneth's fast-talking, smooth voice continues to dominate the conversation. Within seconds my father's agreeing before even finding out the price.

"Fantastic," Kenneth says, clapping his plump hands. "Joshua is dropping off your bags as we speak. We have a variety of amenities for you to enjoy during your time here. There's an on-site restaurant and gift shop, a salon and day spa. Out through the garden doors"—he motions to a set of glass doors—"is a café, and just beyond that are the tennis courts. There's an outdoor pool, a recreation room with billiards, and, of course, our theater. This is a current list of our movies." Kenneth hands my father a brochure and exhales, finally taking a break from his monologue.

"Wow," I say, peeking over my dad's shoulder to look at the brochure. "Why would anyone ever want to check out?"

Kenneth turns slowly, folding his fingers over his chest. "They rarely do, Miss Casella. Now," the concierge says, smiling pleasantly to the three of us. "Here are your keycards and maps. Again, I'd like to welcome you to the Hotel Ruby. I hope you enjoy your stay."

I widen my eyes and reach to slide my keycard off the desk. Kenneth watches me, and then after a moment he turns and disappears behind the small door once again.

"What a weirdo," Daniel says, slipping his hands into the pockets of his zip-up. "Place is great, though. I feel classy as hell."

"It's nice," my father says, and I see the hint of a smile on his face. This hotel has put us all in a good mood. It's almost enough to make us forget why we're here.

Beyond a set of oversize doors in the hallway, music drifts in, soft piano playing and lounge singing. There is a gold stand with a sign that reads ANNIVERSARY PARTY—1937 set out in front. Must be a rager, because I don't know who would be up at this ungodly hour for an anniversary party, or why the hotel would allow it to go this late. Aren't the other guests sleeping?

"I'll see you later," Daniel says, tugging on my sleeve.

Before I can ask where he's going, he crosses the lobby, turning back once to wave to me. My father calls my name from the golden doors of the elevator, waiting.

We ride without a word. It's rare to spend any alone time with my father. Even these few minutes pass awkwardly, as if he were a complete stranger. The bell for the sixth floor dings. My father murmurs his good night and then walks out. He pauses and turns to me. In his eyes is the beginning of an apology, and I open my mouth to ask him what's wrong. But the doors close, leaving me all alone in the elevator.

A nagging starts in the back of my mind like something I've forgotten, but then the elevator doors slide open, revealing the thirteenth floor. I step out.

The hallway, long and ominous, has a burgundy-patterned floor, dark wood paneling on the walls. It's beautiful, but at the same time it feels . . . heavy. Like the air is too thick. At the end of the hallway, above a glass table, is an oversize gilded mirror. I catch my reflection—my light ginger hair tied in a knot, frizzy along the crown from travel, my long-sleeved T-shirt casual and worn; I'm completely out of place among the old-fashioned decor. The familiar image comforts me, I realize, and I battle back the chills that are trickling over my spine.

Room 1303 is at the beginning of the hallway, and I take one more glance around before unlocking the door and going inside. When I flip on the lights, I gasp and

14

cover my mouth. I think I've just won the hotel room lottery. It's gorgeous. There is an elaborate sitting area (is that a fainting sofa?), with vintage furniture in bold patterns, stained-glass lamps, and an intricately carved wood table. The bed in the corner has a fluffy white comforter and large, overstuffed pillows; the posts frame the mattress and curve over the top. I wander around the room, struck again by how incredible this entire hotel is.

When we traveled as a family, *before*, we were thrifty. The only time I've ever stayed in a nice hotel was when Ryan took me away for the weekend. I still loved him then, still thought we'd end up married, high school sweethearts just like my parents. I lost my virginity on the twenty-second floor of a Marriott. This is so much better.

I drop my bag next to the bed and find a single rose lying across my pillow with a wrapped chocolate. The red of the flower is lush against the starched white fabric, and I pick it up and smell the petals. They're sweet and powdery. I wonder momentarily if I'm still in the car, dreaming. After the obligatory bounce on the bed and check of the bathroom, I decide that despite the late hour, I can't sleep. Not when there's so much to explore. I quickly brush my teeth, take down my hair, and reapply deodorant. There was music downstairs—familiar music. There has to be people. I put on some gloss and slip my keycard into the back pocket of my jeans and head to the lobby.

CR     SO

The lobby is deserted when I walk through, but the bored desk attendant has returned to his computer duty. I wonder if he was reprimanded for ignoring us earlier. By his lack of attention now, I guess not. The music leads me forward until I'm at the entrance of the grand ballroom. It sounds like a serious after-party on the other side of these doors. I look around, my heart racing, and then push my way inside.

There is, indeed, a party. And not a few drunken late-night castoffs, either. I spin, trying to take in all the sights at once. The room is three stories tall, with massive chandeliers, golds and yellows splashed through the room, heavy deep-red drapes framing the doorway. On the walls are panels of intricate tapestries, gold frames. There are private alcoves with benches carved into the wooden walls, guests sipping from fancy glasses. All around me are sequins and bow ties. On the low-rise stage a distinguished-looking older man plays the black baby grand piano while a woman in a gold dress sings along. The words seem slightly familiar, although off somehow. But the singer's voice is amazing—haunting and soul scratching. I want to people-watch, so I go to find a space in the alcove, smiling as the world twirls around me.

A server in a black tux comes by and offers me a drink, bending low so I can take the glass from his tray. He smiles at me, much like the valet, and then disappears back into the crowd. This must be how celebrities live—all-night

16

parties, free drinks. I sip from the glass and the champagne bubbles tickle my nose. My father would kill me.

I stop. Would he? Would he even care at this point?

"Is it casual Friday already?" a voice asks. I turn just as a guy about my age sits down. He's wearing a sharp gray suit, and when he crosses his leg over his knee, I see his shoes are impossibly shiny. He's not smiling, not like the others, but there is a definite hint of flirting in his amber-colored eyes.

"Not technically," I respond, sipping from my drink in a movement that I hope looks natural. "But as it turns out, formal wear at four a.m. on a Tuesday is kind of douchey."

The guy laughs, genuine and hearty, and I like the sound of it. In my world of constant faking, he's showing me the first authentic joy I've seen in a while. I sip again, wondering how much champagne I'd need to forget everything but him.

"You win," the guy says, uncrossing his legs to lean forward. "And I have to tell you, I'm quite charmed by your lack of party attire."

"Well, that's good, because I'm super impressed with the fact that you own a suit."

He laughs again, and the skin crinkles around his eyes, his dimples deepen. His smile is absolutely disarming in the most wonderful way.

"Elias Lange," he says, holding out his hand.

"Fancy," I tease, and slip my hand into his. Rather than shake it, he brings my fingers to his lips, kissing them politely. The heat of his mouth nearly makes me swoon, and when my hand falls back onto my lap, I'm entirely self-conscious of it. As if Elias has brought that particular body part back to life. He smiles and gazes out at the party, seeming to realize his effect on me.

"I'm Audrey," I say. "And I didn't know there was a party tonight. What's the occasion?"

"Same party every night. It's what we do here." He loosens his tie and then reaches to grab a glass from the tray of a passing server.

"We? Do you stay here a lot?" I ask.

He sips, looks at me, and sips again. "I do. Want me to show you around? I've about mastered the trust-fund-kid tour. Promise it's more fun than this."

I plan to tell him no because I don't typically run off with complete strangers after a three-second conversation, even if he does own a suit, but my response is cut off.

"Eli," a girl calls loudly, and then pauses to stand in front of me. She pretends I don't exist as she speaks. "I thought we were going to dance," she says. Her pink lips pout in a childish way I find obnoxious, and from his lack of attention I'm guessing Elias does too. Despite her behavior, the girl is stunning, a vision in a white, sparkly dress, with snow-blond hair framing her face.

"You know I don't dance, Catherine," Elias says casually. "I'm sure Joshua would love to take a spin with you. Would you like me to ask him?"

Catherine's small blue eyes tighten to slits. She spins to face me as if I've spoken. Her glare shoots splinters of ice, stabbing me all at once. "Who are you?" she asks.

Wilting, I try to take a sip of my drink without letting my trembling hand spill the champagne. "I'm Audrey," I respond. Elias shifts next to me like he's about to step in. I hope he does before this girl scratches my eyes out.

"You weren't invited here, Audrey," Catherine says dismissively. "Now leave."

Elias leans forward to take Catherine's hand, drawing her gaze back to him. "Cathy," he says softly. I expect her to warm to his voice—I know I would—but she rips her fingers away like she's offended by his tone. Elias's posture goes rigid, his brown hair falling into his eyes before he smooths it back in place. "Go away," he says coldly. "I'm not doing this with you right now."

Catherine bends down, bringing her face close to his. For a second I think she's going to kiss him, and my stomach turns. Instead she smiles. "Eli," she whispers. "Drop dead, darling."

To this, Elias chuckles and lifts his glass. "Cheers," he says, and drinks.

Catherine tosses one more hateful glance in my direction and then stomps her way across the ballroom. I put my hand on my stomach and exhale, happy to have mostly avoided a confrontation. When Elias turns to me, he shrugs apologetically. "Don't judge me too harshly for being rude," he says. "She's an absolute psychopath."

"She's something," I agree, watching until Catherine disappears from the party. The minute she's gone, I relax slightly. Around us the conversations continue; the music plays, and I'm close to figuring out the melody.

"Ready for that tour?" Elias asks, hiding his smile behind the rim of his glass. "I know where they keep the chocolates for the pillows."

I laugh, thinking he's pretty adorable. But still, I'm not an idiot. He's a total stranger, and even if he weren't, I'm not exactly in a dating frame of mind. "No, thanks," I say.

Elias doesn't appear surprised by my rejection; in fact, he seems to appreciate it. He tilts his head, sliding his gaze over me. "How did you get here, Audrey?" he asks.

"The door."

He laughs softly. "Fair enough. I take it, then, that you're not here for the ghosts?" he asks. "Most of them are." He motions to the crowd in the ballroom.

"Really? Is this place haunted?"

"They think so." Elias pulls his tie from around his neck and tosses it aside. His hair has fallen forward again, and I think he looks more casual, more approachable. It makes him that much more attractive—a sneak peek at his real life.

"Who are you without that suit?" I ask. Elias's eyebrows raise, and I nearly trip over myself to explain my words. "I don't mean naked! I mean in life. Not with a suit—oh, God." My cheeks warm with heat, and soon I'm laughing. To his credit, Elias nods along with my words, as if truly curious about my thought process.

"Well," he says, motioning to the rooms above us, "if you'd like to have a look . . ."

I swat his shoulder, and then we're both grinning, oblivious to the concierge until he clears his throat beside us. He shoots Elias a quick frown of disapproval before addressing me.

"Miss Casella," Kenneth says when he turns to me again. "Perhaps you should head up to your room? After all, you're leaving tomorrow and it's nearly four a.m."

Elias sips calmly from his drink. Does he get carded? Does the hotel care if he, any of us, is underage? And then I wonder what business it is of the concierge that I'm not in bed, tucked under the covers.

"You see," Kenneth offers, like he's read my expression, "this party is invite only. And I don't believe you have an invitation." He waits. "Do you have an invitation, Miss Casella?"

I hate being scolded, and this feels very scoldy. "I do not," I respond. I curl my lip at Elias as if asking what the deal is with Kenneth, and then start toward the exit.

"It was nice meeting you, Audrey," Elias calls out. "Maybe I'll see you around."

I half turn, my heart thumping hard. I don't respond, afraid he'll hear it in my voice—the grief, the absolute dread of the next step. I'll only be at the Ruby for a day, and then I'll be shipped off to my grandmother. To be honest, tonight was the first real fun I've had in ages. I don't want to spoil the mood by letting anyone in on how damaged I am. So I just wave and then zigzag through the crowd back to the doors.

As I leave, my eyes are drawn back to Elias. He sits alone in the alcove, dressed the part but still out of place somehow. His mouth is downturned as he stares into the dancing crowd, glass in hand, like he can't stand being here at all.

My hallway is quiet, so stuffed with quiet it's almost hard to breathe. I go into my room, toss my keycard on the dresser, and launch my flip-flops somewhere under the bed. My head is swimming, and I quickly grab the first pair of pajamas I can find. They're soft and worn through the knees, and I switch off the light and climb into bed.

I stare out the window at the golden trees, lit from below by the hotel lights. It's so peaceful here. My head sinks into the pillow, my eyes growing heavier with each blink. I'm exhausted from the trip and have a dull ache in my arm. I reach to rub the underside of my forearm, but the scene is slowly fading away. I think about the party, about Elias. The way he tried to hide his smile behind his glass, the golden hue of his eyes as he slid them over me. I can imagine the sort of tour he would have taken me on. It probably would've ended in his hotel room. I'm not sure I would have minded that.

I curl up and snuggle into the pillow like it's a person holding me. I picture his arms around me, the beat of his heart under my hand. I pretend it's Elias, warm and comfortable. "How did you get here?" he asks again.

The room sways with the beginning of sleep, a deep sleep that's too inviting to resist. I close my eyes completely and answer, "I don't know."

# CHAPTER 2

My room is dark when I open my eyes, drawn awake by the low hum of music. I blink until my vision adjusts; the soft glow outside my window tells me it's not quite dawn. I've been asleep for only a few hours. Light seeps from under my door, and I wait a beat for the music to stop. It doesn't.

Slowly I get out of bed and feel my way toward the door. From the other side I can hear music, faint, but too close to be from the party. I listen, knowing immediately that I've heard the song before. I just can't place it.

I glance back into my dark room and debate returning to bed. Ultimately, the idea that there's a party so close to me is too intriguing. The hinge creaks as I pull open the door, and I poke my head out to see if there's anyone in the hallway. At first my eyelids flutter at the sudden brightness, but I quickly see that I'm all alone. The music seems to be coming from the end of the hall.

*What is that song?*

I open the security latch so I won't get locked out, and then step barefoot into the hallway. I ease my door shut, taking another curious look around. The chords strum, like a guitar, slowly, too slow to make out the melody. When I leave the safety of the vicinity around my door, my heart starts to pound. My throat grows dry.

I study each door I pass, trying to find the source of the music. I'm not sure what time it is, but I know it's insanely late for people to be awake. Late for them to be listening to a song on a loop. *What song?*

The temperature in the hallway starts to drop, colder the closer I get to the last door. I wrap my arms around myself, rubbing my shoulders when I start to shiver. I wish my brother and father were on this floor. I hate being alone. I'm almost to the last room—room 1336—when the music starts to fade, like someone is slowly turning down a knob.

I stop, the sense of being watched freezing me in place. I swallow hard, past the dryness in my throat, and peek behind me. Terrified that I'll find someone (*something*) standing there.

But the music is gone. Now I'm barefoot in the hallway of the Hotel Ruby with uneven breaths and chilled skin. I look once more at the door and then turn to walk quickly back to my room. I slip inside and shut the door, my palm flat against it as I process my fear. For good measure I throw the locks and then move a chair in front of the door.

I stare at the handle and step backward toward my bed, sure I'll see it turn at any moment. But as the time ticks by, as the sun starts to rise, my panic diminishes. *I'm high strung*, I tell myself. *And maybe just a little drunk.*

Eventually, I slide under the covers, exhausted and achy. Soon I'll be asleep, and my real fears will find me, just as they normally do, to remind me of how I ruined my life.

I never got a chance to officially break up with Ryan. For weeks, months really, I imagined all the scenarios where I would say, "Ryan, I don't love you anymore. I want to be friends." He was my best friend, and not even one with benefits. I would shrink away when he tried to kiss me, find an excuse when he wanted to hold my hand. Ryan loved me the same way he always did. I couldn't break his heart.

We were just shy of our two-year anniversary when I decided to finally do it. End our relationship. I'd cried the entire night before, mentally and emotionally preparing myself for what I was about to do. He would come to my house to pick me up for school, but before we left, I would tell him.

Instead, when I got downstairs that morning, my mother was there making breakfast. She never stayed late on school days. My stomach dropped because it meant another day—another day of pretending to be Ryan Martin's girlfriend.

"What are you doing here?" I demanded, bare feet on the cold linoleum tiles, ASU T-shirt clinging to my chest. "You're supposed to be at work."

My mother laughed from where she stood at the stove. That *What drama has befallen you now?* laugh a mom gets when she thinks her daughter is overreacting. "I don't know, Audrey," she said, turning away to pour a circle of pancake batter into the skillet. "Some people call it breakfast. It doesn't always have to come out of a cereal box."

"You can't be here," I told her. "You're going to ruin everything." Tears began to fill my eyes, and my mother pulled the pan off the heat and crossed the kitchen. She put her hands—hands that were always cooler than my skin— on my arms and steadied her gaze on mine.

"What's the matter? What am I going to ruin?"

My mother liked Ryan. No, she loved Ryan. She thought he was sweet, kind. I once told her she should adopt him, because when he was here, she doted on him as if he'd come from her womb. I stared back into her gray-blue eyes, just like Daniel's, and I couldn't gather the courage to tell her that I was changing my life forever. That although I wanted to stay friends with Ryan, realistically I knew it wouldn't happen. My entire identity would change.

"I . . ." I started, unsure what to say to wipe the expression of concern off of her face. The smell of pancakes— flour and butter—hung in the air, mixing with my dread and making me sick. "Nothing," I said, shaking my head. "Ryan will be here in twenty minutes, so you should probably make extra."

She didn't believe the excuse, quirking up her eyebrow as she weighed whether or not to press me. She didn't. Mom went back to the pancakes, and I got dressed, numbly brushing my teeth and hair. Another day of being dead.

Only it was my mother who was dead less than two hours later.

I open my eyes and stare at the ceiling. The memory of my mother's touch, cool and comforting, fades from my arms. I squeeze my eyes shut, missing her desperately. Wishing I'd thanked her for the pancakes and told her stay, stay just long enough.

There's a knock at my door, jolting me upright. I glance around the wallpapered room, momentarily displaced. The white bedspread, the large, imposing trees outside the window; I'm not in Phoenix. It takes a second before it clicks. I'm at the Ruby.

Another knock.

I look for the time, but there's no alarm clock on the nightstand. Only a gold-plated lamp. "Hold on," I call out, my voice thick with sleep. When I stand, my ankle buckles under my weight, and I stagger back onto the bed. I quickly pull up the leg of my pajama pants, expecting to see swelling, but instead I find a perfectly normal leg, bright pink painted toes. Tentatively I put my foot on the carpet, testing the pressure before I try standing up again. I'm fine.

My brother calls from the other side of the door.

"Today, Audrey. My stomach is starting to eat itself."

I stomp my foot a few times, expecting a stinging pain — anything. After a few hops I decide it must have been just a cramp. I move the chair out of the way of the door, embarrassed that I let myself get so freaked out. In the light of day it seems silly.

I open the door and find Daniel wearing the same clothes he had on last night. His hair is disheveled and there's a shadow of blond scruff on his jaw.

"You look like hell," I say. "What time is it? I don't have a clock in here."

Daniel shrugs. "It's morningish. Brunchish. I don't think there's a single clock in this hotel. Not one that I've seen. But who cares? We're on vacation."

I open the door wider and Daniel walks in. He sits on the edge of my bed and rubs his hand over his hair. "I had the craziest night, Aud," he says. "This hotel is awesome."

"Did you go to the party?" I grab my duffel bag from the floor, tossing it next to Daniel. I sort through the mix of clothes, finding nothing I want to actually wear, and then turn the bag over and dump the contents.

"Is that what that invitation was?" Daniel asks. "I just saw it this morning. Did you go? Why didn't you call me?"

I laugh. "Uh, because I only stayed for a minute before they kicked me out." I see a red racer-back tank top and set it aside while I search for a clean-enough pair of jeans. "You got an invite?" He nods and I glance around the room,

29

looking for my own invitation. I don't find one. "Well," I say, grabbing my clothes. "It was in the ballroom—the music was playing when we got here. Not sure how you missed it."

"I wasn't really paying attention," he admits. "And after you got on the elevator, I went to see if they had a gym." He grins. "Met a girl instead."

"Please don't tell me about it." He always tells me, though, especially since Mom died.

My chest tightens and I cross to the bathroom with my clothes. I tell Daniel I'll be out in a second, and he looks offended that I'm not falling over myself to hear his story.

The bathroom door clicks closed, and I rest my forehead against the wood. Lately I've taken to blocking out all thoughts of my mother, distracting myself when she tries to surface. But this time I can't, not with Daniel's puppy-dog expression on the other side of the door, waiting for me to pat him on the head and tell him how great he is.

Daniel and Mom were best friends. Sometimes I'd come home and find them at the kitchen table, just talking. Laughing. He told her everything. He wants me to take her place, and when I understandably cannot, he hates me for it.

I straighten, blinking my eyes quickly to keep back the tears. I have to be stronger than this. The porcelain sink is cold against my fingers as I grip the edge, staring at my reflection until my pulse calms. Daniel's here and he needs me. So I have to be better.

I grab the hotel-provided toothbrush and paste and turn on the faucet. The taste is chalky, like baking soda, and I rinse out my mouth. My reflection stares back at me and I'm surprised by how well I look. Last night was probably the best sleep I've had since—

"Audrey," Daniel whines from the other room. "I'm dying here."

My brother is spoiled, but not altogether terrible because of it. I pull on the jeans and slip the tank top over my head. Now that Daniel's here, I realize I'm hungry too. I haven't eaten since yesterday afternoon.

Daniel's lounging back on his elbows and still grinning. "So it all started with this gorgeous blonde," he says the minute I walk in, as if we were still in midconversation. "I was lost in the hallway—have you walked around yet?" he pauses to ask. "It's like a fun-house maze. Anyway, I'm just trying to find my way back to the lobby when this girl stumbles out of a room and the door slams in her face."

"Sounds promising." I lean down to lift the bed skirt, trying to find my flip-flops. There they are.

"Right?" Daniel laughs. "So she's crying, black shit all around her eyes. But she's beautiful, and I don't mean everyday attractive. She's like a classic painting."

I put my hand on my hip and scoff. "Seriously? Are you drunk?"

Daniel sits up, his eyes wide and earnest. "I'm not kidding, Aud. She was . . . perfect. Blond hair, nice dress—

a classy girl," he adds emphatically. "And even with the smeared makeup, her skin was like one of those creepy dolls that Nana used to send you." He motions his hand for me to remember.

"A porcelain doll?" I ask.

"Yes!"

"Daniel, she sounds horrible. I used to lock those dolls in my closet at night so they wouldn't kill me. You sure you weren't hallucinating?"

He shakes his head, smiling to himself. "Naw. She was real. I went up to her and asked if she was okay. Then she stared at me for a long while, and I thought maybe she was having some sort of a breakdown. Then she told me I was pretty."

I curl my lip. My brother has always had awful taste in girls. It used to be the around-the-dinner-table joke. But this one might be in a category all her own. Obviously someone was kicking her out of the room. She has bag-gage. "And you responded by . . . ?"

"I kissed her," he says, like it's the only logical response. "I don't get called pretty every day, Audrey."

Now I laugh. "Oh, please. You were voted Best Looking in the yearbook. How much more validation do you need?"

"I'm needy."

I slip on my sandals and grab my purse from inside my backpack. I didn't pack much to go to my grandmother's. One duffel bag and one backpack. My entire life could fit in an overhead compartment. Daniel jumps up from the bed, intent on finishing his story.

"So we kissed, and her skin was ice cold. I asked her if she wanted my hoodie."

"Gross, the dirty one?"

He shrugs and holds open the door for me. "She didn't take it. She said she had a shawl in her room." The door slams behind us, rattling the frame. Daniel and I both glance down the hall at the other rooms, the silence so ominous it automatically makes my shoulders tense. "Uh . . ." Daniel pauses, seeming to sense the same thing, and then continues. "And then she took my hand and led me through the halls. God, it felt like we walked for hours."

When we get to the elevator, Daniel reaches past me to push the button a bunch of times. Although his stories are rarely this bizarre, the last few months there'd been a rush of desperate girls. Ones who needed him, when really he was the one in need.

"Then where'd you go?" I ask. The elevator doors open and we step inside. Daniel pushes the lobby button, and I glance in the mirror and smooth down the flyaway strands of hair from my part. I should have grabbed a ponytail holder. What if I bump into Elias?

"We didn't go anywhere," Daniel says, leaning against the shiny gold railing. "That's the thing—we just walked the hallways all night."

"Morning," I correct, and then apologize when he gives me the *Don't be a know-it-all* look.

"Then we were at her door and she asked if I would come in."

"Stop there," I warn, holding up my finger. I'm grateful when the elevator doors open to the lobby. There are guests milling about, chatting and alive. The creepiness of the thirteenth floor fades, and I'm once again amazed by the beauty of the Hotel Ruby. Daniel and I start toward the busy restaurant, and Daniel waves when he sees our father already waiting at a table.

"Relax," my brother tells me when we take our seats next to my father. "Nothing happened. I know how to play hard to get."

I laugh, and my father raises his eyebrows. "Do I want to know about this conversation?" he asks. I turn to him, shocked by how awake he sounds. The dark circles that have become constants since my mother's death have faded.

"Daniel met a girl," I say, gauging his reaction. Mostly to see if my father will just brush us off like usual. Hum a noncommittal reply.

"Surprising," he responds sarcastically, and then smiles. It just about knocks me off my chair. Daniel and I exchange a glance, and then we both turn back to our father to make sure we aren't imagining this. He's . . . Dad. "What's her name?" he asks.

Daniel's eyes light up like a little kid, and it breaks my

heart how much he wants our father's attention. "Catherine," my brother says. "I didn't catch her last name."

My stomach clenches. "Catherine?" I repeat. Daniel nods and then begins to reshare the story with our father. I take a sip from the glass of water on the table, knowing exactly who he's talking about. She is the girl who came up to Elias. She was rude and threatening, and Elias called her a psychopath.

So of course my brother had to go and hook up with her.

I have two options, really. I can tell Daniel she sucks and to stay away, or I can keep my mouth shut. What would my mother do? I think back to the bits of conversations she and Daniel shared. She'd make a joke, but in her jokes would be some truth. Some hidden advice that my brother swallowed down because it came with a spoonful of sugar. Then again, we're leaving today. It probably doesn't matter.

"Tell Dad the part where she looks like a killer porcelain doll," I say, making my brother laugh. He doesn't realize that I mean it kind of literally. Daniel continues the story, sparing us none of the details, including the fact that her hair smelled like peaches. I'm thankfully distracted when the server comes up to take our food order.

"I ordered you a coffee," my father says, pointing at the cup in front of me. There's a sinking feeling as I thank him and turn to the server.

"Can I have a juice instead?" I ask. "I hate coffee."

She smiles, but it doesn't reach her eyes. My mother told me you can tell if someone's really smiling if it wrinkles the skin around their eyes. She jots down a note. "May I also recommend the ham," she says, opening a menu to point to it.

I crinkle my nose. "Ham tastes too much like pig." I smile. "How about pancakes?" I ask, pretending it has nothing to do with my mother. Pretending it's not an attempt to feel close to her. The server scans the menu like she's not sure they have them listed, and I glance at her name tag—TANYA.

"Great choice," she says, snapping the menu shut. It sends a breeze over my face and hair. "And a side?"

"You pick," I say as a peace offering. She stares at me like I've said the wrong thing. The hairs on the back of my neck rise, and I begin to fidget with my napkin to distract myself.

"Fruit, then," she says, and rounds the table toward Daniel. I'm unsettled, but I watch as she takes his order. Her short, curly black hair is pulled back in a headband, her dark skin complemented by red lipstick. As if sensing me, she glances over and I lower my eyes.

"You all right?" my father asks, startling me. "You look pale."

"Just hungry," I say, spreading my napkin on my lap. When the server is gone, I pull my chair closer to the table, to my family. "Did you know this place is supposed to be haunted?" I ask.

Daniel rolls his eyes. "Yeah, Catherine mentioned it last night. I guess it's how they stay in business. We're in the middle of nowhere."

"I've been thinking about it," our dad says between sips of coffee. "How about we stay another night?"

"Really?" I ask, a smile spreading across my face. Another night at the Ruby would be a dream. Not only does it postpone my misery, it'll give me a chance to check out the cute guy from the party.

"How about two nights?" Daniel asks. "I've got plans, Dad. Even I'm not good enough to pull them off in a mere forty-eight hours."

"Until Friday, then," he says, holding up his cup. "We'll be together until Friday." Daniel and I exchange another glance, but I don't let the comment drag me into the possibilities of after. This moment is too good. "Now," my father continues. "Tell me more about this Catherine girl."

Daniel launches into his thrilling plans to woo Catherine, and it's fifteen minutes later when Tanya sets a plate in front of me. There are scrambled eggs with garnish, and on the side is a steaming slice of ham, bright pink against the white plate. I lift my gaze to Tanya's and she smiles.

"Bon appétit," she whispers, handing me a steak knife. I swallow hard, taking it from her hand. I could argue, cause a scene. But Daniel and my dad are so happy right now. I wouldn't ruin this moment for anything. Not even for pancakes.

I saw into the slab of meat, thinking I'll have to choke it down if I hope to curb my growling stomach. I shove a thick chunk in my mouth, readying my hand on my glass. Tanya turns to grab another plate off the tray, and a flash of red catches my eye. I drop my silverware with a loud clang, terrified. Tanya's bleeding—on her side she's got a fist-size splotch of blood. My mouth is full of food as I try to get the words out, pointing my shaking finger in her direction. My father furrows his brow when I get his attention.

"Is it not to your liking?" Tanya interrupts, sounding concerned. I turn back to her; the blood is gone. Her crisp white shirt is stain-free, pressed and neat. My hands are shaking, and I flick my stare between the missing spot and her face. "Is there something wrong?" she asks, her left eye narrowing slightly as she studies me.

"No," I say, putting my palm on my forehead. I run my hand down my cheek and then shake off the nerves. "I must have been imagining things."

Tanya bites her long bright-red fingernail like she's thinking. Then she smiles politely. "It happens to the best of us," she responds. "Enjoy your breakfast." Then she leaves to grab the other plates.

# CHAPTER 3

After I finish eating, I decide to check out the gift shop I noticed when we checked in. I'm thrilled to be staying an extra two nights as I peruse the shop, which is more like a department store than a hole-in-the-wall filled with an array of tourist tchotchkes. There are key chains and shot glasses, of course, but there are also sets of delicate glasses and plates, linens, and plush robes—everything you'd need to re-create the Hotel Ruby experience at home. Weird, sure. But I'm kind of obsessed with the woven scarf hanging on the coatrack.

In Arizona I didn't wear scarves very often, at least not sensible ones. A decorative one here or there with skinny jeans and boots, but this—I pick it up and wrap it around my neck. The fabric is as soft as cashmere, but thick and warm. It'll be perfect for Elko's long winters, the cold days I'll be spending in some converted attic, locked away like my father's forgotten past.

The thought of moving to my grandmother's fills me with dread once again, and I unwind the scarf and loop it on the rack. I walk along a little farther and skim the T-shirts, pausing at a dark red one with THE HOTEL RUBY embroidered on the front. I smile and start to search through the sizes for an extra-large. When I find it, I hold it up, measuring if it's big enough for Ryan. Lately his arms have gotten massive, and whenever I buy him a large, it—

*Ryan.* I drop the shirt onto the pile and take a step back. I've been on autopilot, mine and Ryan's relationship so ingrained in my head at this point that I shop for him without thinking, that I save up my observations and funny stories to share him with later. Even though I have no intention of calling him. For so long I wanted to be free, and now that I am, I don't know who I want to become. I'm not sure what kind of person I really am.

I leave the T-shirts and head toward the candies near the register. There's an older woman behind the counter, reading through an issue of *Entertainment Weekly*, and a guy restocking bookshelves on the far side of the store. The woman glances up from her magazine and smiles.

"Hello there, hon," she says in a faded Southern accent. "Are you looking for something in particular or just browsing?"

"Just browsing," I respond. She nods, but sets her magazine aside like I've captured her attention instead. She's a little older, about my mother's age, polished and put together in an ivory suit with shoulder pads. She looks like she just walked off the pages of a JCPenney catalog. Her smile is wide and genuine, and her perfume reminds me of a grandmother's—albeit a hip, rich grandmother who wears blazers to work a cash register. "Actually," I say, hoping for conversation, "I might want to buy something for my ex-boyfriend."

She chuckles, and slaps her palm down on the counter, startling me. "Now you're talking." She rounds the counter to stop in front of me. I read her name tag: ASTRID. "Thought I'd be spending another afternoon ready to kill myself," she says. "Have you seen these people?" She waves her arms, gesturing to the Ruby itself. "They may as well be dead, they're so boring."

"Now tell me," she continues, her dark eyes round with excitement. "Is this an ex you're trying to win back, or is the gift more of an apology?"

"It's definitely an apology," I say, embarrassment quieting my voice. Astrid's smile fades slightly, and she leans in closer.

"Then I have the perfect thing," she whispers, and starts walking in the direction I've just come from.

I follow her, doubting I'll send Ryan any gift I pick up. But since my mother's death I haven't had another woman to talk to. Maybe for a moment I can pretend that I do. I blink quickly to avoid the onset of tears, sniffing them away before Astrid stops in front of the decorative jars and chocolate boxes.

"He's not really the vanilla-candle sort of guy," I say, glancing sideways. Astrid reaches past me to grab a white box of chocolates from the shelf and then holds it out. I take the box hesitantly but shake my head. "Ryan won't eat these," I tell her. "He's super anal about his diet. High protein. Low carb. No sugar." I put the box back on the shelf and am surprised to find Astrid smiling at me.

"They're not for him," she says, grabbing the box again and heading toward the register with it. "They're for you."

"Me?"

Astrid slides behind the counter and pulls out a paper bag with "The Hotel Ruby" written across it in red. She slips the chocolates inside and then rings them up. I stare at her like she's crazy. When I don't take out money to pay her, she leans against the register.

"You have nothing to apologize for," she says, in way of explanation. "Just let it go, hon."

"Not to sound rude," I begin, "but I actually do owe him a lot. A hell of a lot more than a box of chocolates."

"That may be," she says, her expression growing serious. "But life has a way of balancing things out. Is he here with you?"

"No. I doubt I'll ever see him again."

Astrid reaches to put her hand over mine. "See?" She turns back to the register like she's just made a powerful statement, but I'm a little confused. Forcing a bonding moment with a random cashier probably wasn't an inspired idea.

Well, at least she grabbed the salted caramel flavor chocolates. They're my favorite. I glance around the counter one last time and notice the postcards. One catches my attention, and I pluck it off the plastic rack. It's a painted portrait of the Hotel Ruby, the massive front doors and leaded windows. The golden lights shining on the trees, setting off the entire scene in magic. "Stay Tonight. Stay Forever" is typed in black on the side.

"Astrid," I say, sliding the postcard across the counter. "Can you add this in?"

She flicks her eyes to the picture and then to me, seeming slightly annoyed that I'm not taking her advice to "let it go." She rings up the card and shoves it into the bag with the chocolates, telling me the total. I hand over a few bills, and while waiting for the change, I see the other employee has finished stocking the shelves. There's an empty cart sitting there, but he's gone.

"Here you go," Astrid says, holding up the bag. I thank her as I take my items, then start for the door, already thinking about what I'll write to Ryan on the postcard. "And hon," the cashier calls. I turn back to look at her, and she smiles. "Welcome to the Ruby."

Upstairs I shower and put on makeup. As I get ready, I open the box of chocolates and pop a piece into my mouth. The first bite is sweet and rich, but as I continue to chew, there's an aftertaste that reminds me of turned milk.

"Bleh," I say, opening my mouth to let the chocolate fall into the trash can with a *thunk*. I rinse out my mouth and then inspect the box, trying to see if there's an expiration date. When I find nothing strange, I close up the box and dump the entire thing in the garbage. "That was a waste," I say, clicking off the bathroom light and heading back into my room.

I sit on my bed and bring the room service menu onto my lap. The postcard lies next to me on the comforter. I grab the pen from the nightstand and blow out a steadying breath. Leaning back against the pillows, I move the postcard onto the menu so I can write.

But after close to twenty minutes the words won't come. They're too big, too broad, to fit in the stroke of a pen. Maybe Astrid was right—I should let it go. Every minute I sit here, I regret more, and the guilt is threatening to eat me up. In an attempt to cut off the pain, I quickly scratch a message on the postcard and sign it.

*I'm sorry for everything.*
*—Audrey*

When I'm done, I hop up from the bed, tucking the postcard into my back pocket, and slip on my sandals. I'll take this down to the front desk and have them mail it. And then I'll be done. It'll be over. I'll let it be over.

Afterwards I'll keep my eyes out for Elias, the gorgeous distraction. I have no plans of pulling a Daniel and hooking up with a stranger, but I definitely liked the guy in the suit.

I think he sort of liked me, too. It's nice to feel attracted to somebody again.

I grab my keycard and head out the door.

At the elevator I smooth down my hair, since it's hell-bent on frizzing out and making me look crazy. I'm trying to mat down my part when the doors open. My heart skips. Elias is inside the elevator, resting against the mirrored wall.

"Audrey Casella," he says, stepping aside to make space directly next to him. "You're still here." He darts a look at the floor number and then back at me. "What an unexpected surprise."

"You're telling me," I say, blushing under his attention. "My father's letting us stay a few more days, and normally I would wait until I could crash your fancy party to bump into you, but I've been told I need an invitation. Not at all pretentious." He chuckles, and I glance sideways at him. "Hey. You lost the suit."

"I look great without it."

I laugh, and stare down at the floor—sure that he can tell exactly how thrilled I am to bump into him. My pink toes are neon against the classic colors in the elevator, the grays and reds, and I shift my eyes to Elias's shoes: soft brown moccasins. He has on khaki shorts, a button-down white cotton shirt with the sleeves rolled up. His hair is tucked behind his ears, although a few strands have fallen forward.

He's taller than I remember, and as I continue to check

45

him out, I realize he's smiling and staring straight ahead. I follow his gaze to our reflections in the elevator doors. When I meet Elias's eyes in the shiny surface, he winks. I smile and look away.

The elevator stops and the bell dings for the lobby.

"Where are you off to now?" Elias motions for me to exit first when the doors slide back. "I'm certainly open to changing my plans."

I turn toward him, the rectangle in my back pocket making me feel like I'm cheating. On whom, I'm not exactly clear. "I'm, um . . . on my way to mail a postcard to my ex-boyfriend."

"I'm a little jealous," Elias says, despite the curve at the corner of his mouth that says otherwise.

"Don't be. It's an apology for being a terrible girlfriend."

"That's incredibly polite of you," Elias says with a laugh. We start across the lobby, our steps deliberately slow to draw out our time together. "Can't say any of my ex-girlfriends would have bothered," he says. "Your boy-friend . . ." He pauses, waiting for me to supply the name.

"Ryan."

"Ryan," he continues, "must be a great guy. Either that or you were truly awful."

"A bit of both, I think."

"I hope you never have to be that kind to me."

We reach the deserted front desk, and I flash Elias an apologetic smile. "Don't think I'll be here long enough for us to reach any official status, so you should be safe," I tell him.

Elias turns, resting his back against the counter so he can look out over the lobby. "I'm not afraid of commitment," he says.

"I am."

"Goddamn, you're interesting." Elias peeks sideways at me, a wry smile on his lips. "Let me steal you away for a little bit. Give you that tour."

I'm seriously considering his offer when the door to the back office opens and Kenneth walks out. He smiles brightly, like he's pleased to find us waiting. Elias glances back but doesn't acknowledge him. Kenneth doesn't miss a beat, though.

"Mr. Lange," he says, nodding to Elias. "Ah, Miss Casella. You're still here. What can we do for you?"

This is actually way more awkward than I considered. I take a step away from Elias and pull the postcard from my back pocket. "I was looking to mail this?" I say in a hushed voice. I slide the card across the counter, and Kenneth stares down without touching it. When he doesn't respond, I clear my voice to sound steadier. "I don't have any stamps," I say. "I thought maybe—"

"I'll take care of it right away," Kenneth says, folding his hands in front of him. He doesn't go on, he doesn't check the address. I wait a long moment, but his face is a portrait of pleasantness. I thank him and turn to Elias, widening

47

my eyes to let him know the concierge is being weird.

Elias's lips hint at a smile, but he straightens them and nods to Kenneth politely before taking my hand to lead me away. When we're across the lobby, his fingers slide from mine, the sensation sending chills over my skin. We both look back to where Kenneth is standing. He watches us, but then the concierge picks up the postcard and disappears into the back room.

"Okay," I start, "what is the deal with that guy?"

Elias groans like he has no idea where to begin and really doesn't care to. "You already told me you wouldn't be here long enough to send me a very polite rejection," he says. "So you shouldn't spend your time guessing the intentions of the concierge. What you should do"—he holds out his hand—"is come with me."

"And where are you going?" I ask with mock suspicion.

He laughs and lowers his hand. "To hell, probably. But first I was thinking of sneaking you around the Ruby. Kenneth will hate it."

"I thought we weren't going to spend our time worrying about him."

"I'll do the worrying for us both," Elias says. "Kenneth's only concern is making sure the Ruby runs properly. He also likes to check in to make sure I'm not getting into trouble." Elias purses his lips. "I always seem to find it, though."

"You should try exhibiting some self-control."

"Where's the fun in that?"

Getting into trouble with Elias sounds like an interesting way to spend my Wednesday afternoon. But I don't really understand why he's at the Ruby. Does he live in a hotel?

"What exactly do you do here, Elias?" I ask with a laugh. "Unless you're Eloise, I highly doubt—"

He takes my hand again to tug me forward. "Later," he says with a mischievous smile. "Because right now I have a completely inspired idea, but"—he glances back at the desk to check for Kenneth—"we don't want the concierge to see us."

"Sounds like you're looking for trouble again."

"Indeed," Elias says. We walk into the hallway, and I crane my neck as we pass the restaurant, surprised when I find my father still inside, now talking with Kenneth. How did the concierge get over there so fast?

My dad gets to his feet, his arms gesturing wildly as he and Kenneth engage in what appears to be a heated conversation. My father takes Kenneth's arm, desperate. And then, suddenly, as if he knew I was here, Kenneth's dark gaze snaps to me. Dread falls around my shoulders; my breath catches.

"Come on," Elias says, oblivious to Kenneth's new location. He takes my arm, and then we're next to each other again, starting off down the hallway. I wonder momentarily what my father and Kenneth were arguing about. Was it about me? But then Elias laughs, and his fingers slide down my arm to take my hand. The sensation on my skin makes my heart race, draws me completely into his world. It's been so long since I've wanted something—someone. I forget everything else.

"Don't freak out," Elias says, his dimples deepening with his smile. "But I was thinking we could start at the spa. Namely, the steam room?"

Hot and sweaty while wearing a towel. I can't believe I'm going to agree to this. "Interesting suggestion," I say.

"Yes, I thought it was brilliant." We both laugh, and then he tugs me toward the frosted glass doors at the end of the hallway.

I've been in a steam room only once or twice, after working out at the gym. But the YMCA's white-tiled floors and benches have nothing on this place. The smell of cedar immediately hits my nose as we walk into the small room, a light fog hanging in the air. We have the place to ourselves, and I cross the wet floor to the benches. I sit first, expecting Elias to take a spot next to me, but he goes next to the water bucket and sits down.

When we walked into the spa, the woman at the desk didn't even glance at us, instead smiling at her phone like she was reading a text. I imagined Kenneth wouldn't be at all happy, but Elias only put his finger to his lips and pulled us past the receptionist. A girl in a bright-white dress stopped us then, greeting Elias with a kiss on the cheek. I didn't roll my eyes; my time as Ryan's girlfriend was a crash course in handling jealously. Not that he would have strayed.

Elias asked the girl if we could borrow towels, and she shot him a disapproving look before grabbing a large, fluffy towel and extending it in my general direction. Like Catherine at the party, this girl didn't appear very pleased to see Elias talking with me. I thanked her and took the towel.

I changed in the bathroom and then met Elias in front of the steam room, a little stunned to see him without his shirt. Of course, I was standing in a towel as well, but I could barely formulate a sentence that didn't start with "Wow . . ."

Elias is not Ryan—he's not bulked up, thick and strong. Instead he's incredibly tall and thin, fit, with muscles corded around his frame. I actually like it better. Being with Ryan always made me feel a little self-conscious, like I should be working out instead of chowing down on movie theater popcorn.

I expected some recognition that I was also nearly naked, but Elias only looked me over once and then opened the door to the room.

As we sit here now, the room is certainly warm. I settle back against the heated wood bench behind me, staring across the room at Elias. He takes a ladleful of water and pours it over the hot rocks, the spitting steam hisses, quickly enveloping the room. The vapor reaches me, hard to breathe in. But it's intoxicating, the pure heat licking my skin.

Elias stands and then comes over to where I am, climbing up to take the bench above me. I reposition myself, my elbow on his seat as I rest my chin on my arm. Elias lays his head against the wall and then looks down at me. Moisture has started to gather on his face, his collarbone. I'm feeling altogether seduced.

"Why did you send that postcard earlier?" he asks, his voice rougher in the thickened air. "What exactly did you have to apologize for, Audrey?"

I exhale, my muscles relaxed and loose. "For not loving him enough," I say quietly. "For trying and failing. But worst of all, for not telling him even though I'm sure he knew. I was a coward, and he deserved better."

Elias closes his eyes, his Adam's apple bobbing as he swallows. "Sometimes we're with the wrong people for all the right reasons. Would it surprise you if I told you I could relate? Only I didn't try to love her, and I certainly didn't apologize."

"That sounds harsh," I say, fairly certain he's talking about the girl my brother's been sneaking around with. But since Elias just admitted he didn't have feelings for her, bringing up Catherine seems kind of pointless. "Why were you with her, then?" I ask anyway, hoping for a bit more detail.

Elias is quiet for a long moment, but then he opens his eyes and sits forward, elbows on his knees. His skin has grown pink in the heat of the steam room. "It was expected," he says. "And even when I told her my feelings, she didn't care. She thought we belonged together no matter what." He looks at me, really looks at me. "Now that, Audrey," he whispers, "is a terrible girlfriend."

There's a sudden loneliness in his expression, even with our bodies close together, wet with steam and sweat. I connect to it—his melancholy mirroring my own. For an instant I'm not alone. Not with him. It's weird, because the more Ryan tried to give me, the lonelier I felt. And yet this stranger has broken into my world and taken up space.

Elias laughs, dragging his gaze from mine, and lies back on his bench. "You shouldn't look at me like that," he says toward the ceiling. "It's too soon for me to kiss you. I haven't charmed you nearly enough."

I put my fingers on my lips, covering my smile. "I think you're doing pretty well," I say, making him laugh again.

"Yes, but if I'm going to practice that restraint you talked about," he responds, "then we'd better get out of here before this heat clouds your better judgment. Come on." He climbs down from the bench and then helps me up. I grip my towel, keeping it tight around me, even though a knot has formed in my stomach. I take Elias's arm, ready to pull him back, but as he opens the door, the cool air rushes in, bringing me back to my senses. The steam quickly clears, along with the overwhelming desire, and I find Elias watching me.

"We'll skip the massages," he teases. "You should definitely put some clothes on. Meet you out front?"

I agree, still a little shaken from my brush with complete and utter lack of self-control. And when we part, I head into the locker room to rinse off in the shower, setting the temperature to cold.

# CHAPTER 4

After tying my damp hair up in a bun, I head to the entrance of the spa and find Elias chatting with the girl who gave me the towel earlier. When I walk out, she casts an uneasy stare in my direction, then tells Elias good-bye and leaves to go about her job. Not at all awkward.

Elias smiles broadly as I approach, his hair slicked to the side and his cheeks flush from the steam. "You're radiant," he tells me. "I am completely under your spell, Audrey."

"Uh-huh," I say like he's full of shit. But I enjoy the compliment, especially when I'm feeling just as interested. "Now where to?" I ask. "I'll have to check in with my dad at some point; this day isn't carefree."

Elias pulls open the door and we walk out, energized from our time at the spa. We're paused at the entrance of the lobby while we contemplate our next step, when I see my brother walk out from the restaurant. He's glaring down at his phone, his eyebrows pulled together.

"Hey," I call to him. Next to me Elias straightens, sliding his hands into the pockets of his shorts. Daniel comes over, holding up his phone helplessly.

"I can't get a signal in here," he says. "I've seen other people using their phones. Rot in hell, AT&T." He stops and looks at me. "Why's your face so red? What have you been doing?" He squints at Elias. "Who's this?"

Elias stretches out his hand. "Elias Lange," he says. "And you are?"

"Her older brother." Daniel shakes Elias's hand, clenching his fingers in a way that tells me he's squeezing harder than necessary. Elias doesn't even flinch.

Daniel takes his role of protective brother seriously. Before Ryan, whenever Daniel didn't like a guy I was dating, he'd wait on the porch with a Louisville Slugger resting on his shoulder. But then there was Ryan, and everyone loved Ryan. My brother hasn't had to stand up for me in a while. In a way, I'm touched. I'm also glad he left his baseball gear in Phoenix.

"I'm heading to the pool," Daniel says to me, turning his back on Elias. "Go grab your bathing suit."

"The weather's perfect for a swim," Elias interjects, seeming amused by my brother's lack of manners. "It's sometimes overcast this time of day, but it seems—"

"Now, how do you know my sister?" Daniel interrupts, spinning to him. He's pretending to be confused, which makes him all the more obnoxious. He shoots me the same look and I scoff. I don't know Elias half as well as Daniel knows Catherine.

"We met in the elevator," Elias says. Daniel stares him

down, and then, as if just remembering the true source of his irritation, my brother pulls out his phone in search of a signal. While he's distracted, Elias leans in to me.

"I thought it best to leave out the part where you asked to see me without my suit," he says casually. I push his shoulder, making him stagger a step, and he laughs quietly.

Daniel turns his attention back at us. "I'm going to check out the pool before I grab my stuff. Meet me there?"

"In a little bit," I say. "I'm on a tour." To be honest, I just don't want to spend the day watching Daniel sunbathe.

"Fine," my brother says suspiciously. "But you better meet me later or I'm coming to your room." He starts to pass us, then pauses to look back. "And you'd better be in there alone, Audrey."

"Gross. Good-bye." I wave him off, letting him know he's laying it on a little thick. Elias presses his lips together like he's trying not to smile at my brother's threat, and we watch as Daniel walks out toward the garden.

"Is he always so protective?" Elias asks.

"Mostly, but you seem to especially piss him off."

"I sometimes have that effect. But then again"—he smiles, brushing back a wet strand of my hair that's fallen from the bun—"you do look . . . disheveled. I can see why he assumed I was a bad influence."

I swat his hand away playfully, but his touch has already spiked my desire. "Whatever," I say, pretending he's not driving me crazy. "I'm still waiting to hear why exactly

57

you're the Ruby's most eligible bachelor. Your entire existence is suspicious."

Elias laughs, offering me his arm in a natural movement. His politeness is striking in my otherwise uncivilized world. "I live here," he replies. "And before you jump to conclusions, let me finish showing you around. Maybe you'll understand why."

"Why you live in a hotel?" I ask. "Doubtful. I'd tell you how bizarre that is, but I'm on my way to live in my grandmother's attic. So I'm not sure I'm in a position to make that statement."

Elias looks at me, my admission catching us both off guard. I hate the heaviness that's seeping in, and I bump my shoulder into his. "Let's hurry before I change my mind and go to the pool with my brother."

"We should run, then," Elias says, pulling me ahead quickly. We laugh and then stop in front of the elevator. He presses the down arrow and glances over, his eyebrows pulled together. I can tell the comment about my grandmother's attic is weighing on his mind.

"It's not a big deal," I say quietly, facing the doors. With so many other things to talk about, my future in Elko, Nevada, is not high on the list of things I feel like discussing. Why did I mention it at all?

"Fair enough," he says. "But don't you want to know the next stop on the tour?"

"Is it your hotel room?" I ask, looking sideways. I'm

not serious, but I love the blush rising on his cheeks. I kind of love the idea of seeing his room, too.

Elias chuckles. "That's later. No, I was thinking we should go to the heart of the Ruby herself. And . . ." He pauses. "Well, after your suggestion this is going to sound boring. I was hoping to take you down to housekeeping."

The Ruby has a basement. It's not creepy or haunted, although it does feel dull and cramped after the grandeur of the lobby. The walls are pale blue; the floors are gray with black scuff marks. A girl rushes by in uniform, smiling shyly at Elias as she passes. I turn to watch her and then nudge Elias.

"Do they all know you here?"

"Yep. Take a left." He points down a hallway that's thick with the smell of laundry detergent and dryer sheets. It's a comforting scent—one that reminds me of home. Of my mother.

"How many times have you given this tour?" I ask. My question is harsher than I intend it, but I'm trying to divert my thoughts from my mother. Elias side-eyes me like he's offended.

"First time," he says shortly. "But thanks for assuming this means nothing. Another left." We turn, and the hallway narrows where cabinets line either side of the walls. Elias stops halfway down and reaches over my head to open one. I step aside, afraid I've hurt his feelings.

"I'm sorry," I say. Elias pulls down a tiny chocolate mint and holds it out. He rests his shoulder against the cabinet door, looking down at me. I slowly unwrap the candy and bite off the corner. Like the toothpaste earlier, it has an old, chalky flavor. I rewrap it and slip it into my pocket. "I didn't mean to imply you're a dick," I say quietly to Elias. "I just figured—"

"Figured I was untrustworthy?"

I smile a little. "No. I figured you live in a hotel with a constant stream of strangers. Women. And of course there's the fact that you're . . ." I should stop talking now.

"I'm what?" Elias asks curiously, leaning closer.

"Cute."

"Cute?" he asks thoughtfully. "You think I'm cute?"

My face feels like it's caught fire, but every second I'm with Elias, the more comfortable I am with my attraction to him. Still, I try to play it cool; shrugging like my admission is no big deal.

"I've always thought of myself as handsome," he says. "Thank you. And since we're sharing—I find you intoxicating. Wholly addicting."

Our locked gazes linger, and then I laugh. "Stop flirting with me, Elias," I say to lighten the moment. "Let's talk about something else. Like why you live in a hotel in the middle of nowhere."

"You don't like the Ruby?" He seems almost hurt, but then he looks past me and straightens. His entire face lights up. "Lourdes," he says. "You're back."

I turn and find a young housekeeper, maybe just a little older than us, walking up. "Yesterday," she says. "Seems we have some new guests." She smiles warmly at me, and then fixes her gaze on Elias. The housekeeper folds her arms over her chest like she's waiting for an explanation. I realize then how small the space Elias and I are crammed into is. A tiny nook that could really only be for linens or secret kisses.

Elias puts his hands on my shoulders and ushers me forward. "This is Audrey Casella," he says. "I was just giv-ing her a tour."

"Of the basement?" Lourdes asks. Her eyebrows are per-fectly drawn on, hitched high in a silent-movie-star sort of way. Her hair is short and dark, her skin a deep olive color. "You're not supposed to be down here, Eli," she says, although her voice has softened. "I'll take her back to the lobby."

"Lourdes . . . ," he starts to say, but she shakes her head. "You'll get me in trouble."

Elias quiets, watching her apologetically. His dispo-sition has changed entirely, like he hates the thought of hurting her. "You're right," he says, and then turns to me. "Besides," he continues with a smile, "I don't think your brother would be very fond of me had I finished the tour." I lean against the cabinet, a little breathless.

"Yes, Eli," Lourdes announces, "you're very sexy. Now move along."

Elias chuckles and touches my arm before he slides past me. He walks to Lourdes, towering over her small frame. "We've missed you," he says.

Lourdes lifts her gaze to meet his. "I know." There's a sudden glimpse of loss between them, and then Lourdes pushes Elias to the side. "Now run along," she says lightly. "And don't come back down here unless you plan to fold towels."

"Any time." They say good-bye, and Elias waves once to me and disappears down the corridor. When he's gone, Lourdes lets out a deep exhale.

"Sorry to break that up," she says. Her voice is smoky, and now that Elias is gone, she seems much happier to see me. "It's not a good idea to sneak around with him," she says. "He rarely thinks beyond the moment." My stomach sinks with disappointment, but Lourdes quickly holds up her hands. "I'm not saying Eli's bad. He's not." She smiles reassuringly. "He's not the one you need to worry about."

"Then who is?"

Lourdes presses her lips together, as if telling me she's already said too much. She closes the cabinet with the chocolates and starts back down the hallway, motioning for me to follow. I'm struck with the smell of home once again, but this time the nostalgia isn't as painful.

"My mother used this kind of detergent," I blurt out. Lourdes turns to look back at me, at first confused, but then her expression softens.

"Mine, too," she says, sadness dripping from her voice. "What . . ." She pauses. "What does it smell like to you?"

It's a weird question, but at the same time I don't mind having a memory of my mother that isn't seeped in tragedy. "Tide," I say with a smile. "But I could never figure out what she added to it. All these months I could never get the same scent. I haven't smelled it until now."

"I smell bleach," Lourdes replies. She turns back around and continues down the hall. I search for the hint of bleach but don't find it. "Come on," Lourdes calls. "The concierge doesn't want guests in housekeeping." She glances back again. "Have you seen the pool? It's spectacular."

"Not yet. My brother's going there now. I guess I'll meet up with him."

"You should." Lourdes stops at the elevator and presses the button. "And I'm sure I'll see you around. What room are you? I'll send some extra chocolates."

"Thirteen oh three."

Lourdes's smile drops from her lips. She tries to recover, but I can't unsee it. She presses the button again, trying to hurry the elevator. "Does Elias know where you're staying?" she asks casually.

"Uh . . . no, I don't think so. He hasn't been to my room, if that's what you're asking. Wait, why?" I ask, feeling uneasy. "Is my room haunted or something?"

Lourdes laughs, clapping me on the shoulder just as the doors open. "Not at all," she says. "Not at all."

CR BO

A shadow falls over my magazine as I'm lounging next to the pool in a deck chair. I squint at the gathering clouds and then find Daniel's blond head bobbing in the water. Up until this sudden change in weather, it has been beautiful. Perfect.

There are a few other guests, but they all seem to be wrapped up in their own conversations. A young couple has laid their towels in the grass, resting on their folded arms as they whisper to each other. An old man reads the paper at the table with an umbrella top. None of them even glance in my direction, which is just as well. I'm probably still blushing from my run-in with Elias.

"Audrey," Daniel calls, pulling himself up on the blue-tiled sidewall. "Come in before it rains. I want to show you my dive."

"I can watch you dive from here. You don't need a fan club, Daniel. Sometimes you can just do awesome things for your own enjoyment."

My brother's expression falters, and he drops back into the water with a splash. I hurt his feelings, even though I didn't mean to. Daniel is all heart; he loves me to pieces. But with that love comes his constant need for validation.

On the other side of the pool Daniel climbs up the ladder and then positions himself on the edge. There are three girls on the deck chairs behind him, and they angle to get a better look. Daniel doesn't notice, though—he's hyperfocused on his impending dive. Hoping to get it just right. I sigh and drop the magazine on the chair before going to stand across the pool from him.

"You'd better nail it," I call. The corner of his mouth lifts, and then he brings his arms forward and leaps into the pool. As I expected, he hits a perfect vertical entry and loops back up to break through the rippling surface. He shakes the water off of his face and finds me.

"How was it?" he asks.

My chest aches because I don't react the way Mom would. She would clap and hoot and pump his ego. I only smile. "It was great," I say. "It was really great, Daniel."

He beams and then swims over to the side to do it again. I take up residence where I can watch him, dangling my feet in the water. Some of the guests leave, shooting skyward glances at the thick clouds. On Daniel's third try I tell him we should head in before he gets struck by lightning. He's posing for his next dive when I notice Lourdes, from housekeeping, walking over.

She's no longer in uniform. Instead she wears black shorts and a pale pink blouse, her eyes brightened by thick mascara. She holds up her hand in a wave when I notice her, and I go over to my lounge chair, wondering if she's here to see me.

"Hi," she says, seeming nervous to approach me. "Elias said you'd be here. Do you mind if I hang out for a bit?"

"Not at all," I respond, motioning to the chair next to me. "Although it looks like it might rain."

"It never rains." Lourdes sits, and we both turn toward the pool when Daniel splashes in. He pops out of the water, and notices us. He nods his chin to Lourdes, and she smiles in return.

"Is that your brother?" she asks me as Daniel starts swimming toward the shallow end. I can see Lourdes checking him out, and I want to tell her not to bother. Knowing Daniel, I'm sure he's already plotting how to meet up with Catherine again, especially since their encounter sounded bizarre. He's predictable like that.

"That's Daniel," I tell Lourdes. "We're here with my dad."

"Oh?" She looks genuinely surprised, which is odd. Did she think we'd just come here on our own? Is that what the other guests do? "I hadn't realized," Lourdes says. A shadow of doubt crosses her features.

I lean forward on the chair, noticing the change. Before I can ask her about it, cold drops of water hit my bare feet and I see Daniel standing over me, wiping his hair with a towel.

"Hey," he says to Lourdes. He's charismatic, and I watch as Lourdes practically melts under his attention. "I'm Daniel."

"Nice to meet you." Lourdes stares at him a second and then turns back to me without introducing herself to him. "So, Audrey," she starts, "a bunch of us are going to the roof tonight to celebrate my return." She rolls her eyes, looking embarrassed that she's the center of attention. "You should come too. Meet everybody."

"Oh." It takes me a minute to realize that I'm the one she's inviting and not my brother. "Sure," I say. "But there's a party in the ballroom. You don't go to that?"

"The staff's not invited," she answers quickly. "Which is okay with me, since I hate most of the guests here." She laughs. "Believe me, the roof is better. We go at sundown. You'll be there?"

I don't really have to give it much thought—I'm not invited to the fancy party either. "Count me in. Sounds fun."

Lourdes smiles broadly, standing from the chair. "See you tonight," she tells me. She runs a long gaze over Daniel and then waves before turning to walk back across the lawn.

"She doesn't like me." Daniel pulls his face into an exaggerated *How is that possible?* expression. "I thought everyone liked me."

"They do," I say. "Except for me, right now, because you're being obnoxious."

Daniel laughs and whips me with his towel. "Oh, stop. I'm joking. Mostly." He shrugs. "She liked me."

"I'm going inside," I say, rolling up my magazine and tying my towel around my waist. Daniel joins me on the walk back, and just when we get to the patio doors, the sky starts to clear. "It's going to be a beautiful night," I say, looking up. "Are you coming to the roof with me?"

"Don't think I was invited," Daniel says, not sounding terribly upset by it. The air of the Ruby is chilly on my skin, and Daniel shivers and brings his towel around his shoulders. "I'm going to explore other options." He pauses and points ahead. "Such as . . ."

Across the lobby Catherine waves, pageant-princess style, and starts toward us. She's no longer in a gown, but she's still too fancy for midafternoon. A bright white blouse with layers of necklaces glittering in the window-filtered sunlight. Short cigarette pants with spiked black heels, ornate silver bracelets. I sigh and swing my head toward my brother.

"Are you kidding me?" I ask him. She's over the top, even for his taste. He laughs, fully aware.

"Dan," Catherine says, out of breath when she reaches us. She places her palm on my brother's cheek, dramatic and entirely too affectionate. "I was so worried," she murmurs, letting her hand fall away. "I thought you'd left."

"No," he tells her. "Just found out we're staying until Friday. Isn't that awesome?" She casts an annoyed glance in my direction, speculating what part of "we" I fit into. "Oh, Cathy," Daniel says quickly. "This is my sister, Audrey."

She smiles politely. "Nice to see you," she says disingenuously, and immediately turns back to Daniel.

"Likewise," I say closemouthed.

Catherine runs her gaze over Daniel and then touches the towel at his neck. "The pool is gorgeous," she says. "Were you swimming?" I resist the urge to answer, "Duh."

"Yeah," Daniel responds, a little prideful. "I was practicing my dives, but my sister was entirely unimpressed." He knocks his elbow into my side, and I groan and take a step away. I'd rather be spared their idea of small talk.

"I can't even swim," Catherine says. "I would have been impressed."

"I'll teach you," Daniel says, puffed up and self-important. When Catherine excitedly tells him she'd like nothing more, he pulls her into a playful hug, pinning her under his arm in a way that might suit a campus girl but is out of place in high society.

Catherine turns up her face and they both smile, and I know exactly what my brother sees in her: Adoration. Attention. Catherine's feeding his inner boy, giving him the validation he craves. The idea that he's still so desperate for attention sends me into another guilt spiral, proving once again that I'm not living up to what my family needs. It makes me hate Catherine a tiny bit more . . . although I already summed up how terrible she was within two minutes of meeting her.

Catherine glances behind us and her expression falters. She pulls away from my brother with a longing sigh. "I've got to run." She tilts her head like she hates the idea of leaving him. "Promise me you'll come see me before tonight's party," she says.

"Promise," Daniel responds. Catherine doesn't acknowledge me before walking purposefully toward the garden doors, shooting a quick glance at the front desk. My brother watches her until she's out of sight, and when she's gone, he turns to me with a shit-eating grin on his face.

"Gorgeous, right?" he asks.

I shrug. "For a murderous doll, sure."

"Wish I hadn't given you that description," Daniel mutters.

I shake my head in mock sympathy. "You really didn't think that through."

He laughs, and we make our way toward the elevators on the other side of the lobby. Just when I think I've gotten used to the opulence of the Ruby, I'm dazzled again by a new bit of crystal or a painting I didn't notice.

"Mom would love this place," I say to myself. The minute the words are out of my mouth, Daniel clears his throat, aggressively readjusting his towel.

"It's cold," he says distantly. "I've got to change." He starts ahead, leaving me behind in his silence. I want to yell to him that I miss her too. That it hurts me too. But Daniel hates when I talk about Mom, so I shut up and follow him.

We walk through the lobby, and the concierge is at his desk, typing on the computer. Daniel and I climb into the elevator and press our floor numbers, facing out. Kenneth looks up from the desk.

He's motionless as the doors close to block him out.

# CHAPTER 5

My father orders his steak rare, and I raise the corner of my lip in disgust as the blood flows from the cut in his meat to stain the white dinner plate. He bites a big piece off his knife and glances at Daniel.

"What are your plans for tonight?" he asks him, chasing his food with a sip of red wine. I'm still trying to get used to seeing my father like this. His wavy salt-and-pepper hair is tamed with gel or mousse, making it flat and old-fashioned. He's clean shaven, rosy cheeked. But strangest of all, he's interested in our lives again.

"Don't know," Daniel says, picking up a drumstick of fried chicken. "Might meet Catherine later, but until then I'll probably work out. You?"

"I received an invitation to the party in the ballroom tonight." Our father laughs and takes a sip of wine. "Can't remember the last time I attended a formal event. Probably my wedding."

I divert my eyes to the white linen tablecloth. The way he said it—like his past with my mother was some casual memory—hurts. I wait for Daniel's reaction.

"You're going to the party?" he asks our father with

a strained voice. Daniel is clearly rattled by the mention of our mother, but in typical fashion he's ignoring it. If he doesn't acknowledge that she died, it can't hurt him. That's what he told me once, anyway.

"Yes, I thought I might have a drink or two," Dad says. "You should come. I believe you received your invite?"

Daniel crinkles his nose. "Yeah, but it's not exactly my scene. A bunch of old people, isn't it?"

"Not all of them." Dad laughs. "But I'll be doing my part for the senior citizens."

He's funny. I forgot that about him. Daniel smiles, and suddenly I'm the odd one out of this family-bonding moment. "I didn't get an invitation to the party," I say, feeling slighted.

Daniel smirks. "You must have pissed someone off, then."

"Whatever," I say. "I wasn't going to go anyway. I don't want to be stuck at some stuffy party all night. And that guy Kenneth at the front desk? What a tool. I'd rather find my own form of entertainment."

My father's hand tightens around his glass, and he takes a sip of wine. "Then I should probably alert housekeeping," he says through pursed lips. "Your idea of entertainment involves property damage."

His words are a slap in the face, a harsh dose of reality in the dreamlike peace we've found in the hotel. I blink quickly, humiliated. Angry. My father starts to apologize, but Daniel drops his food and starts to wipe his hands on his napkin, pushing back his chair like we're leaving.

Dad never did wait for an explanation about the house party that got Daniel and me sent away. I figured he didn't care enough for me to offer him one either. It was almost three weeks ago—a Saturday, the day after my birthday. Daniel had brought me home one of those Hostess mini apple pies, tossing it like a football to where I sat alone in the kitchen.

"Happy seventeenth," he said with a smile, his arm around the stray he'd brought home. She snapped her gum, all blond curls and attitude, unimpressed with my existence. I thanked him, though, because Daniel had remembered my birthday and my father had not. He'd stayed at his office the last three nights, and I started to doubt he was coming home at all.

After my brother left, I went up to my parents' room and sat on the bed. My mother's memory had been scrubbed from the house, even her scent. All that was left were a few pictures that stood on the mantel in the family room. I waited on the bed until dark, but my father still didn't come home.

My phone buzzed in my pocket, and I took it out to see Ryan was calling again. I still don't understand why he stayed with me. I had never come out and told him that I wasn't in love with him anymore, but he should have seen it. Instead he treated me like a sick child—his love a chicken soup for my lonely soul. But it seemed too cruel to leave him now. I'd end up married to him someday, I figured. It was the only way to justify my mother's death.

I WANT TO HAVE A PARTY TONIGHT, I texted back, not wanting to actually talk. CAN YOU MAKE THAT HAPPEN?

For my birthday Ryan had skipped school with me and made me breakfast at his house. I spent the day going through the motions with a hollow heart, as an empty vessel. Sometimes I wondered if Ryan's unconditional love could suffocate me.

WHO SHOULD I INVITE? HEY, ARE YOU OKAY? he responded.

NO. AND INVITE EVERYONE.

I didn't wait for him to answer before heading to my room to grab clean clothes from my closet. The next forty minutes were a blur of shower steam and too much mascara. I wanted to forget tonight. Forget him. Forget me.

The party was in full swing, loud and smoky, when I was on the couch, laughing with a stranger. He had shaggy black hair and heavy cologne. He put his hand on my thigh. I told him to piss off. And then Ryan was there, fighting. My head spun with a delicious mix of alcohol and danger, and I stood up and watched—not even telling them to stop.

The couch tipped back, taking the side table with it, lamp busted on the floor. Ryan had the guy by his collar, punching him in the face. I'd never seen him so angry— and in that moment I realized he was really angry at me. At my abandonment.

"Ryan?" I called weakly. All of my guilt, my pain, my

sorrow, cracked the surface. The tone of my voice must have scared him, because Ryan immediately turned toward me, his eyes fearful. The other guy took the distraction as an opportunity, blasting Ryan in the side of the head with his fist—knocking him out.

My entire body stilled as I watched him fall, first his large shoulder connecting with the floor, and then the top of his head with a *thunk*. The party quieted, all except the song playing in the background—what was that song? It was one of my mother's.

When Ryan didn't immediately move, people started to murmur their concern; some went for the door right away. The guy, just some random guy, spit on my boyfriend. He wiped the blood that Ryan had drawn off his chin, shooting me a hateful glare.

"Slut," he said, even though my refusal of his advance contradicted his statement. Then he swiped his hand along the mantel, sending the framed pictures crashing to the floor. Smashing them into tiny bits of sharp glass and paper. I moaned and fell to my knees, my mother's picture, broken.

It was all falling apart. I wanted my mother. I screamed it; I yelled it at the others as they stared at me, wide-eyed.

"*I want my mother!*" I shrieked uncontrollably, breaking the blood vessels in my eyes and tearing at my hair.

And then my father walked in. We never talked about what happened. He never asked if I was okay.

"Not cool, Dad," Daniel says from across the restaurant table. He drops his napkin over his food and comes to take my arm to pull me up. When I blink, tears drip onto my cheeks.

"I didn't mean that," my father says sincerely. "Audrey, please—"

"Enjoy your dinner," I say in a shaky voice, and let Daniel lead me from the room. It isn't until we're in the lobby that my brother gathers me in a hug, squeezing the breath out of my lungs before he releases his grip.

"Ouch," I say, and wipe the tears from my face. "And thanks."

Daniel nods and glances around the lobby like he's not sure what to do with me now. "He didn't know," he says quietly. "I try not to blame him because he didn't know that you were dying too."

"He didn't ask."

Old pain haunts my brother's features. Daniel is the one who saved me that night. He came home right after my dad and drove me and Ryan to the hospital to deal with his concussion. Ryan could barely look at me after that, like he had seen or heard some version of me that scared him. Eventually Daniel was the only person who looked at me at all.

My brother lowers his head. "Maybe one day you'll tell Dad all about it."

I smile sadly and murmur, "Maybe."

In the movies there are always these poignant moments when people work out their misunderstandings, their miscommunications. But that's not real life. In real life it's hard to tell someone you don't love them anymore. It's harder to tell your father you don't know how to live another day. My grief has stolen my voice.

Daniel glances over to the restaurant, probably thinking about his lost dinner. "You can go back," I tell him. "You don't have to starve for my benefit."

He looks doubtful. "Of course I do. I'm your brother. Besides, Dad's credit card can handle a room service charge. I was hoping for lobster."

I laugh, and Daniel and I walk toward the elevators. "Please come to the rooftop tonight?" I ask. "I don't want to meet people by myself." I'm not nearly as sociable as Daniel. I've learned to operate within the buffer of his charisma, avoiding the main focus so I can choose my words. Be funny. Now I'll have to work on the spot.

"What about that cute girl from housekeeping?" Daniel asks, pressing the button for the elevator. The doors open immediately. "You two were getting along famously. Besides, Aud. I wasn't invited, remember?"

"You're just mad she didn't fall all over you."

"A little," he allows. "But it's only Wednesday." He winks, and I push his shoulder, my tension faded. Even with tonight's emotional hiccup, I've been having fun. I can't remember the last time that happened.

The elevator stops on his floor. "You always have plans," I tell Daniel, still hoping he'll change his mind about the roof. He walks out and shrugs apologetically.

"I'm very personable. It's a gift and a curse."

"Uh-huh."

He chuckles and heads down the hallway toward his room. I sigh, my shoulder against the elevator wall. Daniel's pursuits are wasted on Catherine, in my opinion, but I'm not going to bring it up. He seems happy with her, and more than anything I just want to see my family happy again.

It's just after sunset when I follow Lourdes through the metal door onto the roof. The air is warm, humidity sticking to my skin. The music is low and haunting—the slow scratch of violins, an echo of a voice singing. One of the servers from the ballroom walks by and presses a cold bottle into my hand. He's dressed in a white T-shirt and black pants. His hair is no longer slicked to the side, but spiked out and shaggy around his ears. He winks at Lourdes.

"Welcome back, gorgeous," he says. Lourdes flashes him a smile and spins dramatically to watch him walk away. It's flirtatious but playful. Jokey in a way you can only be with your close friends.

"Everyone's really happy to see you," I say, taking a sip of my beer. "How long have you been gone?"

Lourdes slides her gaze in my direction. "A while. I was

suspended." I mouth an "Oh," but she laughs. "It wasn't anything illegal," she explains. "Kenneth and I just have a difference of opinion."

"I can imagine," I say. "He seems like he'd be a terrible boss."

"You have no idea."

I glance around the roof and find the server who handed me the drink. He joins another guy, and they climb onto the edge of the roof, their legs dangling over the side. I point them out to Lourdes. "Isn't that dangerous?"

"Yep. That's why they do it. In case you haven't noticed," she says, motioning around us. "Most everything fun is dangerous. I'm sure Eli has told you as much."

My heart rate spikes at his name, and I turn to her. "I don't really know him that well."

She laughs. "You will—it's Elias. We've all fallen in love with him at some point or another." She leans in like she's telling me a secret. "Our lot has been together for a while, Audrey. It's about time we had someone new to stir things up. I am truly torn about your entire situation."

"My situation?"

"You're leaving soon," she says, taking my drink to sip from it. "But part of me wants you to stay at the Ruby." She hands back my bottle. "Now come meet my friends."

Lourdes starts toward the group sitting on a row of metal cylinders near the wall, laughing and casual in the fact that they do this all the time. I guess if there's a party every night, one you're not invited to, this is a pretty cool alternative. There's an older guy about halfway across the roof wearing a green army jacket, even though the weather has grown muggy. His head is shaved and he's handsome, and he grins the minute Lourdes and I get within three feet of the group.

"Ah . . . ," he says, putting his boot up on a crate, blocking our path. "It's about damn time," he says with a slow drawl. "This place has been torment without you." He darts a look at me. "Now what do we have here? I don't believe you're supposed to bring guests to the roof, Miss Fuller. Is she an exception? What would Kenneth say?"

"I don't really give a shit what Kenneth thinks," Lourdes says sweetly, reaching to run her fingers over his arm. "Besides, Jerome, he's not the boss of her." Her smile fades. "Or me."

Jerome lowers his boot from the crate. "He'd beg to differ. But you know I have a soft spot for you." He waves us past. "Have fun, darlin'," he tells me.

"Thanks." My questions are starting to multiply, but Lourdes walks on and I don't want to get left behind. I jog to catch up with her.

We stop in front of a group of five or six people. The waitress from the restaurant who gave me ham, the valet who flirted with me when I first arrived, even the quiet girl from housekeeping, among others, are here.

"There's our girl," the valet announces, smiling at Lourdes. "Nice to see you again. We've—"

"Yeah, yeah, you've missed me." Lourdes brushes away the sentimentality, humble but endearing. The group watches her with adoration. A hint of sympathy. Then their attention shifts, and they lean forward, waiting for me to speak. I'm suddenly speechless.

"This is Audrey Casella," Lourdes says for me. "Her brother's the hot blond one." The girls and a thin guy sipping from a martini glass all smile and nod to each other. I want to roll my eyes, tired of people always noticing Daniel for his looks.

"He's also a nice guy," I add. They glance around and laugh like I've told a joke I don't know the punch line to. "No, really," I say quieter, turning to Lourdes.

"I'm sure he is," she says. "But we don't really judge people based on how nice they are. The nice ones usually go to the party downstairs." The valet reaches to touch Lourdes's thigh to get her attention, and when she looks down to where he's sitting, he hands her up a bottle. "Thank you, Joshua," she says, then holds up the drink in cheers. "To our new guests," she announces. "May they extend their stay and keep us company."

"Cheers to that," Joshua says with a sly grin before taking a drink. The others murmur their toasts, and then Tanya moves aside for me and Lourdes to sit down. I take an extra sip, trying to calm my nerves. I don't know any of these people—and I'm intimidated, especially when they seem to know everything about each other.

"So tell me, Joshua," Lourdes says, stretching her leg to lay her foot across his lap. He immediately puts his hand on her ankle, stroking his thumb over the skin. "How long have you and Catherine been rekindled? I had to hear about it from the dishwasher." Joshua's fingers still, and my heart sinks.

"Rumors," Joshua says, moving Lourdes's leg off of him. "I know better than to deal with her. Not since the last time she stabbed me."

"Catherine stabbed you?" I demand, my worry for my brother spiking. The group looks over at me, and I earn a few stares from across the roof.

"Shh . . . ," Lourdes tells me. "We're not supposed to gossip about the guests. And Joshua's fine. He's making it sound more dramatic than it really was."

"Yes," Joshua says sarcastically. "I tend to exaggerate when women stick knives into my belly."

"What's funny about that statement," Tanya calls out, "is that 'women' is plural." They all start to laugh, but I'm wondering if my brother is in danger. I want to ask, but at the same time I can't tell if they're joking or not. And I'm not sure how they'll react if Daniel is hooking up with someone's girlfriend. I'll get the details from Lourdes when the others aren't around.

Lourdes swears from next to me, and I turn to follow

her line of sight. Elias, dressed in a pressed black suit, is walking across the roof terrace and heading straight for us. I realize I'm grinning like an idiot, and I try to play it cool before anyone notices.

"For Christ's sake," Tanya says, leaning back against the wall. "This place is going to hell tonight."

"Oh, relax," Lourdes tells her. "It's not like it's his first time up here."

"This can only end badly," Tanya adds. I glance back at her, wondering what exactly she means. Do we have the same idea of what ending badly is? If so, I'm screwed.

"Eli," Lourdes calls. "Twice in one day. This has been quite a homecoming."

Elias reaches our part of the roof, and my momentary doubt is overshadowed. The soft light casts him in a silhouette—tall and angular. His shoes scuff to a stop and his face comes into view, painfully handsome. He smiles warmly, the kind of smile that deserves one in return.

"Just happy to have you back," he says to Lourdes, sitting on the edge of another metal cylinder. "And you know I'd turn up more, but Kenneth can be a tyrant sometimes."

"A true villain," Lourdes adds. She holds Elias's stare until they both break the moment by laughing. Elias shifts toward me.

"I was hoping I'd catch you at dinner," he says quietly. "Caught up with your brother outside the restaurant instead. He wasn't pleasant."

"I can imagine." I sit back, more at ease in the group now that Elias has arrived. He exudes calm, comfort. He's an old friend I haven't gotten to know yet. "And why were you looking for me?" I ask him, leaning closer. "Don't you have a boring party to get to?"

"I do," he concedes. "But I'd much rather follow you around all night." His eyes shimmer, passionate and wild. The pull between us is magnetic, and it's hard not to imagine crashing my lips against his. Around us the group pantomimes conversation, pretending they're not listening. Elias moves closer, and my gaze is drawn to his mouth. "I'll come find you after the party," he says.

"You could just skip it," I suggest. Joshua chuckles from behind me, and Elias looks up, silencing him. "What's so important about those parties?" I ask. "Why do you have to go? And don't tell me it's because of Kenneth. He's the concierge."

Elias folds his hands in his lap, and I watch as he works his jaw, the sharp lines, the tightening muscles. He's laughed off every other mention of Kenneth, but now I see his true resentment. I wonder if it has to do with Lourdes's suspension, or if it goes deeper than that. A hush falls over the moment.

"There are rules," Tanya says when no one else speaks up. "Like any job, if we don't follow them, we're punished. Although I haven't been working here as long as these guys, I know to keep my mouth shut. And if you want to

enjoy your stay, enjoy the sights"—she glances at Elias—
"you don't piss off the concierge."

Her threat isn't leveled at me; I turn to Elias. "Would he
kick you out of the hotel?" I ask. "Is that even a bad thing?"

"Elias's family helped build this place," Joshua answers
for him. The two exchange a heavy look, tense with history. It occurs to me that the history might have something
to do with Catherine. When she asked Elias to dance last
night at the party, he refused but then mentioned Joshua.
I wouldn't be at all surprised if she had created some weird
hotel love triangle. "Elias is never going to leave," Joshua
continues. "Hell, the party is *for* him."

Stunned, I start to ask if that's true, but Lourdes is ada-
mantly shaking her head. "Don't even go there, Joshua," she
says like he's a petulant child. "Eli can't help that he was born
with a silver spoon." She flashes him a playful smile, and Elias
chuckles, his tension fading. "Besides, we know exactly who
these parties are for—Kenneth's enormous ego."

"House rules," Tanya calls out, and the group repeats
it back and then takes a drink. Elias nods, since he doesn't
have a bottle, and although I'm not exactly sure what the
"house rules" are, I sip from my beer.

"Now," Lourdes says, poking Elias with the toe of
her shoe. "You should probably get downstairs before
Catherine comes looking for you. I don't think any of us
want to deal with her mood swings."

Catherine, again they toss out her name. But this time

her clear link with Elias pinches with the beginning of jealousy. So much for mastering that particular emotion. I'm definitely going to ask about her—for both mine and Daniel's sake. I don't know these people. Don't know their pasts, their relationships. I'd rather not stumble into some unseen drama, especially when I have plenty of my own.

Elias levels his gaze at Lourdes. "Take it easy on her," he says, motioning to me, and Lourdes grins her response. Elias stands and brushes off the back of his black pants. I give him a once-over, admiring his suit, his class. Now that he's about to leave, my resolve to avoid confrontation wanes.

"Find me after," I say, agreeing to his earlier suggestion. I'm only slightly embarrassed when I hear one of the others laugh, because when Elias's eyes meet mine, I'm overcome with a sense of comfort, a sense of purpose. I want to spend more time with him. I want him.

Elias's mouth spreads into a broad smile. "I will definitely find you," he says, sounding relieved. He then crosses the rooftop, his shoes clapping on the cement.

My stomach flutters with the sort of nervous energy you get just before an impending kiss. That pull, the quickening heartbeat. The tension. It's been so long since I've wanted to be kissed. I nearly forgot what it felt like. I nearly forgot how to feel.

# CHAPTER 6

After Elias leaves the rooftop, Lourdes leans in to me, the smell of my mother's detergent clinging to her, making me feel as if we've been friends for years. "He likes you," she teases. "Eli is achingly sweet on you."

I bite down on my lip to keep my smile from splitting ear to ear. It could be the alcohol, but I'm dizzy with this rekindled emotion. The flirtation is invigorating.

"It's about time," Joshua says. "And hey, if you break his heart, you can always date me." He tips back his drink to get the last drop. "I like the bad ones."

Although Joshua's attractive, he's also kind of slimy. "Not interested," I reply, making him laugh. He shrugs and tells me it's my loss.

Music continues to play from an unseen radio, and I turn to check out the others on the roof. I recognize a few of them from around the hotel, but it's hard to tell who they are now that they're out of uniform. The door to the stairwell opens and two men walk onto the roof. They immediately stand out—long hair, black T-shirts. Neither talks as they move past the staff and pause at the ledge. The taller of the men removes a pack of cigarettes and shakes two out. The men smoke, chatting as they look over the grounds of the Ruby. I can't quite place what's different about them, but when I turn around, Lourdes is staring at me. She pulls her brows together like she's confused. I look back to the men, but they've already gone inside.

"Do you know the story of the Ruby?" Lourdes asks in a hushed voice. Pink rises high on her cheeks, excitement making her eyes flash mischievously. The other staff members lean in like this is their favorite part. "They say this place is haunted," Lourdes says.

"That's what I heard," I say, intrigued by the eager looks of the others. I've never been a fan of scary stories — life is scary enough — but in a hotel this old there has to be some fascinating history. "What happened here?" I ask.

The housekeeper beams and the others get comfortable. I'd think it odd, but without cell reception or Wi-Fi for distraction, listening to campfire tales might actually be kind of fun. "The Hotel Ruby was built in 1936," Lourdes starts, smiling at the others. "It was a playground for the rich and famous. A stationary *Titanic*. And just as tragic."

The group laughs, but I glance back over my shoulder, feeling more unsettled by the second. Where did those smoking men go? How did they disappear so quickly?

"This place was a legend," Lourdes says. "When it was built, it was said to have the most majestic ballroom in the West. People flocked from all over: senators, actresses, tycoons. Elias's family"—she smiles at his name—"was among the stockholders who pulled together to build the hotel in the first place. In fact, they were being honored in the ballroom the night of the fire."

"Fire," I repeat. "Did they die?"

"Yes. During the first anniversary party the ballroom caught fire," Lourdes says. "Sixty-seven guests in all. No one would open the doors for fear the entire hotel would burn down. So they locked them in."

The crowd quiets around us on the roof, and a sense of melancholy thickens the air. I swear, it's like I feel the Ruby itself sigh. "That's awful," I say, a little breathlessly. Chills crawl up my arms, and I dart my gaze around at the group. They're transfixed, waiting for Lourdes to finish the story.

"The owners quickly rebuilt—same details, almost like it never happened. The building was sold, and then sold again. There is one constant, though: the party. In honor of those who perished, the Hotel Ruby holds a party every night in that ballroom. Guests come from all over the world to spend an evening with the ghosts there." Lourdes whispers the last part and then laughs when she sees that she's actually freaking me out. "It's why Kenneth makes sure everything is perfect," she says, shaking her head. "Otherwise he'll be out on his ass."

"The Ruby is a tourist trap," Joshua calls. "Certain guests are required to attend the parties, to keep up appearances. Mingle and mix for the time of their lives. At the

Ruby"—he smiles bitterly—"where you can stay tonight. Or stay forever."

I didn't get an invite to the party, even though both Daniel and my father did. I don't mention it, though. It's embarrassing. Am I not important enough? Was Daniel right—did I piss someone off? "So do you think this place is really haunted?" I ask.

Joshua opens up the cooler and pulls out another bottle, twisting off the top and then handing it to Lourdes. She thanks him before answering me. "Nearly seventy people were burned alive in the ballroom that night, Audrey. I'd imagine some were pretty traumatized. But don't worry"— she takes a sip—"they're just ghosts."

"House rules," Tanya sings out. Again they respond and then toast. I look at Lourdes and she smiles around the lip of her bottle.

"No talk of work in the off-hours," she explains. "No talk of Kenneth, no talk of our lives outside of the Ruby. Those are our house rules. It makes the job bearable." She reaches into the cooler and pulls me out a drink. Normally, I wouldn't have a second one, but I'm having fun. I like the house rules. I don't want to talk—think—about my life before or after the Ruby.

The music changes and the mood shifts. At first I don't recognize the song, but the group starts catcalling like they've been waiting for it all night. The tune is cheesy, but at the same time I understand why they like it.

"Who even sings this?" I ask. I remember my mother cranking up the song once or twice in the car when it came on the classic-rock station, but I have no idea who the artist is.

"Who the hell knows anymore," Joshua says like it's not important. "It's totally eighties, and to Tanya, that's totally awesome." He smiles at her, but she's already on her feet, swaying to the music.

The chorus begins, and Tanya starts singing, softly at first. I look around at the others, not sure how to react, and they start cheering—telling her to go for it. Then suddenly Tanya clutches her shirt and stretches her other hand toward us, belting out the lyrics.

We all start laughing, and Tanya goes on, rounding the circle of people to offer each of us a partial serenade. She's committed, singing the ballad like it's meant to be sung. At one point she fists her hair and drops to her knees. It's freaking magical.

Eventually the song drifts off into a softer voice, and Tanya, out of breath, climbs to her feet. She bows, looking triumphant. The crowd erupts in cheers, and Joshua puts his fingers between his lips and whistles.

"It never gets old," one girl says sincerely.

"Thank you," Tanya says, and collapses next to Lourdes. "I just love that song."

"I prefer Billie Holiday," Joshua says, grabbing a new drink. "Or, you know, someone with talent."

"Music snob," Tanya says. She leans over and pecks him on the lips, and he licks his lips in response. I'm suddenly and completely confused. Are they the couple? I lift my bottle to take another sip, but find I've finished my drink. Have I been here that long?

"Do you need another?" Lourdes asks when I set down my bottle with a *clink*.

"I'm good," I say. The song changes again, and it's the same one I heard in the ballroom at the party. Same one I heard in the night. Again I can't quite place it. I close my eyes and try to block out everything else, but I can't understand the lyrics. The melody sounds too slow.

"Hey," Lourdes says, drawing me out of my daze. When I look at her, she's electric, pulsing with energy. "Want to see some ghosts?" she whispers.

I'm suddenly and completely sure that I don't, not when it feels like fingers are crawling up my spine. But Joshua overhears, and he's already grinning madly. "I don't know," I say, not wanting to sound like a total chickenshit.

"Come on, Audrey," Joshua says. "You're only here for a few days. Make the most of it. This is the best part." A few others have caught on to the conversation and are already buzzing with excitement. Even though I don't believe in ghosts, not really, the Ruby might just be able to convince me. I don't want to be convinced. I like being a skeptic.

"She's scared," Tanya laughs out. "You can't seriously be scared."

My cheeks warm with embarrassment, peer pressure at its best, and I glance back to Lourdes. She raises her eyebrows to ask if I'm in. The eerie feeling has subsided, and the excited expressions surrounding me have piqued my curiosity.

"Do you ever really see ghosts?" I ask the housekeeper quietly. Lourdes's red lips pull into a wide grin.

"All the time."

I glance around the rooftop to the other staff members beyond our group. They're continuing on in their conversations, their laughter, oblivious to this plan to —

"It's called Wake the Dead," Lourdes says. "And we only play when someone new hangs out with us. Really," she says teasingly, "it's for you. So you can't say no."

"I can," I correct her. "But I won't this time. As long as you promise to save me if I get possessed or something."

"Doesn't work that way." She gives her head a quick shake, and Joshua reaches out his hand to help Lourdes up. Tanya and two others grab their things to join us.

My stomach coils with dread, like it does with the slow ticking of a climbing roller coaster. The few drinks I've had set me spinning momentarily when I stand, but then I'm fine, and following behind Lourdes and Joshua, who has the cooler. On the way across the roof Lourdes pauses at the guy in the army jacket, leaning in close to whisper into his ear. He pulls back to smile at her longingly. She walks on, and the guy offers me a nod, telling me to have fun, as if the roller coaster is about to drop. At the door I glance back over the roof and then at Lourdes, who smiles, and takes my hand to pull me along.

Rather than taking the regular elevator, Joshua leads us through a series of corridors to an elevator at the back of the hotel. There's a sliding metal gate in front of the door, and a dial for the floors that looks like a golden clock hangs above us. The clanging metal is loud as Joshua slides the gate over and ushers us inside. He slams it shut, and I press myself against the back of the elevator, afraid it's too old to operate. The others don't look at all worried.

"Where are we?" I whisper, grasping the golden railing as the elevator shakes to life.

"This is the staff elevator," Lourdes says, running her fingers along the burgundy textured wallpaper affection-ately. "Most people don't even know it's here. It's original to the Ruby."

"It's lovely," I say, although I'm worried this death box won't get us downstairs before it falls apart completely. The ice in the cooler rattles as we struggle along, and I officially meet the two other staff members—Casey, the shy girl from housekeeping, and Warren, who seems nice but wears a perpetual smirk, like he's in on a joke we're not. The six of us are quiet until the elevator shudders to a stop, and I stagger sideways, bumping my shoulder into the wall. Joshua rips open the gate, and the others quickly walk out. I follow them, glancing up at the dial to check which floor we're on. The dial has stopped in the empty space between the lobby and the basement.

This isn't the basement, at least not that I can tell. It's definitely not where Elias took me earlier. I wonder then what time it is, and how much longer it will be until I see him again. There are no clocks, and I left my phone in my room.

Joshua points ahead to a gray metal door and then pulls a key from his pocket, looking back to smile at us. Outside there is a concrete slab patio, green Dumpsters off to the right, the smell of trash blending with the smell of flowers floating over from the garden around on the other side of the wall. The group doesn't stop here, though. Instead Tanya walks to a plastic bench and lifts the lid. She removes flashlights and starts handing them out. By the time she gets to me, all that's left is a small utility flashlight, as opposed to the handled floodlights the others carry.

Once we move beyond the concrete slab toward an area with trees, the air has cooled. We start across the grass, and the night becomes impossibly dark, pure blackness beyond the edge of the garden. Lourdes and the others are giggling, the beams from their flashlights dancing along the trees and grass. I can't remember what the world looked like beyond the wall of the Hotel Ruby. It didn't seem this dark when we arrived here.

"Wait up," I say, quickening my step. My flashlight isn't bright enough to offer me comfort, not when the others dissolve into small circles of light in the darkness. I sidle up next to Lourdes and take her arm. She looks sideways at me, her face half in shadow.

"Who should we meet first?" she asks. "We haven't been out here in months, maybe longer. But I bet we can find Aras—he's an old spirit. Older than the Hotel Ruby, I think."

I gulp, uncertain if she's kidding and then annoyed at myself for falling for this. I roll my eyes and then tug on her arm to stop. "Let's go back," I say. "It's colder out here."

"Just wait," Lourdes murmurs, pulling ahead and ignoring my plea to return. The air has gone quiet, with the exception of Joshua, who I can hear laughing somewhere in the distance. The sound of it is comforting, grounding me in reality.

"We're almost there," Lourdes says, aiming her light at a small, worn path winding through some overgrown bushes. I wrap my arms around myself, the temperature continuing to drop the farther on we walk. It's only minutes, but then the light slides across an empty space, falling on a large object. I stagger to a stop, unsure of what I'm seeing at first.

Lourdes bursts ahead, jogging forward just as Joshua and the others come through from another path, their lights trained on the same object.

It's a fountain, or at least it used to be. Now it's just a stone statue, ivy and moss crawling up the sides and filling the basin to distort the figure. Lourdes and the others go over to set their flashlights in the second tier of the stone, illuminating the area before sitting on the surrounding bench. Joshua already has the cooler open, handing out drinks, but I take a second to look around. The Ruby looms large behind us, although none of the light from its windows travels to where we are.

We may only be just outside the garden area, but it's a world away. The overgrown brush hides us completely from view, and in this small clearing, nature has created our own little playground.

"Audrey," Joshua calls, holding out a drink to me. I smile and meet him at the fountain to take it. The others watch me, and when I take a sip, they seem to relax, saying it's been too long since they've been here.

"What is this place?" I ask, sitting next to Lourdes. The stone is cold through my jeans, and I shiver at the touch. Tanya moves to sit on Joshua's lap, her arm draped over his shoulders. Casey and Warren lounge back against the mossy fountain. Warren pulls a small, clear bottle out of his coat pocket and pours it into his glass, then hands the rest of the bottle over to Casey to swig from.

"The memorial," Lourdes says. She sets down her drink and then turns and grabs one of the flashlights. She begins to pull back the ivy and brush moss from a section in the middle of the second tier of the fountain. "See?" She steadies the light on a small patina plaque.

IN HONOR OF THE VICTIMS OF THE 1937 FIRE—MAY YOUR WANDERING SOULS FIND PEACE.

"What the hell does that mean?" I ask, meeting Lourdes's eyes. "Did they expect them to haunt the place? That's a pretty creepy tribute."

She laughs and returns the flashlight before snatching up her drink. "They didn't put this memorial up until five years later, five or ten," she says, like the difference doesn't matter. "They'd been getting complaints from guests who had all manner of troubles. Broken glasses, missing objects, cold touches on their skin. People stopped wanting to stay here, so the owners put up this memorial in a place where regular guests wouldn't find it, but where the ghosts could. They thought maybe they just wanted some recognition."

Joshua laughs and takes a long drink. "A dilapidated fountain would certainly make me stop haunting," he says. "Much more honorable than, say, a funeral."

I set my drink aside, the mention of a funeral still too fresh to let it slide over me. Sickness starts to twist inside my gut. "What do you mean?" I ask. "Were there no funerals?"

"Not for everyone," Lourdes says. "Some people didn't

have family, no one to notify. Legend says their bodies, or what was left of them, got tossed back here somewhere. They could have built this fountain right over them. Doubt that would offer them much peace."

"They need an exorcism," Tanya says from Joshua's lap. "If they want to get rid of the ghosts, they need to send them on."

The others scoff at her, sounding offended that she even mentioned it.

"What?" she asks, smiling. "Wouldn't you rather watch some weak old men in robes toss holy water on the place? I think it'd be hilarious."

"I wouldn't," Lourdes says, turning back to me. "I like the place just the way it is—ghosts and all." She grins and then holds out her bottle to toast me. "Besides," she adds, tossing a look back at Tanya, "we'd be out of a job if they got rid of the ghosts."

"It's true," Joshua says, shaking his head. I'm starting to suspect they're all a little drunk, and in that moment I realize I'm a little drunk too. "I'm still waiting for one of those ghosts to happen into my room at night," Joshua mumbles. "I don't discriminate between the living and the dead."

"You're disgusting," Tanya says. She must not mean it, though, because she leans in and kisses him. Next to me, Lourdes sighs and rests her back against the fountain.

"So who should we call?" she asks, rolling her head to

face me. "Last time Eli had us summon a little old lady, but she never showed."

"Elias was here?" I ask, surprised. Lourdes bites down on her lip and then gives me a teasing smile. I may have sounded a little overeager at the mention of his name.

"When Tanya became a staff member, he came out to celebrate with us," Lourdes says. "Really, I think he was trying to avoid Catherine. She's a psy—"

"Psychopath?" I offer.

"Exactly. Anyway, we came down here and tried to wake the dead. Nothing happened, though, except Tanya ended up falling in the fountain and busting open her lip. That was a fun explanation when we went back inside."

I look up to find the Ruby, a few lights on in the upper rooms. I wonder what Elias is doing right now—and if he's doing it with Catherine. Disappointment (or is it jealousy?) starts to darken my spirits. But then I remember all the times I wished for Ryan to cheat on me, just so I'd have a reason to break up with him. Jealousy is an interesting change.

"I think we should call on Lennox," Lourdes says definitively. "He was the desk clerk on the night of the fire. They say he actually tried to open the doors to let people out, but the other guests held him back. He ended up getting trampled." Her expression sags. "That's so sad, isn't it?" She glances at me, the perfect arches of her eyebrows pulled in. "He was trying to help."

"It's disturbing," I whisper, feeling all at once the mood has shifted. A prickling of cold air, a cold touch, starts to crawl up my arm. I swallow hard.

Lourdes closes her eyes and tips her head back. "Lennox," she calls. "Lennox, we're here to wake you. Come out, come out, wherever you are."

I don't want Lennox to come out. Not at all. I sip nervously from my drink and dart my gaze in every direction, waiting for a white apparition to float in, scaring the shit out of me. The others quiet, but I wish they wouldn't. I want them to laugh, acknowledge everything is normal and that waking up ghosts isn't an actual thing. Not even at a memorial. I take another drink, and then my bottle is empty. I set it aside in the grass and look over at the others, startled when I find them watching me.

"Do you hear him?" Lourdes asks, her eyes glassy and wide. My entire body has started to shiver, my lips have gone numb. I'm about to tell her I want, no, I *need* to leave, when there's a rustling in the bushes.

I snap my head in that direction and jump up from where I was sitting at the fountain. My heart rate explodes, pure panic rushing in. Before I can even scream, a figure appears and I think I might faint. I smother my mouth and fall back a step, the world starting to spin.

But as the apparition comes into focus, the others start to laugh. The shaved head, the green jacket. It's Jerome from the roof, holding four bottles in each hand. He looks directly at me, smiling broadly. "Did they get ya?" he asks.

I can barely catch my breath, still shaking too hard to talk. I look at Lourdes and she stands, throwing her arm over my shoulders. "I'm sorry, Audrey," she says through her laughs. "We did the same thing to Tanya when she came here. Scared her senseless."

Tanya nods emphatically. "Had nightmares for a week," she says. "This one"—she nods at Joshua—"decided it'd be even funnier if they all turned off the flashlights first. I fell in the damn fountain."

"Blood everywhere," Joshua says, making wide circles with his arms. He notices Tanya glaring at him. "It was sad," he adds unconvincingly. Tanya swats his shoulder and stands from his lap, going over to sit with Casey and Warren instead. She's not mad, though; she's laughing at herself with the others.

"Sorry, darlin'," Jerome says. "Lourdes thought you'd appreciate a little initiation." He leans in to kiss her cheek, attraction plain on his face. Lourdes winks at him and takes one of the drinks he's holding. Jerome walks over to talk with the others, and my fear is fading into an adrenaline rush.

"You're not mad, are you?" Lourdes asks tentatively. She lowers her arm and stands back a step to look me over. "I didn't mean to—"

"I'm not mad," I say. "Honest." Now that I know a real ghost isn't traipsing in to take over my body, I'm having fun again. I grab another drink, and the others burst into laughter every time they look at me, and eventually none of us can keep a straight face.

"Was there really even a Lennox?" I demand, turning to Lourdes.

"No," she says, shaking her head. "I made him up." She pauses, looking at the Ruby and taking a swig from her drink. "No one tried to help them out of the ballroom that night. They just let them all burn."

# CHAPTER 7

I'm not sure how long we're outside, but Tanya and Warren have sneaked off into the trees, while Casey and Joshua are laughing and whispering on the other side of the fountain. Although Lourdes hasn't abandoned me, she and Jerome keep exchanging glances that I'm not part of. She reminds me of Daniel, the way everyone's drawn to her. Only she handles the attention with humility rather than pride.

I wonder what time it is. I never know what time it is anymore.

My drink is empty, and I make the conscious decision not to have any more tonight. As it is, I'm not sure how I'll feel when Elias is done with his party. An ache starts in my arm, deep in the bone. It's the same pain I had before bed. I roll my shoulder.

"You okay?" Lourdes asks, turning to me. From the bushes Tanya and Warren stumble back in, midlaugh.

"My arm hurts," I tell Lourdes like it's no big deal. "I'm fine, though. Probably just pulled a muscle."

Lourdes hands Jerome her drink and climbs to her feet. Joshua leans forward, checking to see what's going on. "Come on," Lourdes says to me. "It's getting late." She turns to look at where Joshua and Casey have gotten close. "And weird." Joshua chuckles. "If your arm hurts," Lourdes continues, "I have some muscle relaxers in my room that should do the trick."

"That shit doesn't work," Tanya says, dropping down next to Jerome. Her face is flush, even in the meager shine of the flashlights.

"It'll work for her," Lourdes responds quietly. "She's not as desensitized as the rest of us."

"Lourdes collects the leftovers," Joshua explains to me. "Clothes, magazines, *pills*—she's her own mini-mart. It's how we stay current around here."

"You'll always be a cad, Joshua," Tanya says. "No amount of culture will change that." She glares at Casey, and the girl shrinks away, obviously intimidated. Warren shoots Tanya a pointed look, and sits next to Casey.

Joshua puts his hand over his heart. "I'm wounded," he tells Tanya mockingly. "Kiss it and make it better." He flashes a devilish grin, but Lourdes takes my arm to help me up before I see if Tanya accepted his offer.

I don't really want a muscle relaxer. I've tried them, tried everything in the medicine cabinet after my mother died. Muscle relaxers just put me to sleep. And I don't want to sleep. I want to find Elias, and kiss him. I put my fingers over my lips, holding back the wild laugh that wants to escape. This is so not like me. Or . . . maybe it is. I'll go

105

with Lourdes to get the medication, but after that I'm going straight to the front desk. And I'm asking for my invitation to the ballroom party.

The elevator whines as it lowers us deeper into the hotel. Lourdes is standing near the gate, and now that we're alone, I can finally find out exactly what my brother has gotten himself into with his latest bad decision. "Can I ask you something?"

Lourdes looks over her shoulder at me, biting down on her lip like she's trying to hold back a smile. "Of course."

"What's the deal with Catherine?" I try to keep the annoyance out of my voice.

"I was wondering when you were going to ask about her," she says, resting her shoulder against the wall. "I noticed you flinched every time her name was mentioned."

"I did?" I'm mortified that I'm so easy to read.

"You don't have to worry about Eli," she says simply. "They've been over for a long time." Despite her reassurance, the comment has the opposite effect. I suspected they'd had a relationship, but I kind of liked avoiding thinking about it. My stomach sinks, and I wonder what Lourdes's idea of "a long time" is.

"And Joshua?" I ask, worried for Daniel. "Is she dating him now?"

"Catherine never dates anybody," Lourdes says. "At least not long-term. Not since Eli."

Oh, this keeps getting better and better. Rather than ask Lourdes for the details, I decide to wait to ask Elias himself. No sense dragging Lourdes into this and furthering my humiliation. If I had any sense at all, I'd walk away from this summer-camp romance with Elias. But having any emotion beyond grief is too enticing. I checked my logic at the door of the Ruby. The elevator shudders to a stop.

"My brother's been hooking up with Catherine," I say simply. "I'm guessing he should stop that?"

"Definitely." Lourdes pulls the gate to the side with a *clang*. I don't ask anything else about Catherine because the fact that my brother is kissing the ex-girlfriend of the guy I'm almost kissing is gross enough for me to tell Daniel to knock it off.

"Sorry to bring you here again," Lourdes says. "I've recently been relocated to the basement." Beyond her the hallway is dimly lit, depressing and lonely.

"Why were you moved? Was it part of your suspension?" I ask. I can't believe she has to live in the basement. It's cold and there aren't even any windows.

"Pretty much. I suck at following the house rules," she says with a smile. Lourdes walks out of the elevator, and I have to jog to keep pace. The gray hallway ends, splitting off in two directions. She takes a right, and the tiles are replaced by dark carpet, red walls.

"So what do you think of the Ruby so far?" Lourdes asks, and stops to motion around us. "It's beautiful, right?"

107

"Sure," I say. "And your creepy story aside, I think it's kind of fun. My dad seems better. Dinner ended with me in tears, but that's not exactly news." I slow as a sense of guilt wraps around me. Can I really blame my dad for his comment about my reckless behavior? Isn't it my fault that we're here in the first place?

Lourdes turns, her eyebrows pulled together. I wave off her concern. "It's fine," I say. "He hasn't really been himself the last couple of months. I don't think any of us have."

"What happened?" She shifts uncomfortably. "If you don't mind me asking."

"My mother died three months ago." The words come out automatically and I hate them. I hate how easy they've become to say. "My father couldn't handle the grief—none of us could." Lourdes makes a sympathetic sound and puts her hand on my arm. Her fingers are cold; the touch reminds me of my mother. Sets me at ease.

"This hotel is a nice vacation from life," Lourdes says quietly. "It can be great—you'll see." She starts down the hallway again. "Just keep off Kenneth's radar," she adds. "Make sure your brother does too. He likes to keep things in order. And if they're not . . ." She trails off, and I'm confused how a concierge can have so much power over an entire establishment.

"You can report him if he's harassing you," I say, thinking of stories where employees banded together to sue big corporations. "You can report him to management—"

"He is the management," Lourdes says, spinning to face me. "Kenneth is the authority at the Ruby, and he can do as he wishes. I've tried everything possible, Audrey. I'm only telling you this now because I like you. And if you stay here, I want you to be prepared."

"Prepared?" I ask. My arm continues to hurt, and I rub at it absently, wondering if the concierge means to hurt me. "Wait," I say. "If I stay? Like . . . beyond my reservation? As a job? I don't think my father would go for it either way. He has other plans for my summer." My heart sinks as I think about my grandmother's attic.

Lourdes's shoulders sag, as if she can read my thoughts. "See," she says, "this is why we never talk about life outside the hotel. Good or bad, it affects us." She turns to point down the hallway toward a room. "That's me," she says. "I'll grab the bottle and be right out."

I nod, rubbing my forearm. Lourdes disappears inside the room, and I lean against the wall, alone. Above me there is a *clunk*, something heavy hitting the floor, and I look up. In the silence that follows, my thoughts turn to my brother.

I haven't seen Daniel in a while. He must be around because Catherine would be at the party. Unless he decided to go with her. Would Daniel go without telling me?

Lourdes's door opens and she walks out, a pill bottle in one hand and a glass of water in the other. As she approaches, I shrug apologetically.

"To be honest," I say, "I don't think I need a muscle relaxer."

"You look miserable," she responds. "You don't have to put on a brave face for me. I know you're tough." She rattles the bottle to entice me.

I hold up my uninjured arm, and Lourdes shakes a pill onto my palm. It's tiny, and I examine it for a moment, trying to figure out exactly what it is.

"Flexeril," she says, reading the label. "But really, it's a mental thing. If you think it's helping, then it will. Here"—she hands me the entire bottle—"in case you need another dose."

I examine the bottle myself, seeing it's over five years old. Still, I'm not sure how much fun I'll be later if this pain gets worse. I shove the bottle into my pocket. "Well," I say. "Hope this doesn't kill me." I toss the pill into my mouth, and Lourdes hands me the water to wash it down. The minute I pull the glass from my mouth, I feel slightly better. A placebo effect.

"Thank you," I say, giving her back the glass. She sets it on the floor, off to the side, and then walks with me back down the hall. "I'll put you in the regular elevator this time," she says with a smile. "I know you're not a fan of the other one." She pushes the button when we get there, and while we wait, she laughs suddenly and leans against the wall.

"God," she says. "I've had too much to drink. You must think I'm a crazy person, talking about ghosts and pills.

Please disregard everything I've said tonight. Wait," she says, holding up her finger. "There was one other thing—is Daniel staying on the thirteenth floor with you?"

"No. Both he and my dad are on the sixth. Why?"

"Just curious," she says. When I continue to stare at her questioningly, she lifts one shoulder. "I'm in housekeeping. I wanted to know where to send the best stuff. You ruined the surprise."

"Hope I still get some chocolates." The elevator doors open and I step inside. Lourdes touches her forehead like maybe she really did have too much to drink.

"I have an early day tomorrow," she says. "But I'm glad you came out with me tonight. You forgive me for scaring you, right?" She scrunches up her nose, not sure of the answer.

"Totally," I say sincerely. "It was fun. Even though I hate being scared."

"We only did it because we like you." She smiles, looking relieved. "Promise. And if you stay awake for Eli, the party in the ballroom can go on until three or four. I doubt he'll leave before then. He'll find you when he's done socializing."

The doors start to close, but I put out my hand to stop them. "Does Elias like the parties?" I ask Lourdes. "He doesn't seem to."

"Maybe once upon a time," she says. "But nothing lasts forever. Except the Ruby."

Lourdes turns to walk back to her room. I lower my arm and the elevator doors close, but rather than push the button for the thirteenth floor, I press for the lobby. If Elias used to enjoy the parties, what changed his mind? I can't help but think it has to do with Catherine. And again there's that spike of jealousy.

When the doors open to the lobby, it hits me how bizarre the night has been. I cross the expansive room toward the front desk, reflecting on my conversation with Lourdes. The story of the Ruby itself. The terror I felt at the fountain. A cold sensation drifts over me, and I lift my head to find Kenneth behind the desk, smiling as I approach.

"How may I help you this evening, Miss Casella?" he asks pleasantly. I look for a hint of the sinister man the staff described, but Kenneth is all business. His uniform is tidy, his eyes curious and helpful. I don't buy his bullshit, though.

"Good evening," I say, trying to sound mature. In reality the muscle relaxer has slowed me slightly. "I was wondering if you could help me." I lean my elbows on the counter, steadying myself. "How exactly does one get invited to the party in the ballroom?" I ask. "Is there a way I can go?"

Kenneth doesn't flinch, only stands there motionless, waiting to see if I'll go on. When I don't, he tilts his head apologetically. "I'm sorry," he says. "The party is invite only."

"I know," I respond. "But I was wondering if I could have one of those invitations."

The concierge turns to his computer, tapping quickly on the keys. He looks at me and smiles. "I'm very sorry, Miss Casella. You're not on the list."

"But my father and brother have both gotten one." My adrenaline starts to pump, and my politeness is beginning to fade away. "We came here together."

"Very sorry," he says again, folding his small hands in front of him.

That's all he's going to say? I'm starting to feel light headed, but I don't want to leave here without some answers. Why would both my father and Daniel get an invitation and not me? "Is there someone else I can talk to?" I ask the concierge. "Who makes the list?" My voice has taken on a hint of panic at the thought of being left out of my family.

Kenneth's face tightens with concern. "You don't look well, Miss Casella," he says kindly. "Perhaps you should return to your room and get some rest." He pulls a handkerchief from his breast pocket and holds it out. I don't take it, and he winces apologetically. "You have a little . . ." He motions to the side of his forehead and then stretches the cloth out to me again. Hesitantly, I press it to the side of my head where he indicated and feel a sudden sting.

"Ow." When I pull away the handkerchief, I see a small splotch of blood on the cloth. My stomach lurches, and I press the fabric to my head once again. "What happened?" I ask, although I don't see how he would know the answer.

"You must have hit your head," he says. "Nasty little gash. Get some rest, Miss Casella. If I see your brother or your father, I'll let them know you were here looking for them."

I'm shaken by the blood, trying to remember when I could have hit my head. On the roof? At the fountain? Maybe I accidentally scratched myself while the concierge was refusing me an invite. My body suddenly sways, and I catch myself by grabbing on to the counter. I want to lie down, even as I toss a longing glance at the closed doors of the ballroom party.

Why can't I go? Without a word of thanks I keep the handkerchief to my forehead and start toward the elevator. Every step is like walking through deep sand—my legs are tired and heavy, my muscles burn with exertion. For a moment I entertain the thought that Lourdes inadvertently poisoned me, but when I get to the elevator, I'm slightly better.

The doors close, and once I'm alone, my heart calms and the ache fades. I turn toward the mirrored wall and slowly lower the handkerchief to inspect my wound. Only there is none. There is no gash, no blood. There is nothing there at all.

I fall back a step, confused and a bit scared. But I saw blood on the handkerchief—felt the sting of the cut. When I go to check the cloth, it's no longer in my hand. I spin, checking to see if I dropped it, but there is only the burgundy patterned carpet.

"What the hell?" I murmur, checking my reflection once more. I even turn around and look over my shoulder to make sure the handkerchief hasn't stuck to my shirt. It's gone.

The elevator doors suddenly open and I jump. I didn't hear the signal for the thirteenth floor. Wait, did I even push the button for my floor? My breathing quickens, and the emptiness of the elevator, the silence, sends a streak of fear through me. My throat clicks when I swallow, and I take a tentative step out of the elevator. I glance down the hall one way and then the other.

Empty. Quiet.

I sway on my feet and reach out to put my hand on the wall. The elevator leaves for another floor, and I decide that I'm being ridiculous. See—this is why I shouldn't drink. And why I shouldn't take a muscle relaxer after ingesting alcohol. What was I thinking? Oh, right. I wasn't.

Annoyed with myself, I head toward my room, my steps slow but steady. When I get to my door, I hear the faint sound of music. It's the song. The same one I can't place. I'm about to search it out when the music disappears entirely. "At least I'm not the only person on this floor," I murmur with a bit of relief, and slide my key into the door.

# CHAPTER 8

I'm jolted awake by the shrill ring of the phone. I sit up, and the room tilts one way and then the other. I'm still in my clothes, the lights on. I don't remember lying down. I vaguely remember talking to the concierge, asking for an invite, but everything goes blurry after that. The bottle of muscle relaxers is on my nightstand, and I groan at how stupid I was to take one. The phone rings again, and I move quickly to answer it.

"Hello?" I say, clearing the sleep from my eyes.

"I'm sorry," a voice says. "I didn't mean to wake you." At first I don't recognize it, but then Elias laughs. "Hello?" he asks, like I might have fallen back asleep.

I smile instinctively, that goofy sort of smile that I'm glad he can't see. "I'm here," I respond. "How was your party?"

He hums out his discontent, sounding tired—which makes me imagine him lying in bed just a few floors from where I am now. "Same party every night. But I'd rather not talk about my evening," he says. "How did you enjoy the rooftop?" His mouth must be close to the receiver; his voice is muffled and scratchy. So damn sexy.

"It was fun," I say. "Although it got a little weird toward the end."

"That sounds about right."

We're both quiet for a moment, and I wonder if he's changed his mind about meeting up. Sure, it's probably 4 a.m., but it's not like I have anywhere to be in the morning. "Elias—" I start to say, but he cuts me off.

"Are you hungry?" he asks. "We can raid the kitchen. Hang out for a while." I think I hear him smile. "See the sunrise."

"I'm starving," I say, unable to hide how thrilled I am. "But will I end up getting kicked out? It seems like every time I see you, one of us is being asked to leave."

"Not tonight. I'll sneak you around, completely unde-tected. We'll grab what we want and then go eat it in the garden. Avoid the lobby altogether." I glance toward the window, remembering how dark it was outside. Remembering the memorial.

"It's dark out there," I say.

"Then we'll eat in my room." He laughs. "And I prom-ise that's not meant to sound at all lecherous. I'll be a com-plete gentleman."

"Your room, huh?" I hope he realizes how attracted I am to him. And I hope his idea of being a gentleman includes a good-night kiss. I reach to grab my cell phone to check the time, but the screen is blank. Dead. Did I check it earlier? "What time is it?" I ask Elias.

117

"Not sure," he says. "But if you'd rather, we can do this another night." His tone softens to an apology, but there's no way I can sleep now.

"I'm not tired anymore," I say. "Actually, I wasn't tired at all. But Lourdes gave me a muscle relaxer earlier and I—"

"Wait, what?" Elias asks, sounding concerned. "Why would she do that? Are you all right?"

"Yeah, I'm . . . fine." I rotate my shoulder, testing my arm, and the pain is completely gone. Like it was never there at all. I swing my legs off the bed. I get up and straighten my clothes, heading toward the bathroom to clean up a bit. I check my reflection; my cheeks are rosy with sleep, my hair tamed and smooth. I smile. "Now," I say, hoping he hasn't changed his mind, "what floor is the kitchen on?"

Elias lives on the seventh floor, facing the gardens. The minute he holds open the door of his suite, I can see the breathtaking view out the oversize leaded windows. The trees and shrubs are silhouettes against the dark blue sky, light blue on the horizon. I think it's almost morning.

If we shut off all the lamps, we could watch the sunrise together. I glance back at Elias as he balances a plate on his glass, closing the door slowly so it won't slam shut. We have peanut butter and jelly sandwiches, glasses of milk. Who needs champagne and caviar? This is much more romantic to me.

"Your place is nicer than mine," I say, setting my dish

and glass on his dresser. I take a bite of my sandwich, nodding my appreciation at his fantastic suggestion involving food. I start to wander the suite, admiring all of the finer details. Elias sits on the sofa and immediately takes two bites of his sandwich.

"You didn't eat at the party?" I ask, trying to remember if I'd seen a buffet table the night before.

"I don't like their food." Elias takes another bite before settling back on the couch and crossing his ankle over his leg. "It all tastes stale to me."

On the corner desk is a watch, stopped at midnight. The metal is heavy, and I slip it on my wrist and clasp it. I turn to Elias and show him how it dangles and slides up to my elbow. He smiles, looking content as I sort through his things. Looking comfortable with me in his bedroom.

"How do you afford to live here?" I ask, setting down the watch before going back to finish my sandwich. "Your parents?"

"Sort of. My mother paid a lot for this room initially. But because of a family tragedy," he says, "I'm grandfathered in. They can never kick me out. Even if I don't pay."

"The fire," I say, earning a surprised look from him. Before I can explain, he nods.

"Ah, Lourdes spun her tale about the Ruby," he says. "She likes to embellish. Did she scare you at the fountain? She tries to make it more terrifying each time."

I take a bite of food, thinking it over. It wasn't exactly scary. "I thought the story was sad," I state, looking at Elias. "It's sickening what happened to those people."

"And yet life goes on," he says quietly, drinking the last of his milk like he's taking a shot of alcohol. "Now what about you, Audrey?" he asks, setting down his glass with a *clink*. "How did you end up at the Ruby?"

"What about the house rules?"

Elias tosses his head back and laughs. "Wow, you fit in amazingly well here." When he looks at me again, his dimples flash. "I hate that rule," he says. "We should break it. I won't tell anyone."

"Our secret?" I ask playfully. "Does that mean you'll tell me your secrets too?"

"If you want." He pulls the knot on his tie until it loosens, and then yanks it over his head to toss it over the arm of the sofa. Again I'm drawn in by the sight of him, casual yet still elegant.

My pulse races with desire, a little bit of fear. It's hard to catch my breath, and I walk to the window. There's a golden glow on the horizon; a new day. A fresh start.

"I came here with my father and brother," I say. Moisture has collected on the outside of the window, and I trace a heart on the cool glass. "My mother died," I say quietly. "She died three months ago, and I didn't know how to handle it, other than badly. I got in trouble and now my dad is sending us to live with our grandmother. This is just a pit stop before my shiny new life starts. A life I don't even want."

Elias is quiet long enough for me to turn back to him. His warm eyes have softened, but he doesn't lower his gaze. He looks right at me—sees me. I wait for him to say he's sorry, to offer his condolences, but he doesn't. He seems to know that that's the last thing I want to hear anymore.

"My turn," I say after the quiet stretches on. "If your family has the money for you to live at the Ruby on a permanent basis, why aren't you in college? Or working the family business?"

Elias smiles nostalgically, flashing his dimples. "I went to college for a bit," he says. "But my family needed me here. The Ruby thrives on tourism, ghost sightings and extravagance, and I'm a connection to the original anniversary tragedy. Attending parties has become my job. Could be worse, I suppose."

"You can't do that forever," I say. "And the good thing with college is that you can always go back. Hell, you can even get a degree online. That's what my brother plans to do. I mean, what's the alternative?"

"The Ruby isn't so bad," Elias says with a shrug. "Like most things, it's what you make of it."

"That's very glass-half-full of you." I shoot him a smile and slowly make my way over to where he sits on the couch. We could have met anywhere—a college campus, some coffee shop in Tempe. But I met him here, and this place suits him, fits around him rather than him to it.

"You know," I say, pausing next to the arm of the sofa. "My ex-boyfriend's cousin ran a hotel. His name was Marco and he was kind of a tool, but he said the job was great. He got discounts at other hotels, even in Hawaii. Maybe you can take this place over. The staff would probably love if Kenneth was fired."

"We all would," Elias says. He grabs a tin box of mints from the coffee table and clicks open the top. After he places one on his tongue, he holds out the box to me. I thank him and put a mint in my mouth and then drop down next to him on the couch.

I bite down on the candy, and a powdery explosion of cinnamon kills off any residual effects of the peanut butter. Elias is staring toward the window now, lost. For a wild moment I consider reaching for him and kissing him. Deep and passionate. But one thought stops me.

"Sooo . . . ," I say, drawing his attention. "You and Catherine, huh?" I wait to see how he'll react, but Elias's expression is perfectly unreadable.

"It was a long time ago."

Well, that was the most frustratingly vague response ever. I tilt my head, looking him over. "She was the girl you were talking about in the sauna," I say, thinking back on our earlier conversation.

Elias readjusts his position to lay his arm over the back of the sofa, fully facing me. "Yes," he confirms. "But Catherine and I were never a good match. Our parents wanted us to date; they had a lot of expectations. The feelings just weren't there between us—although we did hate each other quite passionately for a time. She can be possessive."

"I gathered that from last night's party. For what it's worth," I say, "I'm glad it's over between you two." Elias chuckles like that should be obvious at this point. "But it's not because I don't want to compete with a beautiful, yet vicious, blonde."

"She is quite a force," Elias concedes.

"I'm worried about my brother," I continue. "He's been spending a lot of time with her, and I don't want him to get beat up by the staff or anything."

"You should tell Daniel to be careful," Elias says. "Because if anyone's going to hurt him, it'll be Catherine. She has an ugly temper. Do you want me to talk to him?"

I laugh. "No, he'd take that as competition and probably want her more. I'll try. I doubt he'll listen to me, though— he's an idiot when it comes to girls. But if Catherine does anything to him in the next two days, I'm going to kick her ass. Just putting it out there."

Elias bites down on his lip to hold back his smile. "She should be very afraid," he says, running his gaze over my scrawny arms. He rests his head on the cushion, staring over at me.

"You look out for him," he says admiringly. "You must be very close with your family."

The comment hurts my heart. Up until three months ago the answer would have been an automatic yes. But Daniel and I have stopped talking about the important things. My father and I hardly talk at all. I'm not sure how we messed up so badly.

I blink quickly to prevent the tears from forming. "There was this one time," I say, staring past Elias, "when I was sitting on the roof outside of my bedroom. It wasn't a sunrise" — I motion to the scene outside the window — "but it was a sunset. My mother had taken Daniel out to buy new school clothes, and I didn't want to go. After they left, I climbed out my window.

"When my father came home from work, he panicked because he couldn't find me. Eventually he poked his head outside my window and saw me perched at the base of the steep slope. I was thirteen, and thought I was in love."

Elias sniffs a laugh, and I flash him an embarrassed smile.

"Turns out, so did my friend Kieran," I continue. "She kissed my boyfriend at the buses in front of everyone. I felt betrayed, humiliated. In hindsight, Aaron and I had zero in common, but at the time it was huge."

"Infidelity can wreak havoc on your life," Elias says, more seriously than necessary for a story about a girl and her first boyfriend.

"My father's initial reaction was to call both Aaron and Kieran to tell them off, but I stopped him from making things worse. And then he told me that I deserved better. That I deserved the best. He put his arm around me and said, 'Kid, you're going to get everything you want out of life. Once you get past the parts that suck.'" I stop, sniffling and shaking my head to keep back the emotions. It's been so long since I thought about my dad—my real dad. The one who loved me before Mom died. I don't always remember he existed.

"Here," Elias says, taking my hand to gently tug me forward. I rest my cheek on the collar of his shirt, breathing in the clean, crisp smell of him. Like my mother's detergent. Like home. "I understand grief better than you can imagine," he whispers, resting his chin on the top of my head. "Sometimes the beautiful memories are the saddest ones of all."

I slide my palm onto his chest and find his heart racing. It draws me from my misery, offering me validation. Excitement. Elias wraps his arms around me, and I close my eyes, absorbing the feel of him. The heat of his body. I run my hand up to his collar, playing with the top button of his shirt, listening to how his breathing changes. His arms tighten, and I shift so my lips graze his neck. His jaw. I let my sadness fall away. Let the world fall away.

"I want to know everything about you, Audrey," he whispers near my ear. "I want all of you."

My head spins, drowning out the world as I slide my cheek over Elias's, pulling back to look at him. His eyes are heavy with desire, his skin pink and alive. I thread my fingers through the back of his hair, our lips about to crash together in the most wonderful way.

Elias knots his fist in the fabric of my shirt, like he can't wait a minute longer. He leans in, but just before his lips touch mine, the phone rings from across the room. The sound is like an alarm bell, and instinctively Elias and I jump apart.

It rings a second time, longer and louder, and I have to cover my ears. Elias bolts up from the couch and crosses the room, his posture rigid. He grabs the receiver, shooting me an apologetic look. "What?" he asks into the phone. His skin pales, and he lowers his eyes. "Yes, I know."

Outside the sun has risen, barely breaking over the trees. I was too busy nearly making out to even notice. The spell has been broken now, and it suddenly *feels* like six in the morning. The cinnamon has left a chalky aftertaste, and I want a glass of water.

"I have to go," I whisper, pointing to the door. Elias shakes his head no, his mouth working like he's about to ask me to stay, but I turn away before he can.

"Yes, I understand, Kenneth," he snaps into the phone. "Yes," he says again, sounding resolved. The door clicks when I close it behind me.

The hall is empty and quiet, and I know this is the walk of shame—wearing last night's clothes as I slink back to my room. What I don't expect to find is Catherine striding off the elevator in a glamorous dress, her hair wilting pin curls. She stops dead in her heels and stares at me. Her eyes flick to Elias's door, then back to me. Her lips tighten, and for a moment I think she's going to attack me.

I mentally review everything I was ever taught about self-defense. Thumbs in the eye sockets, knock out the knee. But who am I kidding? I've never been in a fight in my life. My threat to kick Catherine's ass if she hurt my brother was complete bullshit.

"Have a nice night?" she asks instead.

I open my mouth, but I honestly don't know how to answer. To my silence Catherine responds with a laugh and turns to walk back onto the elevator. You have got to be kidding me. I'm going to have to ride the elevator with her.

Elias's room is only four doors down. I could go back there. Then again, I don't want Catherine to think she can intimidate me—even if she does. And ew, she's been sneaking around with my brother all night, I hardly think she's in a position to judge.

I exhale and then walk into the elevator and press the button for the thirteenth floor. Catherine turns to me immediately, and my nerve evaporates. I could confront her— tell her to leave my brother alone. But that would make me sound kind of crazy. I'd rather my brother be the only one who sees me like that. I fake boredom to avoid talking to her, picking the clear polish off my fingernails.

"When do you leave again?" Catherine asks, sounding wistful.

"On Friday," I say, and turn to her. Daniel was right, she does have skin like porcelain. I can't help but think about her and Elias, wondering how I measure up. "We have somewhere to be," I continue. "Daniel and I are going to live with our grandmother." I want to take back the words the minute they're out of my mouth. The vulnerability in them is painful.

Catherine gives her head a little shake. "No," she says simply. "No, you're not."

A chill climbs up my arms, clutches my throat. Her statement is more scary than sincere, and when the elevator doors open, I can't get out fast enough. The minute I'm in my hallway, I expect her to follow me, but she glances at the floor and then at me.

"Night, Audrey." She smiles and takes a step backward in the elevator, disappearing behind the closing doors.

# CHAPTER 9

I wake with a start, the night having bled into morning, into afternoon. I see the bottle of muscle relaxers on my nightstand, and I rustle the comforter sliding over to grab it. I glance at the label again and then shake my head before dropping the bottle into the trash can with a *thunk*. I'm an idiot. My cell phone is nearby, and I pick it up and pull it back into bed with me. The screen says I have no service, not even to check the time, but at least it's turning on now. Weird because I haven't even charged it.

I fall back into the pillow, and a haunting sense of loss comes over me. My fingers shake as I tap the photos icon and find the album titled "No."

To deal with my grief I took all of the photos of my mother, or ones that reminded me of her, and put them in a separate album. I couldn't bear to delete them. Instead I labeled them "No" so that I'd be able to stop myself from staring at them. From dripping tears on my screen. From breaking down in math class because I'd accidentally seen her smile—wide and genuine.

"Don't do it," I tell myself now, afraid of the flood of memories that will follow. My thumb hovers over the album, hovers over my past. "Don't see," I whisper.

I'm not sure how long I sit, frozen, before my hand starts to cramp. I drop the phone onto the bed and cover my face, my body jolting from holding back my cry. But it's a new day. As Ryan said after the funeral, "Every day's a gift, Audrey. Don't waste it."

I still, Ryan's voice whispering in my ear. It wasn't fair, the way I treated him. He deserved better than me; I think even he knew that. But he loved me, and we fight for the things we love even when they're bad for us.

"You're just going to leave?" Ryan asked, perched on the edge of my bed while I packed. He kept his head lowered, as he had since the night of the party. He'd gotten a concussion, the bruise still heavy over his brow. He was suffering headaches, blurred vision in his right eye. Doctors weren't sure when (or if) it would go back to normal. Even after all that he couldn't let me go.

"What am I supposed to do?" I asked him. "Run away? I told you, Daniel and I are going to plan something soon. I'll call you. I'll let you know I'm okay."

"And if I'm not okay?" Ryan asked. I turned from my closet and met his eyes. He looked so sad, so goddamn sad, and all I wanted was to disappear—set him free. But I was too selfish for that. I walked back over to where he sat and paused in front of him, looking down. I put my hand on his head, and he leaned in to rest his cheek against my stomach, his arms around my waist.

130

I closed my eyes and pretended I was already gone. "I love you," I lied. Because I was too weak to tell him the truth: I had stopped loving him months ago, and even if I escaped Nevada, I wouldn't be coming back for him. He would never see me again.

The memory turns my stomach and I force myself out of bed to take a hot shower, as hot as I can handle. I'm ashamed of my behavior. Sickened by the pain I must have inflicted on Ryan. But I couldn't make myself love him anymore, no matter how much I wished for it. No matter how many nights I cried over it. I was the worst thing to ever happen to him.

The shower rains down on me, and my tears are washed down the drain. When I step out from behind the curtain a while later, the cold air is refreshing. Revitalizing.

I take my time getting dressed, putting on makeup, blow-drying my hair. It's all robotic, a way to avoid thinking. But when I'm finished and look in the mirror, it might just be the prettiest I've ever looked. The Hotel Ruby doesn't have hard water like Phoenix. My hair is smooth, my skin soft and creamy. I smile before I even realize.

My keycard's on the dresser, and I grab it before going downstairs. Last night's dinner with my father was a bit of a nightmare, but today is a new day. And I don't plan on wasting any more of those.

CR ℘

The restaurant is crowded when I make my way through the tables toward my father. The room buzzes, and as I pass, I overhear a couple talking about "the ballroom" in a hushed tone. I almost stop to ask for details, but my father notices me and waves. I smile weakly, surprised that he looks downright cheery to see me.

"Hey, kid," he says, resurrecting a nickname from my childhood. "How'd you sleep last night?"

"Uh . . ." I trip into my chair, lost for a response. He's wearing a collared shirt and jacket, more business than casual. He must have gone shopping, because even at his best my father wasn't this formal. I hardly recognize him.

When I don't speak, my father leans into the table, lowering his voice. "I'm sorry about dinner last night," he says sincerely. "I've been on edge, but now I want to make it up to you and your brother. We're still a family, Audrey. That won't ever change."

I'm about to double-"uh" when a server appears at my side. It's not Tanya, but instead Warren from the rooftop. He smiles at me, small and private, as he flips over the glass in front of me and pours water. His coldness tells me our meet-up was secret, even from my dad.

"What I'm trying to say," my father continues like I'm listening, "is that I haven't always been the best father, and for that I'm sorry. I'll be better."

I'm so completely thrown by his behavior; I can't say my true feelings on the topic. He owes us a lot more than

132

an apology. But for now I force a smile. "It's okay, Dad," I tell him. "I haven't made it easy for you." He seems content with our mutual apology, but what I really want to say is, "You abandoned us. And when we leave this hotel, you plan to do it again. How is that being better?"

With a shaky hand I take up my glass of water and sip. The silence between me and my father extends into awkward, and I need to fill the space somehow.

"How was the party in the ballroom?" I ask. "People seem to be talking about it."

The chair creaks as my father sits back, his eyes shining. "The party was wonderful," he says in a quiet voice. "Things have changed, Audrey. For the first time I know we'll be all right. The three of us together. You'll see." He pauses, and a shadow of melancholy crosses his face. I can't quite place it, even though I'm sure I've seen that expression before. "I hope you'll see."

There's a thumping in my chest, an impending sickness at a thought I can't reach. I'm glad my father is optimistic, but I'm not going to buy into the idea that we'll be a happy family by sundown. I'm more cautious than that. I take a sip of water and wait for my nausea to fade. When it does, I talk again, steering us toward lighter topics, trying to shake the uncomfortableness that's sunk into my skin.

"What did you wear?" I ask. "I doubt you packed your Armani suits."

He chuckles, warming considerably. "I did leave those

behind," he jokes. "My polo shirts didn't fit the bill, so the hotel sent up a suit. This, too." He pulls on the lapel of his jacket. "They've practically given me a new wardrobe."

"That's nice," I say. "Maybe mention I could use a dress or two."

"I will. And," he confides, "I met your brother's latest obsession at the party. Cathy is . . ." He widens his eyes.

"A psychopath?" I offer, repeating Elias's description.

"I'd say intense. Sociopathic, possibly. I could be wrong." He lifts his hands in a shrug, and I find myself smiling. The weight lifts from around us for the first time since my mother died. Figures that Dad and I would bond over my brother's terrible taste in women. Speaking of my brother:

"Have you talked to Daniel today?" I ask.

"Not since last night. He left the party early. He and Cathy seemed to be having a fight."

"Daniel was at the party?" I scoff. "What the hell! He told me he wasn't going."

"Language," my father reminds me, and then raises his finger to the server to indicate we're ready to order. "Daniel didn't want to be there," he continues, partly distracted by his menu. "But I'm guessing he was dragged. Either way, it was nice to see him in a suit instead of a filthy sweatshirt. The ladies certainly seemed to appreciate it, as well."

"Overshare," I mutter, and glance at my menu. But I'm not in the mood to eat anymore. Daniel said he wasn't

134

going to the party, that liar. How is it that both Daniel and my father are invited to a party and I'm not? What sort of bizarro world is this?

Warren arrives and my father quietly orders a club sandwich. I order the crepes. I put my elbow on the table and rest my chin on the heel of my palm, looking over at my dad. I still can't believe he went to a party last night. Then again, the socializing could be the catalyst for his change of heart. He wants to be a better father; he seems more confident, less in mourning. Who knows, maybe things have changed. He might not take us to Grandma Nell's at all.

"How did your night go?" my father asks. "I didn't see you wandering the halls, so you must have found some form of entertainment."

"I wasn't feeling great and went to bed early." That's . . . sort of the truth. I leave off the part where I hung out on the roof drinking alcohol, sneaked around with a strange boy who I almost kissed, and saw Daniel's psycho girlfriend in the elevator at sunrise. My father doesn't need *all* the details.

"Not feeling well?" he asks. "But you never get sick."

I turn to him to see if he's joking, but his earnest expression tells me he's not. "Dad, I'm always sick. Mono, pneumonia, chicken pox?"

He presses his lips together, looking embarrassed. "Sorry," he says. "Your mother usually handled that side

135

of the parenting." We're both silent for a moment, letting the words sink in. "How are you feeling now?" he asks to fill space.

"Fine," I say. "Probably just a pulled muscle, but my arm's better now. I'm not even sure how I hurt it. Slept on it wrong in the car, most likely."

Just then Daniel walks into the restaurant—his threadbare T-shirt impossibly wrinkled, like it's been balled up at the bottom of his backpack. His hair is askew, his lips pale. He's obviously hungover. He drops into his chair and then winces and touches his temple. "Shit," he mumbles.

"Daniel," my father warns him. But Dad's face has brightened, and I think he might be truly happy to have us together for a meal. I used to dream about moments like this.

"Coffee, black," Daniel says when the server comes by. He continues to moan until he lifts his head, surprised we're watching him. "Sorry," he says. "I have no idea how this happened."

"Consuming large quantities of alcohol?" I suggest.

Daniel screws up his face in a *You're a comedian, Aud* look. "Of course it was alcohol, but I blacked out. I've never blacked out," he says with irritation. "But the last thing I remember, I was walking out of that party, Catherine telling me not to leave, and then *bam!* I woke up feeling like this. I swear it's like my head is split in two." He turns to point where it hurts.

The ground drops out from under me. I gasp a scream

and jump up from my chair, knocking it to the floor with a clatter. "Daniel," I yell, grabbing my starched white napkin. On my brother's left temple, sliding into his hairline, is a huge crack; brain matter is exposed. Blood runs down his cheek and pools at the collar of his shirt.

Tears stream from my eyes, my heart rate soaring as I fight with shaky legs around the table toward him. I look at my dad, expecting the same horrified reaction, but instead he's staring at me, wide-eyed.

"Audrey," he says in a harsh whisper, glancing around at the other tables like he's embarrassed. "What are you doing?"

I can't even respond, instead I grip my brother's shoulder and press the napkin to his seeping wound. "Stop it," Daniel says, swatting my hand. "Audrey!" He finally succeeds in pushing me back, but I'm hysterical. I can't lose my brother, too. I'll die without Daniel. I'll die.

I rush toward him again, but he puts up his hands defensively. "Stop it," he says, wrapping his fingers around my wrists. The napkin falls into his lap, and I look down at it, surprised it's still white with all that blood. Oh, God. Why isn't anyone helping us?

"Aud," Daniel begs, his voice cracked with worry. It draws me out of my hysterics, and when I focus on Daniel again . . . the blood is gone. The wound, too, as if it were never there. I sob out a relieved sound and take a step back, bumping into the empty table behind me.

I open my mouth to speak, but the words don't find their way past my lips. While Daniel's head is perfectly fine, his expression, and my father's, is one of extraordinary concern. As if I'm the problem here.

*You were bleeding to death,* I think, but can't say. *Your brains were falling out, and yet you were still talking to me. How is that possible?* My face is wet with tears, and I dart my eyes around the room at the people who are staring at me. The moment grows heavy, expectant. But I have no explanation for what I just saw.

I reach a trembling finger to run it over Daniel's forehead, checking to make sure it's really still intact, but he shifts his head away. I've never seen my brother more scared than he is in this moment.

"Jesus, Audrey," he says. "Are you okay?"

"No," I respond hoarsely. "I don't think I am." Yesterday I saw blood on Tanya, and today I imagined my brother's skull was split open. What sort of person does that? What the hell is wrong with me? "I'm going to the bathroom," I mumble, leaving for the back of the dining room.

My body shakes, my jaw quivers, as I try to catch my breath. My left leg is suddenly stiff, and my gait shifts to a limp. I could be having a stroke. *Like my mother*, my mind whispers. I choke back a cry, pushing away the thought — terrified of it like it's a curse.

No. This is probably a reaction from the pill Lourdes gave me last night. It's causing hallucinations.

I push the swinging bathroom door, grateful to find the room empty. There's a wrought-iron bench in the corner, and I go to sit, bending forward with my head lowered in crash position.

What is happening to me?

The door flies open, the handle smacking the white tiles on the wall. I nearly jump out of my skin, and clutch my shirt over my heart. Lourdes stands there in her house-keeping uniform, her hands on her hips. She runs her dark gaze over me, gauging the situation. Then without a word she walks to the mirror and examines her reflection.

"I heard you scream, and your brother said you ran off." She swipes her fingers over her eyelashes to unclump her mascara. "He was worried about you." Lourdes glances back at me. "Should I be worried too?"

"I don't know," I say with a quick shake of my head. Now that I've left the dining room, the image of a bleeding Daniel seems utterly ridiculous. "Did my brother . . ." I pause, not sure how much I should share about my current mental state. "Did he look all right to you?"

Lourdes turns back to the mirror with a devilish smile. "He's hot—even with a hangover." She pulls a compact of foundation and a tube of lipstick out of her apron. "Why?" Lourdes pops the top off her lipstick and rings her lips in red. After smoothing them together, she runs her finger along the lower line.

As I watch her now, the moment is so filled with normal

that my nerves begin to calm. "I've been seeing things," I offer vaguely, and wave my hand. "I'm also losing time — not blacking out, but just . . ." I stop and sigh. "I'm just confused, really."

"Have you eaten today?" she asks casually.

"No, not yet. Do you think that could be it?"

"Well, that and you had alcohol," she points out. "*And* you took a muscle relaxer. *And* you stayed up all night with Eli." She meets my eyes in the mirror and winks. "See where I'm going here?"

I'm feeling more ridiculous by the second. I haven't exactly been making the healthiest life choices the past few days. "Or," she adds, tapping her palm under her curls to fluff them, "it could just be the ghosts messing with you." She laughs before turning around, her hip against the porcelain sink.

"I'm definitely blaming the ghosts," I say, calmed now that Lourdes has shed some light on the situation.

"By the way," she says, "I'm not sure what happened last night, but Eli hasn't shut up about you."

"What did he say?" I'm slow to stand, still a little shaky, and make my way over to the mirror to check my reflection. It's not too terrible, although I have to wipe away a bit of mascara from under my eyes.

Lourdes purses her lips as if weighing how much to tell me. The scale doesn't tip in my favor. "Doesn't matter," she says. "But I told him to be careful. Elias is a really good friend of mine, and I don't want him to get in trouble because of this little thing you have. It is a *thing*, right? Because he seems to think so."

"We're just hanging out," I say. "It's not a big deal." I have a hard time holding back my smile. In reality, I'm only here until tomorrow. Our "thing" is going to be short lived no matter what.

Lourdes watches me, and a slow drip from the faucet echoes in the silence. "He's in the garden," she says. "I can't remember the last time I saw him outside." Her expression softens, and I can see how much she cares about him. "He's worth it," she adds quietly. "If it were me, I'd think he was worth it."

"Worth what?"

The door opens and two older women with fur shawls stagger in as if their shoes are painful. One woman moves to the sink nearest Lourdes, knocking her compact into the sink without apologizing. Without acknowledgment. Lourdes quickly snatches up her supplies and shoves them into her apron. She's flustered, and I expect her to confront the woman, but instead the housekeeper rushes out without another word.

The gray-haired woman glances at the powder residue spilled from Lourdes's compact. "The help in this place is disgusting," she murmurs to her friend. "Absolutely worthless."

"Report it to the front desk," her friend replies, hobbling

141

over to the stall door. "They'll straighten them out. This place does have a reputation, you know."

How dare they? "You're the one who knocked it over," I say, grabbing a paper towel from the dispenser and tossing it at her. "Report that."

The woman gasps, looking offended that I'd even suggest she clean up after herself. She stares at where the paper towel landed on the side of the sink. She straightens her back, skin paled, and then goes to enter the stall next to her friend. At first her voice is shaky, but then she and her friend continue talking between stalls, complaining about the food, the service. I stare at their closed doors, wondering how they could be so rude.

I'm angry, and I want to kick open their stalls to tell them they're not allowed to treat people like this. That money doesn't buy class. I'd tell them not to report it to the front desk because Kenneth is an asshole and the staff is afraid of him.

Instead I pull open the main door and then flick off the light, submerging the room in darkness. The women yelp and howl for help, but I pretend I don't hear, and shut the door behind me.

# CHAPTER 10

I'm not hungry when I return to the table. Dad and Daniel seem to be at the tail end of an argument I luckily missed, and my plate of crepes are pale and withered. I tentatively sit down, anticipating their questions. Daniel is the first to look over, and my breath catches but is soon replaced with a sigh when his head is still wound-free. I imagined the entire thing.

"You all right?" he asks, halfway between panic and annoyance. I nod and then cut a piece of crepe and shove it into my mouth. If starvation is the cause of my hallucination, I'm going to ensure I'm well fed through the rest of this trip. The food is dry and cold. I take a sip of water and force down another mouthful.

"Your sister said her arm's been hurting," my dad says for me, then shoots me a worried glance. "Could this . . . outburst be related?"

*He's thinking stroke. I know he is.*

"I'm fine," I reassure him, sipping from my water before taking another bite. Lourdes already placated my fears, and I don't want to think more about it. See the flaws in her logic. "Probably need to eat more," I add, and smile unconvincingly, judging by the looks on their faces.

"Lay off the drugs, sister," Daniel mumbles, drinking from his coffee. I laugh, but Dad has turned his attention to my brother. He folds his hands on the table with a show so parental it seems fake.

"Now let's talk about you," he says in his new-and-improved Dad voice. "Drinking? Blacking out? Daniel, this isn't acceptable behavior."

My brother straightens in his chair, knocked sideways by the fact that our father would criticize him now. He clenches his jaw, and leans his elbow on the table. "Dad, we've been past acceptable behavior for a long time. Starting with you. Don't think you're fooling either of us with this father-of-the-year bullshit."

"Daniel," I whisper, stunned that he would confront our father so plainly. Normally, he'd storm off and then vent to me later. But right now his cheeks have gone red, his fist curled up. I repeat his name and he looks over at me. The fight evaporates from his expression.

The three of us stay silent for a long moment, digesting the new dynamics. I watch my father, waiting to see his reaction. See if he really is the doting man who showed up for lunch today. My father picks up his water and takes a calm sip, then sets his glass down with a *clank.*

"You're right," he says calmly. Daniel and I exchange a look, unsure if he's just being passive-aggressive. "I've changed, Daniel," he says. "I'm finally seeing clearly again.

And I'll do anything to keep this family together. Forever."

*Okay, then.* My dad's eyes are sincere, which only succeeds in making him sound and look like a deranged cult leader. Now that our conversation has taken a turn into the truly bizarre, I stand up from my seat at the table.

"Thanks for lunch, Dad," I say, "but I have to go. I'm meeting up with my friends at the pool. Find you later?" Daniel pushes his cup aside, standing as if I've made an excuse for him to leave too. Smooth.

"I'm happy to hear you're making friends," my father says. I wait for a dig at my past, the mistakes I've made since my mother died, but no insults follow. He might actually mean it. "Let's meet for a movie later," he suggests to me and Daniel. "Around six?"

"Sure," I say. It's been years since I've been to a movie with my father. A wave of nostalgia sweeps over me, and I smile at my brother. Daniel rolls his eyes, still skeptical of my father's sincerity. He hums something noncommittal, and then he takes my arm and tugs me toward the exit. Since arriving at the Ruby, Daniel's been standing up more to our father. There's a new resentment there, anger.

"You didn't have to be so mean," I say when we get out into the crowded lobby. The light filtering in through the windows is blinding at first, setting the room in a haze. Little specks of dust float around us. When my eyes adjust, the people are gone, leaving just me and Daniel in the large room. Confused, I glance around before my brother is talking again.

145

"Does he think he can erase what he's done?" my brother asks. "That we'll just forget after a movie? No. How stupid does he think we are?"

"He doesn't think we're stupid," I tell him. "He's probably having second thoughts about Grandma Nell's. I mean, wouldn't you after spending more time with us? We're kind of awesome." I smile, trying to lighten Daniel's mood. I know it's naive, but part of me wants to believe that my father really can change.

My brother scratches his head, right where I thought I saw the crack, and I look away. For all its grandeur, the hotel lobby has taken on an eerie quality. Where did everybody go?

"Look," Daniel says apologetically. "I'm not ready to forgive him, okay? But you and me"—he waggles his finger between us—"we're okay. Always."

*"Forever,"* I say in a spooky voice, imitating our dad's strange statement earlier. Daniel laughs, pushing my shoulder like he's mad at me for cheering him up.

"It's all *Poltergeist* up in here," he says with a grin. He exhales heavily and glances back at the elevator. "I'm going to grab a shower," he says. "And I'm sorry, but you're going to have to count me out on that movie date. I'm not in the mood."

"I get it," I say. "Although . . ." This is probably not the time, but I can't stop myself. "Are you going out with Catherine?"

He nods. "Yeah. Why?"

Is he already defensive? I keep talking anyway. "Well," I say, "she kind of sucks, Daniel." I hold up my hand, counting off the reasons why on my fingers. One: "She's rude to me, borderline threatening." Two: "Joshua—the valet—actually said that she stabbed him in the gut—like with a knife. And I'm not sure he was joking." I hold up a third finger. "And she's Elias's ex. He says she has a bad temper and that you should be careful."

Daniel is so still for a moment that I think he didn't hear me. But then I notice the anger welling up, and I swallow down any more reasons I was about to give.

"That's awfully convenient, don't you think, Aud?" he asks. "The guys are the ones saying this about her."

I laugh off the beginning of his argument. "Sure, Daniel. She's the toast of the Ruby and everyone's in love with her. Or," I allow sarcastically, "she's a whack job who's going to murder-suicide you in a jealous rage before we check out. Sleep with one eye open."

"You don't know her like I do," he says, ignoring my joke. "She's not that person anymore. None of us are the same anymore, Audrey. Things change."

"What?" I curl my lip. "You're starting to sound like Dad. Look, how do you know she's not just—"

Daniel puts his hands on my upper arms, bending so he can look me in the eyes. "Stop worrying about me," he says. There's a sharp pain—rejection. Even though he

147

doesn't say it, he's telling me I'm not Mom. He must notice the hurt in my face, because he forces a smile. "Besides," he adds, "I can handle myself in a catfight if I need to."

I groan and brush his hands away. He's not going to listen to me about Catherine, and I guess it doesn't really matter. Tomorrow, Daniel and I will be on our way to our grandmother's. *Or back to Phoenix,* I think hopefully.

"Fine," I tell him with an exhale. "Do what you want. I'm going to wander for a while. But if you change your mind about the movie—"

"I won't," Daniel says quickly. He winces and rubs at his scalp. "Plus my head is still killing me," he mumbles. "I'll see you later." Partly dazed, he turns to leave. I watch him walk away, looking unsteady as he gets into the elevator.

The hallway is wide, with gold-framed pictures, quiet and still. Peaceful. I pause in front of a picture labeled THE HOTEL RUBY, 1936. There, in black and white, is a wide shot of the building itself. Possibly more impressive than it is now, if only because of its age. Standing in front is a crowd of people, well dressed and smiling. Are they the stockholders who helped erect this place? I lean closer, trying to find one who might look a bit like Elias, a peek into his past.

"Now it just looks like I'm stalking you."

I jump, and laugh when I find Elias resting his shoulder against the patterned wallpaper a few feet away. "Are you?" I ask. He shrugs, admitting that maybe he is. He holds up a rose, and I'm ten shades of flattered as I take it and smell it. Light and powdery. Utterly charming.

Elias smiles, and it's the strangest thing—I know we're both embarrassed, shy, about our almost kiss in his room, but I don't think either of us plans to stop meeting like this. With my heart thumping, I go to stand next to him against the wall.

"How are you today?" he asks. "I was absolutely miserable after you left last night."

"I'm sure," I say teasingly. "If it helps, I had a nice chat with Catherine in the elevator, so I think I beat you out for biggest buzz kill."

"Ah, yes. You win." His glance drifts past me, and it's clear that he doesn't want to talk about Catherine. I'm glad we can agree.

"I've actually had a terrible day," I tell him, still trying to process what happened at lunch. "I think I'm having a bad reaction to drinking, or to searching for ghosts, or"—I smile—"to staying up with strange boys until dawn."

Rather than laugh, Elias shifts in concern. "What sort of reaction?"

I wave my hand to let him know I'm not taking it too seriously, or at least, that's what I want him to think. "Cracked skulls, blood, the usual," I say, immediately filling with unease at the memory. *It wasn't real,* I tell myself. *Daniel was fine just a second later.*

149

Elias widens his eyes at the gory details, and I quickly change the subject. "So I have nothing to do," I say, twisting the flower nervously between my fingers. "Planned to spend the day exploring. Would you . . ." I tilt my head, waiting for him to agree before I have to ask.

"Like to sneak around with you?" he offers.

We've both inched forward, and the warmth of his body radiates to mine. I smile my response, totally crazy about him. Addicted to our attraction.

"You're giving me that look again," he warns, his gaze lingering at my lips. "I hope that means I've convinced you my intentions are mostly honorable."

"Mostly?" I smile. "I'm leaving tomorrow. I can handle mostly."

"That's good, I suppose. But the truth is"—his body comes maddeningly close to mine—"if we keep at this, I'm not sure I'll want to let you go in twenty-four hours."

"It's more like twenty-three," I whisper, grinning as he leans in and slides his palm over my cheek.

"Yes, then we should start now," he murmurs. Elias presses his lips to mine, and I melt into him. The heat of his mouth, the feel of his arm as it wraps around my waist, pulling me closer. I part my lips and his tongue touches mine, a soft sound escapes my throat.

My mind spins, and I knot my fingers in Elias's hair. He growls out his approval, but then he pulls back and glances behind me. Before I can look to see if anyone is there, he takes my hand and pulls me down the hall, backing me into a small alcove between rooms and kissing me again, harder, more passionately. My entire body has caught fire, and I'm not even thinking when I slip my hand under his shirt to feel his skin. Elias curses, and then we're moving again, farther into the recesses of the hotel. The hall has gotten darker, but every few feet we end up kissing, breathing heavily like we can't get enough of each other.

"We should go to your room," I say into our kiss. Elias shakes his head and then trails his mouth along my jaw; his tongue tickles my neck.

"They'll find us there," he murmurs.

"My room, then," I say. My thoughts are swirling, nearly lost in my desire. I want him; want to remember what it's like to *feel*.

Elias pulls back, his face close to mine. His cheeks are flush, and I think then that he's the most beautiful thing I've ever seen, wild and sexy. He clenches his jaw, setting it at sharp angles, looking me over like he wants to devour me. I want to be devoured.

"Elias," I plead, grabbing his shirt to draw him to me once again. He kisses me but then stops and buries his face in my hair instead. "I can't go to your room," he says miserably. His body crushes me against the wall, but I like it. I like everything about him.

"Christ, Audrey," he says painfully. "You're making me crazy."

151

"Me?" I laugh, running my fingers over the back of his neck. His heart is pounding against mine, and it takes a moment for me to realize we're still in the hallway. Although it's darker, it's certainly not private. I furrow my brow, stunned that I would lose myself so completely. In fact, now that I think about it . . .

I put my hands on Elias's shoulders, gently pushing him back. My rose is gone, a casualty of the hottest kiss ever. Elias seems to realize just how out of control we were and runs his hand through his hair, flashing me a sheepish smile. I take a second to make sure my clothes are still on after basically attacking him. Or did he attack me?

"This is seriously going to affect my day," he says, and then laughs. "Maybe even my week."

"Yeah," I agree, rubbing my lips together. They feel swollen, sore in a way that makes me want to kiss him all over again. I'm invigorated. Alive. "Those twenty-three hours just got a whole lot shorter," I say.

Elias's smile fades, a touch of sadness seeping in. I hate the mood shift, and I step forward to drape my arms over his shoulders. I get on my tiptoes and kiss him quickly on the lips.

"Let's go to the café," I say, and kiss him again. "Do something respectable with our afternoon."

"Why?" He tries to deepen the kiss, but I laugh and back out of his arms. I'm charmed when he grabs my hand and brings it to his lips, kissing it, before sliding his fingers between mine. "Fine," he says with a dramatic sigh. "We'll go, but I'm going to be thinking about that kiss the entire time."

"I'm glad I made an impression."

He hums out an agreement, and we start down the hallway, back to civilization. I expect Elias to drop my hand before anyone notices, but he doesn't. He only squeezes it tighter.

We're all hormones as we sit at a small table on the back patio, gazing stupidly at each other. Elias keeps hold of my hand, sliding his fingers along mine, teasing me with the sensuality of how he's touching me.

"I don't want you to leave," he says, smiling sadly. He reaches for his white porcelain cup and sips his coffee. "But I know you don't belong here."

"Oh?" I ask, part flattered and part lonely at the thought of not belonging. "Maybe you don't belong here," I suggest, looking down at our intertwined hands. "I hear my grandmother's attic is nice."

Elias laughs and lifts my hand to kiss my fingers once more before letting them go. I wrap my hands around my glass, missing Elias's warmth. I told him about how much I'm dreading going to my grandmother's. How I won't know anyone but Daniel.

"I'd take you away from that house," Elias says quietly, staring into his cup. "I'd take you anywhere you wanted to go, Audrey." He lifts his head, sympathy darkening his expression. "I'd be your family."

There's a puncture in my heart as Elias zeroes in on everything I've wanted to hear for the last three months.

"We'll run away together," I joke, although neither of us is smiling anymore. "I'm thinking California would be nice."

"It is," he allows. "I grew up there." Elias sets down his cup, pushes it aside, and leans his elbows on the table. He turns to look at the garden, the neatly trimmed shrubbery, the mountain view in the distance. Flowers—roses of several colors, vibrant and fragrant even from here, crowd the landscape. This is easily the best view in the house.

After a few minutes of comfortable silence Elias looks over at me mischievously. "I think I've changed my mind," he says.

"About what?"

"Taking you back to my room. I'll leave the phone off the hook."

I laugh, considering the offer. The butterflies in my stomach, the twist of desire. I can't even believe when I hear myself decline. "I can't," I say, lowering my chin onto my folded arms on the table. "I shouldn't," I say instead. "No matter how badly I want to."

"We still have twenty-three hours," he says, disappointed but not put off. He opens the black bill holder and signs his name with a quick swipe of the pen.

"Twenty-two," I respond, laughing when he narrows his eyes.

"Come here," he whispers, tossing the pen aside to lean closer. When I do, he kisses me, sweetly, teasingly, over the table. He runs his lips over mine, and then there's the soft touch of his tongue, the warmth of his mouth. My head spins and I grasp his shirt, to pull him closer still.

"Sorry to interrupt."

Elias and I jump, and I look up to see Joshua, dressed in his Hotel Ruby uniform, not looking at all sorry. He shoots Elias a smug smile and then turns back to me. "The front desk sent me over," he says. "Your brother is looking for you, Audrey. Probably a good thing that I found you first." He snorts a laugh and then turns on his heel, heading back inside.

"What is it with you and Joshua?" I ask, sitting up and feeling slightly embarrassed to be caught kissing. I glance around, glad when I see the other tables empty. I didn't even think to look before. Although Joshua was right— I'm definitely glad it was him and not Daniel. That would have been awful.

Elias leans back in his chair, exhaling heavily. "Back when Catherine and I were miserable together, Joshua provided her with a much-needed diversion. I may have punched him in the face a few times because of it." Elias lifts one shoulder. "It was a long time ago. Sort of comical at this point."

"You're frenemies," I tease, but Elias looks confused. An older couple walks onto the patio, and sits at the next table over. They don't acknowledge us, even though Elias nods politely at them.

I want to spend more time outside, carefree with a hot guy and no responsibility, but I shouldn't leave Daniel hanging. I stand, and Elias reaches out to pull me close when I start to walk by. I lean into him, thrilled as he gazes up at me adoringly.

"Come back when you're done?" he asks.

"Are you going to try to convince me to go to your room?"

His dimples deepen, his lips pulling into a slow, sexy smile. "Do you want me to?"

I give him a quick kiss and then hold myself just above him. "Kind of," I whisper, knowing it's true. And really, who cares what I do with Elias? I'm being hauled away to Elko, Nevada, for the foreseeable future. Why not enjoy my last moments of freedom?

Elias groans, rolling his eyes like I'm the biggest tease to ever live. "Hurry," he says, and then drags his coffee cup in front of him.

The front desk is empty, so I look for Daniel in the restaurant, but both he and my father are gone. I see Warren busing the table and walk over to meet him.

"Hey, Audrey," he says, his voice soft and comforting. "You rushed out of here earlier. Everything okay?"

"Fine. I'm looking for my brother, though. Have you seen him?"

Warren glances around, as if Daniel just switched tables without him noticing. Then he snaps his fingers. "Try the ballroom. Your father was talking to another guest about it after you left. Not sure what that was about, though. Other tables." He motions around the room to prove his point. I thank him and let him get back to work, and then I take the turn down the hall toward the ballroom.

When I get to the double doors, they're closed. I doubt my brother is inside, but my curiosity gets the best of me. I saw the room in all its grandeur two nights ago, but I wonder how it looks without the glittering gowns. I decide to find out. Slowly I pull open the door just a crack and lean my head in to see first if Daniel or anyone else is inside. The room is too dark to see anything beyond the light that's seeping in from the hallway.

No Daniel, but I slip in the door anyway, and find the main light switches on the wall next to the entrance. I flip them on and the center of the room explodes in brilliant color. The reds ooze opulence; the chandelier sparkles, casting rays of light in patterns on the floor. It takes a minute for me to catch my breath, completely charmed by the space. Even so, it's lifeless without the party. A beautiful, dead room. Lonely and tragic.

I think for a moment about Lourdes's story. I have no reason to doubt it, but the tragedy is suffocating, especially

157

now that I'm in the ballroom. No one tried to save those people, and I almost feel their sadness hanging in the room. They must have fought to live, to get out. What did they think when they realized the doors were locked?

My skin prickles, and I glance around, taking in more of the adornments. Lourdes told me that people come from all over to hang with the ghosts that reside here. The corners in the back of the ballroom are still heavy with shadows. Suddenly this entire place feels like a grave.

Behind me is the soft click of the door shutting, and I turn, startled. My heartbeat starts to hasten, ticking in my ears. I want to blame the wind, but I feel none. I'm sure as hell not going to blame the ghosts.

"Still interested in the party, I see," a voice calls from across the room. I yelp and spin around, nearly tripping over my crossed ankles. Kenneth stands at the back of the room, and I'm alarmed to think he's been here the entire time. At least, I assume that's Kenneth. His burgundy suit and frame are a match, but his face is hidden in the darkness. I can make out the shape of his bald head, see his pudgy fingers folded in front of him where he rests them against his chest. But not seeing his eyes makes him seem . . . sinister.

I take a step back.

"I'm sorry to inform you," he continues, not moving any closer, "that an invitation has not become available to you. And as I've told you, the parties are invite only."

Agitation nudges me. "How did Daniel get one, then? Or my father?"

Kenneth unclasps his hands to hold them out apologetically. "It's up to the Ruby," he says, as if that makes any sense at all. "Perhaps after you leave, you'll understand their reasoning."

"Mm . . . perhaps," I respond sarcastically. I'm about to walk out, chalking this up to *creepy-interaction-with-concierge day*, when Kenneth calls my name. I glance over my shoulder at him, more intimidated than I want to admit. "Yeah?"

"I've noticed you consorting with the staff. Thought I'd mention that interaction between staff and guests is frowned upon. They face reprimands if you keep them from their work."

"Are you spying on me?" I demand. "And besides, I don't think you can make that rule. They're not your property. They're your employees."

"As such, they abide by the rules of the Ruby. I enforce them. They will be punished for their disregard. It may be best if you spend the remainder of your stay in your room, Miss Casella. Out of trouble."

"It may be better if you back off before I report you for harassment to your management company, Kenneth. And just a heads-up, I will let them know how shitty you treat your staff. Have a great day," I say, mock-saluting him.

I turn back to the door, and behind me there's a sudden and terrifying breeze. A dark, impending echo, like

159

the rush of an animal behind me, ready to attack. *To eat me alive*, I think. My hand shoots out to grasp the door handle, scared it will be locked somehow, but it turns easily. I yank it open and dart a quick look back at Kenneth, mostly to see if he's still there.

The concierge stands, still half in the shadows, hands folded over his chest again. He steps forward, flooding his face with light to finally let me see him. He smiles pleasantly.

"Give my regards to Elias," he calls dismissively. Kenneth turns on the heel of his shiny shoe and walks to a round table. He runs his palm over the white cloth to smooth it down, tugging aggressively on the hem.

Any confidence I faked dissipates, and my stomach knots. Okay—I get it. Kenneth is totally scary. I quickly leave the ballroom, set on finding my brother. Once I tell Daniel about the concierge, I'll let him deal with it. Now I wish he'd brought his bat after all.

# CHAPTER 11

I walk directly to the elevator and then take it to the sixth floor. In the hall I cast looks behind me, afraid Kenneth or an unknown monster might attack at any moment. There are noises in the other suites as I pass—life, unlike the dead silence on my floor. When I get to Daniel's room, I press myself against the door and bang on it. Unease settles over me, and I replay my conversation with Kenneth in my head.

He was threatening me. The concierge told me to stay in my room for the rest of my stay. He can't do that. That has to be some sort of violation.

"Daniel," I call out, banging on his door again. When he doesn't answer, I consider heading over to my father's room to let him know about the situation. But then the door opens suddenly, making me stumble inside. I quickly catch my balance, then launch myself against the inside of the door, throwing the latch to lock it.

My brother stands there, his skin pale and his eyes wide. "Where were you earlier?" he asks. "I had the front desk call your room."

"I was at the café with Elias," I respond, pushing past him into the room. I'm surprised to find his clothes strewn about, the blankets piled on the floor next to the bed. I quickly smooth the bottom sheet and sit on the edge of the mattress. My hands are shaking and I clasp them in front of me. "Why were you looking for me?" I ask.

Daniel looks me over quizzically, then takes a long pause before speaking. "Why are you freaking out?" he asks. "Did something happen?"

"Yeah. I need you to kick someone's ass for me."

"Done," he says automatically, and crosses the room to sit next to me. "Tell me what's going on. Was it that guy?" He waits a beat. "Was it Dad?"

"No. It was the concierge."

"Kenneth?" he says. I'm surprised he knows his name, but it's possible he's met him several times by now. It's just that Daniel isn't normally the observant type. "Is this about the party?" he asks.

"Sort of," I say, "but that's not what scared me. He's terrorizing the staff here, and when I talked to him in the ballroom just now, he . . ." There's no real explanation for my fear—none that would make sense. What can I tell my brother? That it felt like he was running up behind me, ready to attack me, even though he hadn't moved? That he mentioned me talking with the staff, proving he's been watching me? "The guy's a creep," I say finally. "He abuses his employees and he's trying to intimidate me—I think we need to get out of here, Daniel. And then I want Dad to report his ass to his supervisors."

Daniel lowers his eyes with a pained expression. "That's what I wanted to talk to you about." His voice is low, making him hard to understand. He gets up and walks to his dresser, his back to me, his posture rigid. "I didn't see it before," he continues, "and then all of a sudden, right after I left you downstairs, I . . . remembered."

"Remembered what?" I ask. I can't explain the tightening in my chest. *I remember, too,* I think. Only I don't. I have no idea what my brother is talking about. "Daniel, we have to go. This place is too weird."

My brother turns, his features shifting into a gloom I haven't seen on him before. "We're not leaving," he says. His words stick in my brain. He didn't say "early." Daniel didn't say, "We're not leaving early." He said, "We're not leaving."

Once again that impending presence, the sense that something is close to me, makes the hairs stand up on my arms, goose bumps ripple my flesh. The hotel is listening to us.

"What the hell are you talking about?" I ask, my heartbeat pounding in my ears. "Of course we are. Even if Dad decides he wants to spend his retirement playing tennis or going to ballroom parties at the Ruby, that doesn't mean we're stuck here. We can just take his car. We can leave whenever."

Daniel curls up his lip, shaking his head. "I knew you wouldn't listen. You never listen, Audrey." He turns away and grips the edge of his dresser, his body rigid as silence fills the space between us. Panic and worry swirl inside my brain; my hands tremble.

"What's going on?" I ask him. "I don't understand what you're—"

"Do you remember your birthday?" he asks quietly, ignoring my question. At first I think it's a dig, but he goes on. "The one before Mom died. You didn't want a party, but she decided to throw you a surprise one anyway. She wanted to do something special even though she knew you'd hate her for it."

He devastates me. The entire world breaks open and hurt floods in. Daniel doesn't talk about our mother. I didn't know he still could. For the longest time I thought I wanted him to mention her in some way, acknowledge her. But I didn't consider how desperate it would make me feel when he did. How much it would make me miss her again.

"It was the worst birthday party that's ever been," I say with a rush of sentimentality. We both choke out a laugh, but there's agony in the sound.

"Seven of your closest friends," he says, looking back at me. His face is wet with tears, his pale eyes bloodshot. He sniffles hard and brushes his fist over his cheek. "Which basically meant Ryan and a group of kids you hadn't spoken to since junior high."

"I still don't know how she found their numbers," I say, and then bite down hard on my lip to keep it from quivering. Is this therapeutic? Can it be when it hurts so much?

Daniel leans back against the dresser. "I was bringing you home from a driving lesson—which, by the way," he adds, smiling, "you were horrible at. Then we walked in and everyone jumped out. Mom's face . . ." He squeezes his eyes shut, tears streaming down. I start to sob. "She was so happy," he says. "She was so proud of herself."

For a moment mine and Daniel's cries are the only sound in the room. We're heartbroken. We're lost without her. I gather myself, swallowing down thickening saliva. "I turned and walked back onto the porch," I say, continuing the story. "I was embarrassed. She followed me out and asked if I was mad at her. I said yes. I told her I was going to murder you both."

"You had fun, though," Daniel says. "After you came in, after Ryan calmed you down. Mom had been prepping lasagna because she knew it was your favorite. Only she forgot there was still a pizza box on the rack from the night before, and when she tried to preheat the oven, she nearly burned down the entire kitchen."

"Do you remember the flames shooting out of there?" I ask, laughing through my tears. "Ryan and I spent fifteen minutes waving a dishcloth in front of the smoke alarm, until you finally came in and hit it with the broom to knock it off the wall."

"The oven was ruined," Daniel says. "So she dumped

the lasagna in the trash and ordered another pizza. Deep dish, so the candles would stand up in it." He smiles sadly. "But she forgot to buy candles, and the only one she could find was a half-burned number eight that was in the junk drawer for years. But we lit it. And we sang.

"Best birthday you ever had," he says. "Hell, best birthday I ever had."

I close my eyes, the ache bleeding from my heart down to my toes. We both know my mother wasn't perfect, even if the memories I've allowed the past few months portray her that way. She would yell, that completely unhinged kind of yell that would rattle the glasses in the cupboards. One time during a heated argument she asked if I was stupid, and I slammed my door in her face. And there was that time she called my dad an asshole in the car, when we were on our way home from dinner, because he had criticized her father.

But then she was wonderful. She'd instinctively know when to make brownies or pick us up from school to go to a movie. She'd give Daniel dating advice and taught me how to put on mascara so I didn't get spider lashes. She was my mother. She was my mother and I'll never see her again no matter how badly I want to. I don't think there is a more helpless feeling than that.

"Why are you doing this, Daniel?" I ask finally. "Why talk about her now?"

"Because I want you to hold on to those things," he

says. "I don't ever want you to forget that it was good sometimes. It was perfect. And no matter what happens, that won't change."

I start to wipe away my tears, my adrenaline rushing in. "What do you mean?" I ask in a hoarse voice. "What's going to happen?"

Daniel puts his palm over his eyes for a moment; his shoulders sag. By the time he straightens again, his face has hardened. Gone cold. The air in the room deflates. "I'm not going to Elko with you, Audrey," he says. "I'm staying at the Ruby."

I should ask him if he's joking, because in the regular world my brother wouldn't abandon me. He would stick with me even if it meant a few months in our grandmother's house.

"You can't," I say weakly. "You can't do this to me."

He tightens his lips, taking too long to answer. "It's done."

"But *why*?" Tears sputter between my lips. I'm going to completely lose it—this isn't possible. He wouldn't do this! "Is it because of Catherine?" I shout, jumping to my feet. "You don't even know her! I won't forgive you," I say, nearing hysterics. "I'll never forgive you if you do this!"

"This isn't about Catherine," he states. "You're leaving, Aud. Dad wants you to stay until tomorrow, but then you're out of here. Without hesitation. Do you understand? You'll be fine at Grandma Nell's—you'll start over. It's time to let go of all of this. You don't have to—"

"Stop being an idiot!" I scream. My head aches from crying, my body is trembling. I'm afraid I'll hyperventilate if I don't leave soon. Of all people, I never thought Daniel would leave me. "You can't stay here!"

"You're not my mother," he says darkly. "Stop acting like her."

*Silence*. I sway on my feet, bulldozed by his words. Too sickened to be angry. Daniel exhales, seeing the hurt on my face, and takes a step toward me.

"I'm sorry," he says quickly. "But if I—" The phone next to the bed rings loudly, startling us both. Daniel makes no move to answer it, and the ringing comes again—longer and shriller. My brother clenches his jaw and turns away.

"You'd better go," he says coldly. "Go before I say something worse."

"Daniel—"

"Go," he growls. "I don't want to fight with you." He pauses. "Don't make me."

"I'm not going to fight with you," I say miserably. "Like you said, I'm not your mother." He winces, hating his own words. I walk to the door, a mixture of grief and anger now bubbling over.

The phone continues to ring like an alarm, and just as I open the door, Daniel calls my name. I look back over my shoulder, and Daniel's head is down. "Don't trust

Dad," he says quietly. "Don't trust any of them."

Words that aren't an apology are just another slap in the face. "Yeah, well," I say. "You betrayed me. So it seems you're the one who can't be trusted, Daniel."

He shoots me an annoyed look and then walks to the window with his arms crossed, staring over the grounds and shutting me out completely.

I slam his door and then jog down the hall, checking once to see if he's going to run after me to say he changed his mind. I press the button for the elevator and watch his door. He doesn't come for me. The hallway stands empty, the corridor endless from this angle. A hush has fallen over the world, a weighted pause that feels like it's about to explode.

"Come on," I murmur, pressing the elevator button again and again. When the doors finally open, I sigh out my relief and then let them close before selecting a floor. I should go to my father, tell him not only about the concierge, but about Daniel, too. Catherine has obviously clouded my brother's judgment, but I can't accept that he would let a girl destroy our relationship. We depend on each other. He wouldn't abandon me without a good reason. At least . . . that's what I've always thought.

And if I tell my father that, what would he say? He's finally talking to us again. Will I screw that up if I go to him ranting about Daniel and the concierge? My father doesn't exactly have a history of being understanding.

I take a steadying breath, trying to calm myself. Daniel said not to trust our father—anyone—but he's the one acting crazy. My father will probably be waiting for me at the movie theater. I can head down there, check his temperament. I don't have another choice. Now that Daniel has abandoned me, my father's all I have left.

Kenneth isn't at the desk as I come out of the elevator into the lobby. My nerves are shot, my head spinning with different explanations for my brother's behavior. Ways I can convince him to leave with me anyway. There's a crowd meandering outside the theater room, and I crisscross through the bodies until I get to the door. An attendant, more like a guard, stands near the entrance. He's large, with dark hair and dark eyes, and he seems to grow bigger as I pass him. I can feel the weight of his stare on my back, and I wonder if all of the Ruby is watching me now because of Kenneth. Is this the sort of thing Daniel warned me about?

I let out a held breath when I enter the theater, struck all at once by the elegance surrounding me. A screen stretches the length of the back wall—at least twenty feet, with red velvet curtains draped at either side. The walls have burgundy and gold patterned wallpapers, sconces directing the lights into the perfect shadows, adding to the ambiance. Rows of plush red seats lead back from the screen, and are filled with people—many of them in shawls and dresses. I didn't know this was a formal event.

Self-conscious, I smooth back my hair and glance around for my father. There is the smell of popcorn, and I turn toward the small bar set up in the back of the room. About a dozen stools sit at the counter, with important-looking men sipping from short glasses. There's a popcorn machine and a rack of candy, little dishes filled with pretzels on the bar top. I expect to find my father there, but he's nowhere in sight. I do, however, see the woman from the gift shop. She notices me and smiles brightly. Astrid wears a different blazer, with thick shoulder pads, and I offer a curt wave. After all, she did sell me those disgusting chocolates.

I start down the aisle. A few guests look at me and then whisper to whoever's next to them. Some people don't look at me at all. I'm being paranoid, but who wouldn't be after Kenneth's threats? After Daniel's warning? I'm halfway to the screen when I hear my name, and I turn to the left and find my dad sitting in the middle with an empty seat next to him. He looks elated to see me. I don't plan to stay, but I murmur "Excuse me" and shimmy past the legs and laps of the people in the row.

"Hey, kid," my father says when I reach him. "I'm glad you could make it!" He holds down the seat of the chair, and I sit next to him, glancing behind me to see if anyone is listening. In the back of the room the guard has come in and is standing at the end of the aisle. He looks directly at me, and I turn away, my skin chilled under his watchful stare. If I pull my father out of here, will he report it to Kenneth? Is this how the concierge has been keeping tabs on me?

"Are you okay?" my father asks, sounding concerned. "You're so pale."

"Dad," I say quietly. My father furrows his brow, reading my fear. "Dad, I have to talk to you about this hotel."

His easy smile falls away, and his eyes lose the warmth they had when I first arrived. "Kenneth warned me about your behavior," my father says in a disappointed voice. "Have you done something to upset the Ruby?"

There's a wave of unease, my dad's demeanor mimicking the sketchiness that happened in Daniel's room. Do they already know Kenneth is a creep? Or has he brainwashed them? I take in a harsh breath, my entire body starting to tremble. "We have to leave, Dad," I say as calmly as possible, but my voice wavers. "You, me, and Daniel have to get out of here before Kenneth does something to us."

At the mention of our family his expression softens slightly. "Why would we leave, Audrey?" he asks. "Things are better here. *We're* better. You just have to give it a chance."

"A chance?" I repeat, incredulous.

"This is our opportunity to start over. Isn't that what you want?"

I stare at him; the color's returned to his cheeks, his hair is well kept, and his clothes are stylish. I haven't seen him like this since Mom died, and I've missed him. I've missed having a father. "It is what I want," I say, confused. "But—"

"Then it's settled," he says, the rest of my sentence unimportant. "Popcorn?" He outstretches the bag in my direction. "They have candy, too. This is supposed to be a great movie, but the summary was pretty vague. We'll see, I guess."

I take the popcorn even though I'd choke if I tried to eat anything right now. I don't understand what's going on with him and Daniel. The concierge is spying on us, threatening his staff. Am I the one overreacting?

The lights in the room go dark and I gasp. The popcorn falls from my hands, sending white kernels scattering across the black floor at my feet. Right then the screen illuminates and previews start. Patrons lean forward to watch, smiling and content. I ease back in the chair.

My father looks down at the floor and reaches to pick up the bag I dropped. "I'll go grab us another popcorn," he whispers. "Be right back, kid."

People laugh at something on-screen, but I can't pay attention. My mind keeps turning back to Daniel. Why did he bring up my mother? And exactly how long do he and my father plan on staying here? Living at a hotel may be okay for Elias, but I don't want to spend my life wandering around the Ruby, terrified of Kenneth. I glance at the door, considering leaving, but before I can make the decision, my father is scooting back down the aisle. He hands me a new bag of popcorn as he passes.

"Got you Junior Mints," he whispers. "They're your favorite, right?"

My automatic response is to say no, because my father hasn't guessed a correct thing about me in a long while. But this time . . . "Right," I say, taking the white box from his hand. "They are my favorite."

I look down at the candy, still afraid, but maybe a little less so. I turn to my father as he sits down and settles in, smiling before taking a handful of popcorn and shoving it into his mouth. I watch him until he laughs, pointing at the screen, and then I turn away.

When my fear has faded enough, I take a few bites of popcorn and open my Junior Mints. In a way my father's right—maybe we are better here. At least for another night. I sit back and watch the show.

# CHAPTER 12

The movie ends. My father looks over at me as the lights come up. "That was actually funny," he says. "They need to hire better people to write those descriptions. I wouldn't have even stayed if I weren't meeting you."

I return his smile, his affection feeling genuine though it still catches me off guard. The room starts to empty, and my father and I walk toward the exit, tossing what's left of our snacks in the trash can near the door. I pretend not to notice the guard, even as he watches me.

"Where are you heading to now?" my father asks, holding open the door for me to leave first. "We could probably grab dinner if you're hungry."

Distracted, I keep a careful eye on everything around us. "Uh . . ." I'm considering fried chicken when the crowd in the lobby suddenly quiets.

"Mr. Casella," Kenneth says. My stomach sinks, and I turn slowly to face the concierge as he stands next to my father. Kenneth glances at me. "Miss Casella, nice to see you enjoying the Ruby."

"Whatever," I say, annoyed that he'd pretend to be polite to me in front of my father. For his part, my father tenses like he's expecting bad news. Does he really think I'm acting out? He turns to Kenneth, but instead of apologizing, he stoops his shoulders.

"I need more time," he says quietly. Kenneth is unmoved, lifting his chin in a pompous way to look down his nose. "Please," my father goes on, "just another few days."

"What?" I demand. First of all, I just finished telling my father that I wanted out of this place, and now he's begging the concierge to let us stay? Is he nuts? And what gives—did my dad run out of money? I hardly think this is Kenneth's call.

"I'm sorry, Mr. Casella," Kenneth replies, ignoring me. "But this is the final warning. You remember what we talked out, yes?"

My father touches his throat, a sudden flinch of pain. My anger is quickly replaced with fear, terror reverberating from my father to me. Whatever they've talked out— it's not good. I step in and take my father's arm.

"Believe me," I tell Kenneth, trying to act brave. "We're out of here in the morning. You can count on that."

Kenneth flashes me a look of disdain and then sets his eyes on my father. I swallow hard, my dad's arm shaking beneath my hand. "See to it," Kenneth tells him. "Otherwise there will be repercussions." He turns on his heel and walks back across the lobby.

My heart thuds against my ribs; the crowd starts talking again. My father pats my hand like the exchange never happened, and looks down at me, smiling gently.

"Now, about dinner," he says.

"Seriously?" I ask him. "We're not going to discuss the psycho who just threatened you? What is he talking about, Dad? Do you owe him money?"

My father shakes his head. "It's nothing like that, kid. Promise. Kenneth . . . he's uncomfortable with some of the choices you've made. He'd prefer if you left sooner than later."

"Likewise. I think he's an asshole."

My father's mouth twitches with a smile. "I won't even correct your language on that one." Surprised, I laugh. "I just wish we could stay longer," my father continues. "This has been wonderful, having us all together." He looks over at me, his eyes glistening in the lights of the chandelier. "But after tomorrow you'll never have to deal with Kenneth again," he says. "I swear it."

He puts his hand to his chest like he's making an oath, and his expression is no longer frightened. I wonder if I read the signals wrong in their conversation. Kenneth clearly has it out for me, but my father might have been speaking on my behalf. Standing up for me. It reminds me of how much he's changed since we've arrived here.

Dad and I both sigh, turning to look over the gathered crowd. For the first time since my mother died, I feel like we're on the same team. We're about to discuss our dinner plans again when I see him. My heart leaps.

"Elias," I call a little too loudly, startling several people around us. Elias looks up from where he's standing across the lobby with two older men, white-haired types with tuxedos and substantial mustaches. Elias himself has changed into a gray suit and bow tie, his hair combed smooth. His face clean shaven. He tilts his head to say something to the men and then starts through the crowd in our direction.

"Is that Elias Lange?" my father asks, sounding impressed. When I nod, he slips his hands into his pockets and smiles broadly. "That's wonderful," he adds. "I met him at the party the other night. Nice guy." Dad looks sideways at me. "Although your brother doesn't much like him."

"Daniel's predictable that way," I mumble. *At least he used to be.* No, I stop the negative thoughts. My brother will regain his sanity. Once he sees how Dad's acting, how happy the three of us can be in Phoenix, he'll come back to his senses.

My dad shifts, anticipating Elias as he gets closer. I watch with nervous tension, realizing that I never went back to meet Elias at the café. He's probably wondering what happened to me. God, I hope this isn't awkward. My shoulders fall—of course it will be. I'm standing here with my dad.

Elias is taller than most of the other guests. Warm and charming, he murmurs hello as he passes them, clasping their shoulders or shaking their hands. My pulse continues to climb, and when he comes to stop in front of us, he nods politely to my father. "Mr. Casella," he says, outstretching his arm. My dad chuckles, not used to the politeness and respect he's been receiving here at the Ruby.

After what feels like a long pause, Elias turns to me. We stare for a moment, and then he smiles. "Audrey," he murmurs, holding out his palm. So. Damn. Charming. I slip my hand into his, and he lifts my fingers to his lips and kisses them. "You look lovely," he adds, and winks.

"Thank you," I say, probably turning about a million shades of pink. Although Ryan would occasionally hug me in front of my parents, he'd never kiss my hand. It's so . . . intimate.

Elias looks past us to see the emptying theater. "How was the movie?" he asks my father, already on his good side.

My father begins to retell his favorite parts, but I've stopped listening, instead checking out Elias in his suit. There's a swell of affection at the way he seems to say just the right things, how he flashes me a smile every now and then to let me know that he hasn't forgotten I'm there. When the conversation starts to run long, I decide I want him to myself. He's the only thing that makes sense anymore.

"Sorry to interrupt," I say, moving to take Elias's arm. He slides his hand over mine and turns to me. "Can I talk to you for a second?" I ask, earning a chuckle from my father.

"Uh-oh," my father says to Elias. "That's a loaded question."

I roll my eyes. "Way to minimize my feelings, Dad."

"I'm sorry," my father starts, but I wave it off.

"I was just kidding," I tell him, earning a relieved smile. "I'll see you later tonight."

"I hope so, Audrey," he responds with a sudden bout of sadness. "Today was a good day. I've missed those. I have the Ruby to thank for that."

There's a sudden feeling of abandonment, like I'm losing him all over again. My unease returns, and I back away from my father. "Let's go," I whisper to Elias, pulling him toward the hallway. Confused, Elias says good-bye, and then we're walking swiftly out of the crowd toward the hallway. I'd just started to accept that our lives were getting back to normal, or at least on the outskirts of normal, and then my dad had to go and act all brainwashed again.

"You plan to tell me what's going on?" Elias asks curiously. "I spent an hour longer than necessary at the café." Last he knew, we were making plans to spend a sportive evening in his room. Unfortunately for both of us, things have changed.

A couple appears at the end of the hallway, falling into each other and laughing. The woman is wearing an elegant green dress, but judging from her and her companion's wobbly steps, they've spent the better part of the evening at the bar. Neither of them notices us, and Elias puts his hand on the small of my back.

"In here," he says, moving us to the other end of the

hallway near a large wooden door. I didn't notice this entrance before, and as we walk inside, I watch the people go by. They don't even glance in our direction. Elias calls to me and goes to sit in one of the oversize leather chairs in the corner.

"Whoa," I say, looking around. There are tall bookcases and an enormous gray-stone fireplace. Above the mantel is a green and brown painting of a field, muted and masculine. There are several pool tables on one side of the room, near the oversize leaded windows, and dark brown leather furniture. Now that we're away from the lobby, I'm calmer. Or maybe it's Elias.

"This used to be the gentlemen's room," he says, crossing his foot over his knee. "Now it's the billiard room, but most people forget it's here."

"Boys' club, huh?" I ask. I wander over to a shelf and run my gaze over the spines of the books. They're old, some antique, but I recognize the titles from English class.

"Audrey," Elias says softly. "Although I love being dragged away, I can tell something's bothering you. Care to elaborate?" Elias's face has grown serious. Almost expectant.

"Will you think I'm overreacting?" I ask.

"Probably not."

He lives here. Would it surprise him if I told him that I think the Ruby has brainwashed my family? If I told him that I think Kenneth means to hurt me? As I decide where to begin, Elias grows more worried. He comes over and stands facing me, his arms crossed over his chest.

"It's the hotel," I start. "It's affecting my father and brother, changed their personalities."

Elias tilts his head curiously. "How so?"

"Daniel isn't going to our grandmother's anymore," I say, sick at the words. "He abandoned me, and he was cruel. He said not to trust anyone, and that no matter what, I have to leave tomorrow. Like, what?" I ask, confused. "No offense, but my brother can't *live here*. I went downstairs and told my dad that I wanted the three of us to get out now, but he blew it off. He said we were better here — and in a way he might be right. But . . . I don't want to stay at the Ruby anymore. I'm scared of this place. I'm scared of what's happening." I roll my eyes, aware of how insane I sound. "I think my family's possessed," I add, wanting Elias to laugh. But he doesn't. He lowers his eyes.

"They looked happy, Audrey," he says quietly. "When I saw them last night at the party"—he lifts his gaze to mine—"they were both happy. Isn't that a good thing?"

"Uh, sure. Except for the fact that they aren't actually happy. They're grieving—we're all grieving. And although I'm all for denial, this is different. I think it has to do with Kenneth."

Now, this seems to surprise Elias. "What does Kenneth have to do with this?" he asks. "Did he say something to you?"

"More like threaten."

Color blazes on Elias's cheeks and he steps closer, taking my arms. "Tell me everything," he says. "When did this happen?"

For a moment I'm reminded of Ryan and how he tried to fix things for me. In the end I nearly got him killed. I don't want to drag Elias into the same trouble I continually find myself in. I slide my hands along his chest and drape them over his shoulders. "Never mind," I say, wishing for his easy smile to return. "Forget I said anything."

It doesn't work. "Audrey," he says, staring down at me. I get on my tiptoes, tempting him to kiss me instead of scold me. He does, but only briefly. "Tell me what happened," he murmurs, kissing me again like he can't help it.

I sigh, tilting my head as Elias's kisses trail over my jaw, my neck. My tension starting to ease now that I'm preoccupied. "He cornered me in the ballroom," I say, closing my eyes. "Kenneth told me to stay away from the staff, that they'd be punished for consorting with me. Like he's the —"

Elias pulls back so quickly, so violently, that I stumble and have to catch myself on the mantel of the fireplace. "What?" he demands. "Did he tell you that—that they'd be punished?" Elias's eyes have gone wild, his body poised to leave.

"Yes, he said he was enforcing the rules of the Ruby and that I should spend the rest of my time in my room."

Elias curses and bolts for the door. Alarmed, I chase

after him, and we're running, full-on running, down the long hallway. "What are you doing?" I shout, too caught off guard to process the fear bubbling up.

"I need to get to the basement." His voice is rough, and I can barely keep pace with him. The hallway is darker than it was when we came in, the pictures blur as we run past. It hits me—Lourdes is in the basement. Elias fires me a look. "Go back," he orders, although he's obviously not going to stop to force me.

"No," I gasp out, worried for my friend. If Elias is scared, there must be something wrong. "The elevator's the other way," I tell him.

"The Ruby will slow us down," he says, taking a hard left and throwing himself against a metal door. We're in a back stairwell. White walls, gray concrete steps. Elias takes the stairs two at a time, and I can't keep up any longer.

"What do you mean?" I call out, tramping behind him as quickly as I can. "What does that mean, 'The Ruby will slow us down'?"

Elias rounds the next level and shoots me a terrified glance as he continues to race toward the basement. I understand the expression, what it conveys, and my entire body tenses. Kenneth is going to kill her. That's why Elias is freaking out. Kenneth is going to kill Lourdes. I renew my speed, and I'm nearly caught up when Elias grabs a fire extinguisher from the wall and then rams his shoulder into the door, exploding onto the basement level.

"Stay behind me," he says, slowing down and testing the weight of the extinguisher, as if he plans to use it as a weapon. The walls are red, and there are sounds echoing down the hall. Grunting. Crying. At about three doors from Lourdes's, Elias stops to look back at me. "You're not part of this," he says calmly. "Your brother's right, Audrey. You leave tomorrow no matter what. Even if you have to let us all burn."

The words are similar to what Lourdes said at the fountain last night. How no one tried to help the victims of the ballroom fire, no one tried to save them. The sentiment is devastating, especially in a moment of complete panic like this. Elias doesn't appear willing to move until I agree, so I nod weakly, not sure what I've just promised him.

There's a loud crash from Lourdes's room, and Elias jumps forward. He stops at Lourdes's door, and then, without a word, he hikes the extinguisher above his head and slams it down, cracking off the handle and sending it flying across the hall.

I press myself to the wall, the scene in front of me too crazy to be real. Elias kicks in the door. I cover my mouth when I catch sight of what's going on inside. Lourdes is in uniform, sprawled out on the bed, her skin purple and her eyes bulging. Kenneth is straddling her body, his thick hands around her neck. Even from here I'm sure she's dead, and yet the concierge doesn't let go. He doesn't even look at Elias as he stomps in.

Without a word of warning, Elias swings the fire extinguisher, slamming it against Kenneth's head with a sickening thud. The concierge's body goes rigid and tilts to the side, he's completely unconscious when he hits the carpet. Elias drops the extinguisher on the floor and runs a shaky hand through his hair.

I'm stunned in place. I don't know if Kenneth is dead, if Lourdes is dead. Elias stands in the middle of complete mayhem, his shoulders stooped in exhaustion. "Move," I whisper to myself, knowing I have to check on Lourdes. Call the cops and get help. "Move," I say again, pushing off the wall and into the carnage. I go immediately to Lourdes, surprised when she turns to her side, coughing. Her skin is blotchy and the blood vessels in her eyes are broken, blood seeping over the white.

"I'm going to get help," I tell her, fighting down my panic. I can do this. I'll be better than I was with Mom. I'll save Lourdes.

There's a groan from the floor, and Lourdes and I see Kenneth writhing. Blood pours from the gash in his head, but he doesn't seem to be dying. Even though he's a tyrant, I'm grateful. I wouldn't want Elias to face a murder trial, to possibly go to jail for saving his friend.

Elias backs up, leaning against the interior wall of Lourdes's room. He drops his arms to his sides, like he's giving up. The hero who broke in minutes ago is now defeated. He glances at Lourdes and shrugs helplessly.

"I'm so sorry," he says, fighting back a cry. "I tried to save you this time."

*This time,* I repeat in my head, knowing now why the staff fears the concierge. This has happened before.

"I know," Lourdes says to Elias, gasping in a breath. I help her as she struggles to sit up. From the floor Kenneth gurgles, and a thick choking sound fills the room. I turn to Elias.

"We need an ambulance," I say. "Can you call from here?"

Elias doesn't acknowledge my voice, only stares down at Kenneth. The concierge is rolling from side to side, desperately in need of medical attention. In my arms, Lourdes trembles uncontrollably. Her color is returning to normal, but she's mumbling under her breath. It takes a few times for me to catch what she's saying.

"He never dies," she whispers in a broken voice over and over. And then, in reaction, Kenneth's head snaps to us, his eyes staring directly at Lourdes. His face is covered in blood, his head deformed from the impact of the extinguisher. Half dead, he smiles. I scream.

Lourdes jumps from the bed. Bent over and clearly in pain, she stands above Kenneth and shouts at him, "Die! Just die already!" The world has erupted into chaos, and I look at Elias, wanting him to stop it. But he only watches in despair, in complete hopelessness.

Before I can process what's happening, Lourdes grabs a

steak knife from a dirty room-service tray. My eyes widen, and I scream for her to stop, but it happens too quickly. She falls to her knees next to the concierge and buries the knife to its hilt in his chest. He moans, and Lourdes rips the blade out, splashing me in warm blood splatter, and then drives it into his chest again.

The screech that escapes my throat doesn't sound human. In that moment it's like I leave my body. The horror, the heat of the blood on my face, has broken me. I run from the room. "Just die!" Lourdes continues to shout. I'm blinded, wiping frantically at the salty tears and blood near my eyes. I head toward the stairwell, reminded of Elias's words that the Ruby will slow me down.

They just murdered someone. Oh my God. They just murdered someone. I shout for help, running up the stairs as fast as possible. Nothing will ever be the same again. Am I an accessory? Is this my fault because I talked to the staff?

I burst out of the stairwell and into the brightly lit hallway. I'm running for the lobby, glancing down to see my clothes are awash in blood. "Help!" I scream. I take the turn into the lobby and slip from the blood on my sandals. My knee hits the marble floor, sending a vibration up my leg. I call for help and scramble to my feet again, moving toward the desk.

But no one responds. A few people stop to stare at me, watching with curiosity rather than concern, and others ignore me altogether.

"What is wrong with all of you?" I shout, spinning to look at them. "We need help! Get an ambulance!"

"Miss Casella," a voice calls from behind me at the front desk. In that moment life stops. The faces of the people around me blur together and what's left of my sanity shatters completely. *It can't be. It can't. . . .*

Slowly I turn to face the front desk. Standing there in a burgundy uniform, his hands folded on his chest, is Kenneth—smiling pleasantly. I gulp in a breath of air, sure I'm going to faint. Just as things start to go fuzzy, Kenneth holds up a black envelope.

"Good news," the concierge says pleasantly. "You've received an invitation to the party."

# CHAPTER 14

My mother died three months and eleven days ago. Some nights after she was gone, I'd search my memories for the bad times, thinking that if I could realize something horrible about her, it'd make accepting her death easier. Prove she deserved it somehow. It was sick — I knew that, but I also knew that most days it hurt too much to live. I couldn't let go. I didn't know how to move on. But like Daniel showed me, those negative thoughts only made her more real. More *mine*. And so I tried to stop thinking of her altogether.

It wasn't fair that it had been such a normal day. Her death should have been an international disaster — the world sharing in my misery. Instead it was a Wednesday. I had just arrived at school, and Ryan was next to me as we entered the front doors into the main hallway. Normally, the jocks would call out to him, fist-bump him on his way past. But not this time. The first moment I noticed something wasn't right was when we passed by the office. Through the glass partition I could see the teachers crowded around the main desk. No one was crying, that would have given too much away. It was Mr. Powell, my science teacher, who betrayed the controlled group. His stern face had gone slack, his jaw hanging open like it had come unhinged. He was mouth-breathing, hunched slightly forward as he stared toward my mother's open office door.

I followed his line of sight and saw that my mother wasn't in her office. She wasn't with the group. Mom had left for school a half hour before Ryan and I did; she should have been there. But my mother never made it to school. She had stopped to pick up coffees for the office, something she did when she was in a good mood. At the counter of the Coffee Break my mother had a stroke. She stumbled a few steps before collapsing in a heap near the trash can. She was in a store full of strangers, but I was told that several of them tried to help her. One older lady held her hand even though she was unconscious. That same lady came to my mother's funeral, but I didn't thank her. I should have thanked her.

The school had been notified right away. My father was on his way to the hospital, and it was up to the staff to break the news to me. Looking back, I like to think that I sensed her pain, had a small headache of my own—but I know that's probably some psychosomatic bullshit.

I stopped in the middle of the hallway, my stomach lurching. I quickly scanned for my mother's messenger bag on her office desk, any sign that she had arrived. The smell of floor wax was thick in the air, filling my nostrils as I started to tremble.

"Audrey, what's wrong?" Ryan asked, touching my arm. Before I could answer, Mr. Powell turned, his eyes locking on mine.

His jaw snapped shut, but then he covered his mouth with his palm, as if he'd seen a ghost. He must have murmured something, though, because the entire room of teachers turned to look at me. The Spanish teacher squeezed her eyes shut, and the coach put his hand on her shoulder to comfort her.

*I'm not imagining this,* I told myself as the principal rushed toward me. *This is really happening.*

And as I stand here now, in the lobby of the Hotel Ruby, I'm telling myself the same thing: *This is really happening.*

Kenneth's smile widens, splitting wider than possible — a Cheshire cat. I scream, loud enough to crack my voice; the sound sputters away. My head spins with horror and fear. The people around me stare, and yet others continue by as if it's completely normal for a girl to be standing here covered in blood.

Unable to comprehend, I feel my natural instincts kick in and I bolt for the front door. My feet can't carry me fast enough, and my sandals flip off, my arms pumping at my sides. I have to get out of here. I have to find help!

I expect to be attacked at any moment, and I launch myself against the door, sending it flying open as I rush through into the fading sunset. But the minute I cross the threshold, I skid to a stop, tearing flesh from my bare feet on the marble floor. I'm just inside the door of the lobby. How . . .

Kenneth chuckles, and I see one of the other guests put her hand over her mouth to hold back her own laugh. I turn, frantic. Did something push me back inside the hotel? I have to get out of here!

I open the door, running out, but once again I find myself running *into* the lobby. As if the door only leads one way. The door only leads into the Ruby.

My body shakes uncontrollably, my sobs nearly silent and my throat aching from my screams. I cry, and when I wipe my cheeks, my hands are smeared in blood — Kenneth's blood, even though he's standing before me, perfectly intact.

This time I don't run. I walk hesitantly to the door. "Please," I whimper. I pull the handle and look outside, at the world beyond. I see the roundabout for cars, the long driveway that brought us here. I cast a glance back at Kenneth, who is waiting patiently. I walk out, but the world spins, sending me right back inside the door once again.

Tears drip over my lips. "I want to go home," I say, earning a sympathetic tsk from a woman sitting on a chair near the fireplace. Kenneth is no longer smiling. "Please let me go," I say, although my voice is only a strangled whisper.

"That's not up to me," he says curtly. "Now, if you're

quite through with this tantrum, I believe you have a party to get ready for. I'll send your invitation up to your room."

I need to find my brother. My father. I trip forward, catching myself. I stare down, surprised there's blood on my feet. My pants and my shirt. The room starts to swirl, or maybe that's just my mind. People appear and disappear from my vision, and I blink my eyes quickly, trying to get my bearings. "Daniel?" I call, even though I don't see him. My arm begins to hurt, and I rub it absently and take a few steps forward. Words are too big, and too few, to work for me. A shadow passes over the room, and I'm afraid it's Kenneth, growing larger, looming over me with a sinister shade. I start to fold in on myself.

There's a whistle, a sharp whip through the air, and I dart my eyes to the other side of the lobby. Joshua stands there in his valet uniform. He has one arm outstretched to me, while the other is holding open a door that reads STAFF ONLY. He nods his chin, urging me forward, before he slides his eyes in Kenneth's direction, looking ready to run if he has to.

Is this a trick? Another trick that will spin me back into the lobby? But when I turn to Kenneth, he's staring at Joshua, his mouth pulled taut and strained. Kenneth doesn't approve, and that alone is enough to send me running for Joshua. I expect Kenneth to yell for me to stop, but there isn't a sound behind me.

When I reach the other side of the lobby, I peer through

the doorway, finding a narrow hall instead of a room. I want to ask what's going on, but this is the time for action, not explanation. My thoughts are starting to clear, and I regain control of my limbs and mouth. The pain in my arm fades away.

I don't look back at the front desk; I rush inside. The door slams shut behind me, and I jump, terrified. But then Joshua is next to me, pulling me by the wrist, and then to the side. The hallway has deep red carpet and is impossibly long and windy; every turn exactly the same. There are no doors. No end in sight.

Joshua's fingers are wrapped tightly, crushing my wrist as I continue to run with him. I stare at the side of his face, and I must be slowing us down, because he shoots me a look and then slows. "What?" he asks, slightly out of breath.

"Are you like him?" My voice is still a whisper, burning my throat with every syllable.

"Kenneth?" Joshua spits out. "Hardly. But we have to keep moving, Audrey, or the Ruby will start rearranging things. Then we'll never get to the fifteenth floor."

I pull my arm out of his grip and swallow down a shaky breath. "Why are you taking me to the fifteenth floor? What's going on, Joshua? Please tell me I'm not crazy." I stop. "Or tell me that I am. None of this is possible."

Joshua rolls his eyes and roughly grabs my wrist again. "Not now." He yanks me forward. We're running again, and I contemplate how I can escape, get my father and my brother and leave this place, when I can't even get out the front door.

Joshua and I reach the end of the hallway, and the valet lets go of my arm. I rub my bruised skin and turn to find the front of the old-time elevator we took last night. I have no idea how we got here. We ran for too long to end up in the same place we found so easily the night before. Joshua slides the gate over and puts his palm on my back, pushing me inside. He climbs in after me and slams the gate closed once again. I press myself against the back of the elevator as he operates the gear.

"Why didn't he die?" I whisper to myself, grasping the golden railing. The elevator shakes to life. "I saw her kill him. I have his blood on me." I lift my hands, spreading my fingers to prove that there are splatters of red everywhere.

The first floor passes, and Joshua turns to me. He takes a moment to evaluate my appearance. "I know you're terrified and probably have a million questions, but I assure you, I don't have the answers. I just work here. I do know that we have to keep moving, because if Kenneth catches me when he's this pissed off, I'll end up worse than Lourdes." He turns away. "I don't intend to let him catch me."

Beyond the gate, I realize, the hallway lights are going out the minute we start to pass the floors; the darkness is racing us to the top. I'm scared we won't make it. I'm worried that we will.

"So this place is haunted," I state. "By Kenneth? Is he the one who can rearrange things?"

Joshua shakes his head. "Kenneth is the asshole in charge, but the Ruby runs the place. She decides who to take in. This is a hotel," Joshua says, adjusting his uniform. "It's meant for guests. But sometimes the wrong people slip in. You should have just kept your mouth shut and enjoyed yourself. Now you might be stuck here."

I want to laugh, his statement's pure madness. A hotel can't keep me. Then again, I just watched my friends murder a concierge, only to find him smiling moments later behind the front desk. I tried to leave and ended up reentering the lobby, over and over. I'd be the mad one if I denied any explanation at this point.

The elevator jolts to a stop and I stagger sideways, bumping my shoulder into the wall. Joshua rips open the gate and quickly walks out. I follow behind him, glancing up at the dial to check which floor we're on. The dial has stopped on the fifteenth floor. Joshua points ahead to a gray metal door.

"Back entrance," he explains. "Now hurry before Kenneth shows up with a dagger of his own."

My fear once again spikes, and then Joshua is waiting for me, holding open the door. His stance is impatient, and I pause across from him in the doorway. I peel my hair back from my forehead, the strands stiff with blood.

"Will he really stab you?" I ask in a weak voice. "And . . ." *Do you want to ask this, Audrey?* I wait a long beat and then swallow hard. "And what happens to you if he does? Will

197

you die?" I'm scared of the answer. Joshua may not be like Kenneth, but it doesn't mean he's like me, either. His dark eyes hold mine, unflinching.

"You're not asking the right questions," he says calmly. Then he pushes past me and calls for me to come on. I'm going numb; whether from shock or crazy, I'm not completely sure. But it's offering calm when there shouldn't be any. When we stop at room 1525, my body is shivering, even though I'm not cold at all.

The door pulls open dramatically, making me rock on my heels. I snap out of my false calm and take a step backward, bumping into Joshua. "Catherine," I whisper, gulping down a breath. I look behind me, afraid Joshua's set me up. "Why did you bring me here?" I demand. "She hates me!" I've blamed Catherine for convincing Daniel to stay, but now I realize her intention may be much more sinister than that. Frightened, I move to run off, but Joshua grabs me around the waist and holds me fast. I scream, but he smothers my mouth with his palm.

Rather than hurt me, he whispers for me to calm down. To please calm down. He works my body through the door, and I watch as it slams, trapping me in the room with Joshua and Catherine.

# CHAPTER 15

I'm frantic, afraid they're going to tie me up and torture me. Do terrible things that I can't even comprehend. I thrash and dig my nails into the back of Joshua's hand. He yelps, pulling away, and I fall a few steps onto the bed. Joshua shakes his hand, cursing at me.

I quickly take stock of the suite. It's twice the size of my room with a view like Elias's. The entire place smells of flowers, hints of perfume. There's a bright purple and pink bouquet on the dresser, gowns hanging on the outside of the closet door like she was trying to decide what to wear. And then there's Catherine herself, sans makeup. She's not made of porcelain. Tiny freckles dot her nose and cheeks, making her all the more real. She stands there, dressed in a white sequined dress and bedroom slippers.

"Don't come near me," I say in her direction. "I want to go home." I'm completely caught off guard when Catherine lunges at me, dress and all, and grabs me by the upper arms to drag me to my feet. Her sharp red nails bite into my flesh.

"Are you trying to get him killed?" she shouts in my

face, her eyes wild and her curls framing her face. I'm so startled by her ferocity that I don't respond, even as her grip tightens.

"Cathy," Joshua says softly, taking her arms to pull her back. I flash him an accusatory look, angry that he put me in this position in the first place. Catherine tears herself away from him and points her finger in my face.

"Your little stunt with Lourdes is going to get him punished. You knew he would try to save her. How could you put him in danger?"

"Elias?" I ask, suddenly terrified that something's happened to him. That Kenneth has happened to him. "Is he all right?"

"He won't be for long," Catherine says. Her face twists in disgust; her hatred devours me. "At the very least Kenneth is going to kick him out of the party, and then he'll be stuck with the help."

Joshua's lips tighten, and Catherine looks sideways at him without apology. She crosses her thin arms over her chest, turning back to me. "You don't understand," she says. "He can be locked away for a long time, just like that goddamn housekeeper." She stops, slitting her eyes. "Did Lourdes put you up to it?" she asks suddenly.

"What do you mean?"

"Did she ask you to get Eli? I swear"—Catherine shakes her head—"that maid has been trying to steal him for as long as I can remember. She's obsessed with him.

She doesn't care who his family is. She doesn't even care about what Kenneth will do to him."

"You're being paranoid," Joshua says, watching the door like he's waiting for Kenneth to walk in at any moment. "Maybe you're the one who's obsessed."

"Go to hell," Catherine says, barely acknowledging him. Joshua shifts his eyes to her.

"I think I'm already there," he mutters.

The first hint of a smile crosses Catherine's lips, and she quickly tries to hide it before speaking to me again. "Have you seen him?" she asks, less hostile. "Since Kenneth returned, have you seen Elias?" Her voice is heavy with concern.

"No."

Catherine's reaction is immediate and she looks pleadingly at Joshua. He's quick to console her.

"I'm sure he's fine, Cathy," he says. "Kenneth will still want him at the party. He's too important."

"He won't let this go," she says, her beautiful face pulled in agony. "And if he knows I'm talking to *her* right now—"

"Yeah, about that," I snap. "You brought me up here. You know Kenneth is . . ." It's too crazy to say out loud, but I do it anyway. "Kenneth is a ghost or something. And Joshua is talking about the Ruby letting people leave." Catherine appears bored while I'm trying to put together the pieces in any sort of coherent explanation. Helplessness sinks my stomach. "But I couldn't get out the front door," I say. "Can you?"

Catherine's posture dips, caught off guard by the question. "No," she responds quietly. "None of us can leave. If you go out through the garden, you can get as far as the back wall. Joshua can make it to the driveway—but guests stop at the door. Unless you're one of the other ones. They come and go as they please."

"Other ones?" My heart leaps.

"The ones who don't notice us. They're on their own plane, kept separate. I'm sure you've seen them: stuck up and rude? The Ruby doesn't touch them. But to us"—she looks over to Joshua, despair tainting her features—"she can be a real bitch sometimes. We don't try to leave anymore. We're all trapped here together, Audrey, so quit causing a stir. Play your part and you may even get to go home."

"And what is my part? How long have you all been here?" I ask. "How long will I be here?"

"Forever," Joshua says.

I gasp. "Forever? I . . . I can't stay here. I'm not staying here!"

Catherine shakes her head. "Audrey's on the thirteenth floor," she points out. Joshua raises his eyebrows in surprise and then mutters something under his breath. Catherine turns back to me. "Kenneth can't hurt you so long as the Ruby protects you. Follow the rules, eat dinner and swim in the pool, run around with Eli all you want. But you don't belong here, Audrey," she tells me coldly. "Hopefully, you'll be gone by morning."

"I'm not waiting until morning," I tell her. "Listen, I don't know what my floor or any of you have to do with this, but I'm getting my family and I'm getting out of here. Tonight."

Catherine groans like I've just said the most annoying thing possible. "Yeah, well, good luck with that. But if you're going to be reckless, keep Elias out of it. You have no idea what Kenneth is capable of."

"I saw him choking Lourdes!"

Catherine laughs. "That's a slap on the wrist. You haven't seen the pain he can inflict. You'd better hope you never see it. Now," she continues, "you look horrid. I hope you didn't get blood on any of my things. Wash up and I'll give you something to wear." She puts her hand on her hip and surveys her room like a curtain might be a good choice. "I'm embarrassed for you," she adds.

I scoff, not worried so much about my appearance as I am about surviving. But Catherine turns around, leveling her icy stare at me. "I'm not kidding," she says. "If you show up like this, covered in . . . is that a piece of skin?—your father will panic. Daniel will want to help. Other guests will notice. Act like a civilized person or you'll be assigned somewhere else."

"And believe me," Joshua says, running his hand through his dark hair. "There are worse places than the basement."

"Much worse," Catherine agrees. "Now go before I

have Joshua bring me a fire hose to spray you down."

Joshua sits in the chair, putting his feet up on the desk. "That could prove entertaining," he says wryly.

I shoot him a disgusted look and then turn to walk into Catherine's bathroom. Before I close the door, she passes me a pile of things and I set them on the counter. I slam the door in her face and lock it.

This is ridiculous. I don't think anyone will care what I'm wearing when I'm trying to—

I stop short, seeing my reflection for the first time. I'm a horror show, bloodier than I realized. There is an arc of bright red blood across my cheek and eye, a smear of it across my forehead. My hair is matted and stiff, and left-over mascara has blackened beneath my eyes.

"Play your part," Catherine said. Maybe if I do, I can go home. Then again, maybe none of this is even real. I turn toward the door. Maybe they're not real.

I listen at the bathroom door, and although I can hear both Catherine's and Joshua's voices, I can't make out their words. I walk over to the shower and turn the dial as hot as it will go. I'm still barefoot, my sandals lost somewhere in the lobby, but I peel off my shirt and jeans, wincing at how revolting they are. I want Kenneth's blood off of me.

I get under the spray of water and adjust the temperature. I use my nails to pick through my stiffened hair, then shampoo and condition as quickly as possible. When I'm clean, I turn off the faucet, wondering what exactly

Catherine expects me to wear. I climb out of the shower, checking the still-locked door, and then wrap myself in a towel.

I hurry and change into a pair of too-tight jeans and a blouse with strained buttons. Catherine's a bit thinner than humanly possible, I decide, and I quickly use her comb to untangle my hair. When I'm done, I wait, surrounded by the quiet of the bathroom. Once I step outside, I don't know what I'll find. I don't know who I'll find.

"You're getting out of this hotel," I tell my reflection, and then slip my feet into a pair of heels. I stand there feeling absurd, but if you didn't know me, this outfit might be normal. But I'm not even sure what the hell normal is anymore.

I'm startled by a knock on the door. "Do you mind?" Catherine calls. "I'd like to finish getting ready for the party. Unlike you, I actually try to appeal to the opposite sex." She laughs, and I walk over to unlock the door and open it. Catherine studies me and then hitches up her eyebrow. "It's an improvement, if you ask me."

"I didn't ask you," I say, and push past her back into the room. Joshua nods and agrees with Catherine that I'm definitely improved, and I turn to both of them. "So what am I supposed to do now?" I demand.

Catherine sighs and motions for Joshua to answer me instead. I know she told me to run around and act like nothing's wrong, but I can't do that.

Joshua presses his lips into a sympathetic smile. "You live," he says simply. "You live, Audrey. The Ruby will do the rest." He and Catherine exchange a look, and then Catherine strolls into the bathroom.

"Oh, wait," she says, poking her head back out. "If you see Elias, will you be a dear and tell him I'm looking for him?" I don't respond, still not clear about what I'm supposed to do. Catherine motions to the door. "Run along now. And whatever you do"—she pauses, apologetic and regretful—"stay away from that party." She tightens her jaw and shuts the bathroom door.

Unable to bear another second with her, I leave the room and let the door slam shut behind me. Now, in the deserted hallway, I stand, afraid and confused. Catherine said Kenneth couldn't hurt me—but do I believe that? I've seen him attack Lourdes, seen how terrified of him everyone is. Would he have already done something to me if he could have? And what does any of this have to do with the thirteenth floor?

I can't stay here and go along—*live*, as Joshua said— knowing this place is honest-to-God haunted. Knowing that Kenneth is in control of my life. And then there's my family. They plan to stay here—do they know already? Did they try to leave and couldn't? But more disturbingly, if they know the truth about this place . . . why won't they tell me? Why won't Daniel?

I get into the guest elevator, scared but determined.

Even at my worst my brother didn't desert me. He stuck with me while our dad evaporated, made sure I held together when I found out we were moving. Until today he was the person I trusted most in the world, the only one who truly understood my grief.

And so I press the button for the sixth floor. Daniel told me he didn't want to fight—well, too bad. Let's have it out. But when it's done, we're getting out of here. We're getting out of here together.

# CHAPTER 16

Daniel doesn't answer his door. My knocks turn to panicked thumps, and I'm not sure if he's ignoring me or truly not here. He wasn't with Catherine, I know that much. He could be with my father. With that thought I walk down a few doors to my father's room and start the banging process all over again.

I've lost track of time. How long since the movie ended, since lunch? How long have we been at this hotel? Time is a blur. I rub my hands roughly over my face and rest against the wall. I've been telling myself for months that I was alone, but now . . . I truly am. And I'm terrified.

I take a moment to pull myself together. I look down at Catherine's clothes and smooth back my hair. My father is probably at dinner, and he plans to be at the party. I have to find them both, and then I'll drag them out of here if I have to.

A plan starts to formulate. I'll ask Daniel if I can talk to him outside with Dad. And then I'll convince them to leave. We came here together; if we try to leave together, we'll be able to. It makes sense. In my scattered and frightened thoughts it makes a little bit of sense.

I walk purposefully back to the elevator, and the doors open like it's been waiting for me. My heart crawls up into my throat and I step inside. When I turn, I see that every button has been pressed already, lit up and every floor a stop. The elevator doors close, and although it's not dark in this space, the air itself seems to dim.

*The Ruby will try to stop you.*

The bell dings for the next floor. I press myself against the mirrored wall, afraid of who's waiting for the elevator. It feels like an eternity, and I moan out my fear as the doors slide open. No one is there. I bite hard on my lip, scared to peek into the hallway. I wait. *Please, hurry. Please, hurry.* The doors finally close, and I squat down, my legs shaking too badly to stand. It's the same on every floor, and my sanity wavers, until finally the elevator doors slide back at the lobby.

The space is bright and grand in front of me, light glittering from the chandeliers, people happily walking about. I let out a shaky breath and step forward. The scene is one of ease, and I leave the elevator and look around. Is this happening?

My eyes dart to the desk, expecting Kenneth, but he's not there. *Too busy trying to murder his employees,* I think. No one walking around seems even the slightest bit interested in me. But my eyes feel too wide, my skin too cold. My lips are parted, shaking as I breathe erratically. I start toward the ballroom, mentally reciting the different ways I can tell my family that the Ruby is haunted, that it's brainwashing them, and that we have to leave—that we have to try. It's not going well, even in my head.

I pause when I notice two men in tuxedos standing at the doorway of the ballroom. They weren't there when I sneaked in that first day. Is this added security a new development? Is this because of me?

The men nod their hellos to every person who walks in the door. They're not turning anyone away, but will they let me pass? Just then one of the men lifts his head and meets my eyes, like he's known I've been here the entire time. His expression is stern but not altogether scary. If I hope to pass through, I'll need my invitation. Proper attire. I'm sure I could dredge something up in my room, and then I'll come down and . . .

It's then that I hear it, the soft sounds of piano keys; the song. The same song I've heard over and over since I've been here. I turn and follow the melody, my pulse pounding so fast I'm afraid I'm going to have a heart attack. But the *song*. I feel like I should recognize it, that I need to remember it.

The people begin to fade away as I turn down the empty corridor. I'm no longer scared, I'm determined. I have to find the source of the music, and then maybe I'll figure out what the hell is going on here.

I end up at the door of the billiard room. It's partially ajar, the lights blazing inside, but I'm scared to walk in. What if Kenneth is there? What if he's waiting for me?

"Hello?" a voice calls from inside, as if noticing me linger. I push the door open more to find Elias standing at the leaded window. I sway with relief. *He's okay. Thank God he's okay.* When he sees me, he puts his hand over his heart.

"I called your room," he says breathlessly. "I've looked everywhere." His hair has fallen onto his forehead, disheveled, but he's still painfully handsome in his gray suit. He checks me over, and the corner of his mouth tilts slightly. He must recognize Catherine's clothes.

I stare at him, not sure where to start. "Did you hear it?" I ask, my voice hoarse.

"Hear what?"

"The music," I say. "Did you hear the music?"

Elias's face pales and he shakes his head no. "I'm sorry," he says eventually. "I can't hear it, Audrey."

"But . . ." I spin around, taking in the room. Looking for a piano or a radio. "I know I heard it coming from in here." Tears start to blur my vision. "I've been hearing the same song for days," I tell him. "I thought maybe it would lead me to an answer. Everything is so messed up," I choke out. "Elias, my brother's gone crazy, my dad's gone sane. I watched you nearly kill someone." He lowers his eyes, but I go on. "I can't leave the hotel," I say. "I can't even walk out the goddamn door. I just want to go home. I want my family and I want to go home."

Elias's expression weakens. "I know," he murmurs. He takes a step toward me, but nervousness replaces my

211

initial relief at seeing him. I'm overjoyed that he's okay, but I watched him hit a man—or what I thought was a man—and crush his skull. What else is he capable of? What is his part in all of this?

He pauses when I take a step back from him. "Audrey," he says, pained. His entire posture sags, and I see that I've wounded him. My chest aches at the thought. Because when I'm with him, I'm not overwhelmed by grief. My heart is somewhere else entirely, and I didn't think that was possible. I didn't think I would ever love anything again.

"I can't stay here," I whisper. His eyes glass over, and he swallows hard. I'm leaving him—we both know it's going to end that way. "How do I get out?" I ask him.

"The Ruby has to let you go," he says quietly. "You just have to wait."

It's not the answer I wanted to hear. "Wait for what?" I ask. "For Kenneth to kill me?"

Elias's eyes flash. "He won't touch you," he growls. "It's not his place."

"This makes no sense!" I say, raising my voice. "What? Am I like the others, then?"

Elias stares at me a long moment, taken aback by the question. "How did you . . ." He stops and looks over my outfit again. "Catherine," he murmurs to himself. Tentatively Elias moves toward me. I don't shrink back this time. "No. You're not exactly like the other ones," he says. "Except in the fact that Kenneth can't hurt you. Not physically."

I think about that. There was a moment last night, when I went to the front desk to get an invitation. Kenneth implied there was a cut on my head. I felt the sting, saw the blood. But then it was gone. I remember now. I don't know what it means, but I remember.

"This can't be happening," I say, still clinging to the notion that there's a rational explanation for all of this. Elias comes to pause in front of me, and I tilt my head to look up at him. His eyes are desperate and lonely. Sad and loving. It's hard for me not to reach for him, and I ball my hands into fists at my sides. I didn't notice, but there's a fire crackling in the hearth across the room. The sound of voices down the hall. We're not alone, but our connection isolates us from everything else.

"I'm sorry," Elias says. "I . . . we all hoped you'd enjoy your stay and then leave, like the other ones. A fond memory. But I should have told you what Kenneth was, even if I would have ended up locked away like Lourdes."

"Her suspension," I say, putting the pieces together. "What happened?"

"The Ruby doesn't reveal herself," he says. "Or at least she shouldn't. Kenneth has strict rules to keep guests happy, including the others. If you had known what you had walked into"—he lowers his eyes—"you would have made trouble for him. Been disruptive. Lourdes broke the house rules once before. She told Tanya the truth and ended up locked away where we couldn't find her. She was gone for so long." He puts his fingers over his lips, holding back. He takes a breath and continues. "Kenneth doesn't have the power to get rid of us," he says, "but he can punish us. For you I should have taken that chance."

"Maybe," I say, even if it's not what he wants to hear. "But I can tell you that I wouldn't want you to suffer, to be locked away." There's a fine line between self-preservation and protecting the people you care about. Now that we can't change it, I wouldn't have wanted him to sacrifice himself.

"This is my fault," he says miserably. "I couldn't stay away from you. I dragged you into this."

"And what if you had stayed away?" I ask. "My family and I would have vacationed for a few days, played tennis, and then gone on our way to Elko? Where does that leave you? Why can't you get out?"

"I belong to the Ruby now," he says. "But you don't. You still have a chance."

His words leave no room for argument—he's a prisoner here. I'm no longer scared of Catherine, or Joshua, or even Elias. I'm scared I won't be able to get out of this place. That I'll be trapped in the Ruby forever.

"I have to go to the ballroom," I say. "I have to talk to my brother and father." I turn to leave, but Elias's arm shoots out to stop me. I gasp in a breath and turn to him. His cheeks are flaming red, his chest rising and falling.

"No," he says definitively. "You're not going to the party. I won't let you."

"Why not? I have an invitation."

"Because that party's not for you, that's why," he says. Despite his harsh tone, Elias's fingers press gently into my skin and draw me closer. "I know you love your family, but this is about you. You don't belong there," he murmurs.

"People keep telling me I don't belong," I say like it's a rejection. "But I belonged with you. You understood me." Even now my desire for him is overwhelming, madness twinged with desperation. "But we can't be together," I say, wanting to cry at the truth in it. "And you always knew that."

"You're breaking my heart," he responds immediately. His other hand slides over my waist, and when he looks down at me, my legs go weak. I don't want to leave him. Even though I have to.

I wrap my arms around his neck, and then our lips crash together, our mouths hot and frenzied. I get on my tiptoes to be closer, and the buttons on Catherine's shirt pull open. Elias backs me into the wall, kissing my neck, murmuring my name as his hand slips over my thigh. I'm completely lost in the passion, the contact of his body against mine. I forget my pain and my fear.

I can just feel. With him I can feel.

"I've always hated this shirt," he says, peeling the fabric off my shoulders to kiss my skin. The danger, the terror—it feeds this fire between us. Elias and I are almost over. The thought is palpable.

He makes me moan, pressing me into the wall. I kiss

215

him harder, whispering between his lips for him not to stop. I shove his suit jacket open, my hands everywhere. I'm obsessed with the heightened senses. I want more of everything. More of him.

From the door someone clears their throat.

I jump and push Elias back, adjusting my shirt to pin it closed with my fingers. Elias doesn't react nearly as quickly, watching me a beat longer like he's still lost in the moment. But then he drags his gaze to the door, and I turn and see her.

"Oh, for Christ's sake," Catherine says with a long sigh. She's positioned against the frame, bored and disgusted at the same time. "There are more . . . pressing issues than your sexual frustration, Audrey," she continues. "If you wouldn't mind, I'd like to speak with Eli. It's urgent."

I hate her so much. Elias tries to help me refasten the buttons of the shirt, holding back a smile as he does. I swat his hand away, already embarrassed. Elias turns to Catherine.

"You ruined that shirt on purpose," she calls to him. Elias adjusts his suit jacket, crossing the room. "I'm surprised you didn't throw it into the fire," she says.

"You came in too early," he teases. He stops in front of her, and I expect him to send her away, but instead he smiles warmly. "Shouldn't you be at the party?"

Catherine's bitchiness fades, and she reaches to put her palms on his cheeks, examining to see if it's really him. "I was too worried about you," she whispers, her blue eyes misting over. "I thought . . ." Her voice trails off, and Elias puts his hands over hers, a tender moment passing between them.

"You never have to worry about me, Cathy."

"I always worry about you because you're senseless." She sniffles and then lets out a quiet, self-conscious laugh. She wipes at her cheeks and I realize that she was crying. There's a small stab of sympathy, but it mixes with jealousy and I look away. I'm suddenly the third wheel, and it brings me back to my senses. I need to go. I need to get out of here.

Catherine's voice lowers and she starts to whisper, clear I'm not part of their conversation, but it's the distraction I need. Without a word I steal past them. At the door I turn back. Whatever it is that Catherine is saying, Elias's brow is furrowed as he listens intently.

"He's going to retaliate," I hear Catherine say. "You have to . . ."

But I don't listen to the rest. Without either of them noticing, I slip out the door into the hallway. I shouldn't worry about petty things like boys or relationships—Catherine was right, I have bigger problems. But it doesn't erase the fact that Elias is different. Hell, he dated Catherine. The horrible things I've done since my mother died pale in comparison to her temperament. He'd accept my mistakes.

There's a deep sense of loss as I start back toward the lobby. Loneliness is a pit in my stomach, empty and void.

I want what I have with Elias to be real, but it can't be. I'm leaving this place, leaving with Daniel and my father. I can't save him. I'm not sure I can save myself.

When I reach the hall leading to the ballroom, I glance again at the staff members guarding the door. I'll have to get my invitation from my room, find something to wear. I'll get past them, and once inside I'll find my family. And then we're out of here. I just have to hurry.

The elevator signals my floor, but I'm only a few feet down the hall when my legs become heavier with each step. An ache starts in my arm, then continues to crawl over my chest, onto my neck. "Ow," I moan, putting my hand on the wall for balance. Pain, like a tightening vise, starts across my forehead, making my eyes blur with tension. The air has a dreamlike quality. I look ahead to my room, and the walls of the Ruby expand and contract, like they're breathing.

Is the hotel trying to stop me? I consider turning around to make my way back to the elevator, but it's so far—and I'm so tired. So weak. And then it starts: the soft music. The slow strumming of a guitar. The haunting melody, drawing me to it. I rest against the wall, rife with pain and longing for escape. I roll my head to the side and see a light underneath the door of room 1336. The music played in there before but then stopped. If I'm not alone on the thirteenth floor, who else is here?

"Hello?" I call, and push myself off the wall, stumbling forward. My ankle turns and the heel snaps off Catherine's shoe. I stagger forward, the weight of my right leg causing it to drag behind me in a limp. "I need help!"

Instead of opening the door, they turn up the music—louder, until it's on full volume, rattling the mirror hanging on the wall. Are they trying to block me out? What sort of person ignores a call for help? Are they the others? I'm only a few doors away when a terrifying thought hits me: What if this is Kenneth? Or what if it's a trick the Ruby is playing on me?

But the song—the song is so familiar. Around me the temperature starts to drop, colder with every breath. Along with that, my skin feels wet, and I lift my uninjured arm, surprised when I see moisture gathered, like dew on the morning grass.

"What?" I murmur, stepping forward again until I reach the door. I fall against it, my legs finally giving out. I'm slipping toward unconsciousness; I'm slipping away and the terror is crushing. "I'm dying," I breathe out. "I'm dying."

I reach behind me, sliding my hand along until my fingers wrap around the metal handle of the door. I pull it down, my eyelids too heavy to see any longer. The pulsing of my heart pounds in my temples. And then, all at once, the door opens and my body is falling backward.

# CHAPTER 17

My eyes flutter open, and at first the world is blurry. Above me is a light—far, far up in the sky, the world black beyond it. I start to ask where I am, but there is a gurgle and I choke. I turn my head to the side, spitting up blood onto a black ground. I try to take in a breath, but it's difficult. More blood comes up.

I'm cold, and the minute I sense it, the cold is followed by the most immense pain I've ever felt. My entire body is wracked with agony, like it's been dropped from a three-story building, smacking me onto pavement. I moan, struggling to breathe, to comprehend the pain. Then in the background I hear the song again. Only now I can understand the melody. My eyelids flutter again, and I see more light, two round lights below me.

The world is too difficult to understand, and then, slowly, clarity and focus return.

At my side my arm is pinned beneath my hip, a smashing ache at the bone. The fingers on my good hand slide over the ground, touching pebbles and grit and rock. Feel asphalt. A whimper sputters blood from my lips, and I press my cheek to the road and look at the two lights of my father's car, overturned in a ditch about twenty yards away. The song still plays on the radio, the same song from the CD that we were listening to just before the accident.

The accident. It rushes back — the last moments in the car. Daniel taking my Snickers bar, my mother's CD in the stereo. I was tired and reclined my seat. I'd forgotten the rest. I'd forgotten my father mumbling under his breath, how he couldn't do it anymore. I turned to him, tears glistening on his cheeks.

"Dad," I said, startling him. He jerked the wheel.

The car began to slide, my weight throwing me against the door, my head cracking the glass of the passenger window, and I reached for the door handle. The music continued to play, but over it I heard Daniel scream my name. I heard him scream, his body flying forward. The world upended as the car rolled; my door opened and there was a *whoosh* as I was sucked out by gravity. Then . . . nothing. We were arriving at the Hotel Ruby.

I'm a broken pile of bones on the side of the road now, unable to move my legs. The song from the car reaches the end and then loops, playing the same melody. "Dad?" I call, although it's only a thick whisper. *We've been in an accident and I'm nearly dead.*

I blink, my eyelids stiff, and warm tears rush over my face. I lift my hand to wipe them away, and when I lower it, it's smeared in blood. I need help. I look at the car again and then see, just beyond the smashed-out windshield, a body.

221

I see my brother's body. Daniel is turned away, but I can make out his profile, the dried blood staining his blond hair, the wound in his head.

I'm in so much pain, but no amount of physical agony can equal what I feel when I see my brother. "Daniel?" I call, even though I can tell from here he's not breathing. "Dan!" Sobs overtake me, and I try to roll to my side, feeling a pop in my shoulder when I do. I scream and bring my fist to my mouth, biting down on the flesh to keep from passing out. "Daniel!" I yell again, crying too hard to be understood. My body won't cooperate, it's too heavy, and I drag myself, nails snapping off on the pavement as I pull forward.

"I won't leave you," I say to him as if he can hear me. "I'll never abandon you. I never will, Daniel." I sob. "I never will."

I've only made it a few feet, if that. I won't be able to reach him down in the ditch, not with my injuries. I stare at my brother's face, noting his skin has gone gray. In his hair, brain matter has seeped out. The crack in his skull is just like it was at lunch this afternoon. This afternoon . . .

At the Ruby. Adrenaline surges through me, and I take a renewed look around. Clear vision doesn't return to my right eye, but I'm trying to figure out where I am. How can we be here now? We were just at the Ruby. Are Daniel and my father still there? *Is* there a Hotel Ruby?

222

Frantic thoughts, crazy breaks from reality, drag me in and out. My gaze falls on a signpost on the other side of the road: THE HOTEL RUBY—2 MI. Eventually help will arrive, but what does that mean? They won't be able to save my brother. They can't save him because he's still at the Ruby.

My lips pull apart with another heavy cry. In reality I know we may never have walked in those doors. I know it. But I can't accept it. I can't accept a life without my family. I can't leave Daniel. Maybe he's dead, but maybe he's at a party in the ballroom waiting for me. Waiting for Dad.

What would he think if I didn't show up? Would he think I'd abandoned him? Is that what he wanted when he told me I had to leave? Had he figured this all out, kept it from me so I wouldn't stay?

"Too bad," I call to his body. "I won't walk away from you." Madness seems to overtake me, and I laugh. "I won't crawl away," I correct, rolling onto my back to stare up at the streetlight. I can't wait for a passerby to help, or even an ambulance. Because when they show up, they'll take Daniel from me. They'll cover him in a white sheet and I'll never see his face again. His pale blue eyes, just like our mother's. My brother will be dead.

And I can't let that happen.

I stop fighting to breathe, letting out a staggered sigh as my eyelids start to flutter. Heaviness weighs on my chest, and I imagine I'm filling up with blood. I have to get Daniel the hell out of there.

"I'll bring you back," I mumble, fluid running from the corner of my mouth. I look over one last time at his body, at the car where the music plays. Behind the wheel I can finally make out my father's silhouette—the angle of his broken neck. I'm the only living soul here. "I'm coming, Daddy," I whisper, slipping away. I close my eyes.

The music stops.

My mother's funeral was the worst day of my life. I only remember it in bits and pieces, the entire affair a haze of grief. I didn't have anything black to wear; I couldn't even bother with matching socks. In the end, Ryan came over with something of his mother's and helped me into it, dressing me like a limp doll as I cried until my eyes burned. I hadn't seen my father all morning. In fact, I hadn't seen him since the hospital when they told us my mother didn't survive the stroke. They had tried their best, they told us. As if that would somehow temper our grief.

And then I was walking down the aisle of the church, gripping Daniel's arm so tightly he was left with bruises. His blue eyes were bloodshot, the tip of his nose red from crying. He kept trying to hold it in, though, pressing his lips together so hard it looked like it hurt. My mother's friends burst into tears at the sight of him. Daniel being strong—that was more heartbreaking to them than if he'd just crumbled.

I didn't speak at the funeral, and I only vaguely remember seeing my grandmother and the older lady who had held my mother's hand in the coffee shop. When Daniel and I got back to the house, I went upstairs. Ryan came by to check on me, and even he gave up after a while, leaving me with just a kiss on the side of my head.

"Every day's a gift, Audrey. Don't waste it," he said.

I've wasted all the minutes since my mother's death, wishing for an escape. And now all I want is an escape back to that life. We can't stay at the Ruby; I realize that. But I won't leave without my family. Without Daniel.

I open my eyes, stunned at first, still in pain. But as the hurt fades, the scene becomes clearer. The red and gray colors of the Ruby, the thick carpet underneath me where I'm lying against the door of room 1336. I don't hear the music anymore.

At first I'm not sure I can move or if my body is paralyzed. I test my leg, choking out relief when it obeys my command. I grab on to the doorframe and pull myself to my feet, stumbling to the side with one broken shoe before I regain my balance. I swallow hard and look around. All of the pain is gone, but the memory of it haunts me. *Haunting*. My eyes widen and I spin around, seeing that the Ruby's walls indeed seem to be breathing. Are breathing. But it's all changing.

As I watch, the colors of the thirteenth floor are getting dimmer, the carpet draining of color. It's subtle at first, but now I notice everything. I think about my body on the side of the road. About the help that will arrive. Time is slower here. I couldn't have survived on the side of the road for two days. But how long was I there? How much longer will I be here?

I look back at the door of 1336. If I got Daniel up here, could he return with me? Could he still wake up? I sputter out a cry, picturing him alone on the side of the road. Cold. Dead.

And my father, still in his seat belt trapped inside the car. I put my hands over my face, the despair surrounding me, choking me. My father, however unintentionally, caused the accident. Is that what Daniel remembered today? Is that why he told me not to trust Dad? Our father brought us to the Ruby . . . is he trying to keep us here?

I drop my arms, newly determined. I'm shaky, but I don't have time to feel sorry for myself. To retreat into the same self-pity that caused this family trip in the first place. I start toward the elevator, set to storm downstairs, but then I catch sight of my reflection in the hallway mirror. I'm still in Catherine's clothes—broken heel and all. They won't let me into the party like this, and definitely not without my invitation. If I cause a scene, I might get locked away, and I can't take that chance.

I hurry to my room, and when I open my door, I'm stunned by what I find. My lights have been dimmed, candles lit on the dresser. It smells of vanilla and home—the same scent from that first day in the basement. On my bed is a big white box, a bloodred bow tied neatly across the top. I let the door slam behind me, and take a tentative step inside. What the hell is this?

With a trembling hand, I pull the ribbon and untie the bow. Fear threatens to derail me, but I push it down. Crush my fear for right now. I have to keep going and let this play out.

I slip the lid off the box and fold back the tissue paper to reveal the most beautiful red dress I've ever seen. The fabric shimmers, even in low light. The sweetheart neckline, the flowing twists of material. Strappy heels at the bottom of the box.

Next to the package is a simple black envelope. I imagine it's my invitation to the party. Kenneth said he'd send it to my room, but I guess it came with the proper attire. My dad told me that the Ruby had provided his suit as well. And probably Daniel's. I'm slow to pick up the envelope, handling it carefully.

My name is written neatly across the front in white pen. Elegant. Old fashioned. I slip my finger under the lip and open the letter. There is no personal writing, just a printed invitation.

*Black Tie Event*
*You are cordially invited to the Hotel Ruby*
*First Anniversary Party in the ballroom,*
*tonight at 9 p.m. Invitation is required.*

"Yeah right," I mutter, and drop the envelope back onto the bed. I pick up the dress and hold it against my body, looking in the mirror to gauge if it'll fit. It seems to, which doesn't surprise me. I wonder if anyone's worn this dress before. If they were once on the side of the road like I am.

It occurs to me that I'm a ghost. I'm the ghost of someone who's not even dead. What does that mean for everyone else? For my family, or Elias? What are they?

Somewhere in the hall there is the hint of music, beckoning me back. But I shake my head, staying focused on my purpose. "Not without my brother," I say. I look around the room, feeling the presence of the Ruby.

"You can't keep him," I say to the walls. "You can't have me, either." The music in the hallway quiets, replacing my anger with grief. I might not get back home. The real possibility of that is terrifying, and I quickly strip down and step into the red dress. I smooth it along my hips, slip on the shoes. I teeter on the heels, higher than Catherine's, the minute they're on my feet.

After a long pause I turn to the mirror, speechless at my reflection. Despite the lack of effort, my image is flawless. I've

never, not even at prom, after hours of primping, had this complexion. Hair this luxe. I start to smile, but then I take a step
back from the mirror, glaring around the room accusingly.

"Is this what you do?" I call out. "Corrupt the images?
Make it perfect when things are so clearly not." I stare
at my reflection, waiting for the real me to appear, bat-
tered and bruised. But nothing happens. Well, I won't be
seduced. I grab my phone off the bedside table and hurl it
at the mirror, sending shards spitting across the room.

I heave in a breath and look down. My phone is lit
up—even though it hasn't been charged. How could it be?
I'm not really here. In the top left corner of the screen is
the photos icon.

My eyes begin to water, and I pick up my phone and sit
on the edge of the bed among pieces of glass. *Don't see,* my
mind whispers. My thumb hovers for a moment, and then
I open the album titled "No."

The first image that pops up breaks me down, and the
tears flow. Two weeks before she died, my mother and I got
our hair done at the mall. The picture is us in the front seat
of the car, me holding out the phone with my right hand, our
heads pushed together. Mom's pursing her mouth, doubtful of her new, slightly darker hair. My lips are rounded in
an *Oh, snap!* exaggerated expression. When I turned the
phone around to show her the picture, we both cracked up.
She made me promise not to post it on Instagram. She said
she looked awful.

"I will disown you," she said, still laughing. "I look like a Muppet!"

"You're beautiful," I say now, reenacting the conversation. Lost in the memory, I can smell her perfume, hear her voice. Like I'm there. Like she's here. "You're still way hotter than Ryan's mom," I add.

She tsked. "Stop it," she said, even though she knew I was only joking. "Do you think your father will notice the change?" She glanced in the rearview, brushing her fingers through her fringe.

"He never notices anything," I whisper, tears wet on my cheeks.

"Cut him some slack," she said, turning to smile at me. "Your father loves you to pieces. You have no idea how many times he's talked me into something on your behalf. So whether you know it or not, your dad spoils you."

"Only fair, because you've made Daniel rotten," I say. She laughed and then nodded that it was mostly true.

"I don't know how I got so lucky," she said with a sigh, smiling at her reflection. "I just don't know."

"Me either," I whisper, and close my eyes as my soul aches. When I reopen them, the hotel room is still and silent. The echo of my mother's voice is gone. The smell of her perfume replaced with vanilla candles. Glass glitters all around, sparkling in the flickering light.

My body is numb, heavy with loss. My father didn't notice her hair, even though he complimented her almost

230

every day. Like Daniel, he was never observant. I'd grown used to it, considered it one of his quirks. Dad retelling the same stories, mispronouncing names even after he'd been corrected.

I sink lower into grief. My father brought us to this place, and I can see now that he's trying to keep us here—extending our stay. Wanting us together. It's selfish and horrible, but I can understand. If he didn't think we could leave, he just wanted our family back together. He wanted to fix us.

My cries start again—thick, choking betrayal. I scream my anger and hurt, dropping the phone and slamming my fists down on the bed. There is a biting pain, and I yelp. Hazy with tears, I lift my hand and see a triangular shard of glass sticking out of my skin. I quickly yank it free and toss it aside. I gather Catherine's shirt from the floor and wrap it around my hand. I wince at the sting—the pain bringing me back. Focusing me.

I stand and grab the invitation from the bed, shaking off the bits of glass. I leave my keycard on the dresser because I won't be coming back to this room. Instead I'll grab Daniel and my father, and we'll head to room 1336. We'll wake up. We'll be together there.

At the door I see I've bled through the shirt wrapping my wound. I unravel the fabric carefully to check the cut, and I'm stunned when I find my skin smooth. Unbroken. I open and close my hand a few times, completely healed, although the shirt is stained with blood.

Both Elias and Catherine told me that Kenneth couldn't hurt me, and now I know why: I'm not really here. But if that's true, how can Kenneth inflict so much pain on Lourdes? Terrify the other guests? What's different about them?

My telephone rings from the nightstand, startling me. I don't wait to find out who it is. I yank open my door and rush toward the elevator, invitation in hand. I'll play their game. I can fake dead better than anyone. I've done it for the past three months.

I think about my mother, and for the first time since she died, the thought of her doesn't weaken me. It gives me strength. I'm brave. I'm courageous. I'm—

Sick.

Because when the elevator doors slide open, Kenneth is standing there, waiting for me.

# CHAPTER 18

I see you're dressed for the party," Kenneth says, folding his hands over his chest. I glance sideways at him, his short arms and pudgy fingers. The normally pleasant face that now represents oppression and torture. "I must say you are a vision in red, Miss Casella," he adds politely. "It was a good choice."

I scoff, and roll my eyes to the ceiling, not willing to accept his compliment with grace. "I'm not scared of you," I lie. "You can't hurt me."

Kenneth glances at my invitation and then lifts his chin, murmuring out a "Hm . . ." that manages to be both condescending and menacing at the same time.

The elevator is painfully slow, to the point that it stops moving. Sweat gathers at my temples, but I try to stay calm. From what I've already learned, I'm guessing this is Kenneth's doing. His manipulation. I turn to him again, the taste of disgust thick on my tongue.

"We're leaving," I say, folding my arms over my chest in an attempt to look stern. I'd rather have armor. "You can't keep us here."

"I'm merely the concierge, Miss Casella," Kenneth

says. "I have no authority over whether you remain at the Ruby." He runs his gaze over me, weighing out his words. "My guess is the decision will be up to you. How eager are you to get to your grandmother's house?" His lips twitch with a smile, and he turns to face the elevator doors like my fight to survive bores him.

"How do you know about my grandmother's house?" I ask, although I've already guessed the answer.

"Your father has been very forthcoming with his problems," Kenneth replies. "It's therapeutic for him, you see. He's lost and overwhelmed. Luckily for him, unruly children tend to behave in the Ruby. He begged me to let you stay longer." He glances over with an amused expression. "Perhaps he likes you better this way."

I swallow down the comment, unable to argue the truth in it. But what Kenneth doesn't know is that I've already seen my choice. I woke up cold and alone on the side of the road and came back for my family. The fact that he's unaware must give me an advantage somehow.

"Does my father know what you are?" I ask bitterly. "What you really are?"

Kenneth lifts one of his hands in a *Who knows?* motion. "Your father is quite deft at denial. I suspect he needed someone to talk to, and I was more than happy to fill the role. He's enjoying the freedom the Ruby provides, the respite from his grief. I do believe he's forgotten all about your mother's tragic death. All about your tantrums and parties. All about his pitiful life beyond these doors," he snarls, and straightens his posture. "Your father will never leave the Hotel Ruby, Miss Casella," he says. "You should probably begin to accept that."

I step back, and the fabric of my dress makes a swishing sound against my legs. Kenneth's threat only succeeds in solidifying my bravery. "You're not keeping him," I say, pointing my finger in Kenneth's face. In my other hand the invitation crumples in my fist. "No matter what he's done, he's my father. And I'm getting him and my brother out of here. You won't stop me. You can't." I have the vague sense that I'm full of shit, but I'm too angry to stop now. "I'm going to walk into your precious party and grab them both. And then you'll never see us again."

Fueled by my rage, I step closer to him, closer than I'd ever normally want to be. "We're leaving, Kenneth. And I'll burn this place to the ground if you try to stop me."

Kenneth's eyes widen, and I can see the hatred seep out. His arms fall to his sides, and he lowers his chin slowly, his mouth puckered and turning white. He's terrifying.

"You should be careful of the things you threaten, Miss Casella." He hisses out my name, and I step back. "Your friends will be very sorry that you'd make such a callous claim."

I furrow my brow, about to ask him what he's talking about, but the elevator bell dings for the lobby. Without another word, Kenneth walks promptly through the doors and disappears into the crowd moving toward the party.

What did he mean about my friends? Is he going to hurt Lourdes again? Elias? I start to walk out, when Catherine appears at the elevator entrance. At first she looks dumbfounded by my appearance, but then she spins inside and presses the button for the basement.

"Stop," I say, darting forward. I push past her to hit the lobby button, but the doors close. "Damn it, Catherine. I have to get my brother!"

"Daniel is perfectly safe," she says, casting a look at the invitation in my hand. She adjusts her stance, gorgeous in her white dress and perfect makeup. "Your dysfunctional family dynamics can wait."

I notice that she's shaking, and my anxiety spikes. "What happened?" I ask. "Where's Elias?" Is Catherine like me too—caught in some in-between? Or is she just a person who's trapped here, talking to ghosts? The elevator stops and signals the basement floor.

Catherine walks out into the hallway and then pauses to look back at me. "You need to see this, Audrey. You have to know this part of the Ruby before you go blindly into that party." She groans when I don't immediately move. "This is ironic, you know," she says, clearly irritated. "I'm trying to save you, but it's not because I like you, or even because I like your brother. I'm doing this because Eli cares about you. Even if I think he can do better."

Elias must not be injured; otherwise, Catherine would

be running to him. But the image of them in the billiard room is still fresh in my mind. The gentle way they spoke to each other. The way they touched. I freely admit to my jealousy, and I'm pitiful when I ask, "Do you love him, Catherine?"

She smiles softly. "Always."

"Does he love you?"

"Never." Her response is immediate but not cold. She states it as a simple fact—a painful one, judging by the way her eyes glass over. She could have drawn out the moment and tortured me, but she didn't. She may not be completely terrible after all.

"Now," she says, sniffling. "Unless you'd like me to tell you you're pretty, too, I suggest we hurry up before the rest of us are set on fire."

My stomach drops. "What?"

Catherine slips out of her shoes, hooking the straps over her finger to carry them, and starts to dash down the hallway. I have to run to catch up with her, tottering in my own heels. Catherine, of course, is the picture of elegance, even when she's jogging in a sequined gown. We turn the final corner, and my worry deepens when I see several staff members gathered outside Lourdes's door. They shrink away as we approach, avoiding eye contact with Catherine.

"The concierge doesn't want guests in housekeeping," Lourdes told me when I first met her. More than ever the staff are frightened, and I can't help but to absorb some of their worry. I can barely catch my breath when I reach the doorframe, petrified to peek inside the room. But Lourdes is my friend, and I won't walk away from her if she needs me.

I steady myself and then look inside. The first person I see is Elias, positioned on the edge of the bed with his elbows on his knees, his face in his palms. The room is dimly lit, blood soaked into the carpet where Kenneth died, lamps and dishes broken. It takes a moment for me to understand the rest, and I recoil in horror, dropping my invitation.

Lourdes lies in bed, only I wouldn't recognize her if it weren't for her hair. Her skin is burned, so horribly burned that I scream and trip over my heels backing out of the door. I hit the floor hard but keep sliding back until I bump the wall. I smother my mouth to quiet my screams, my eyes fixed on the terrifying scene in front of me.

Lourdes's charred skin is black as charcoal, bits of red muscle peeking through the broken edges. Her fingers are gone, her arms lie limply next to her, her nose and lips decimated. Her eyes rest wide and unblinking because the lids have been burned off.

I cover my face, my head between my knees as I sob. Kenneth did this. I told him in the elevator that I'd burn this place down to get out, and now he's burned my friend. This is my fault. This is how he's punishing me.

A warm hand slides over my arm. I yelp, struggling

until I realize it's Elias. "Audrey, you shouldn't be here," he says, taking my elbow to help me to my feet. "You . . ." He stops when he notices my dress, and shoots Catherine a questioning look. She avoids his eyes and walks inside the room. I'm half out of my mind and clutch Elias's white shirt for balance. "You have to go back to your floor," he tells me firmly.

I throw myself into his arms, hugging him tightly. "I already did," I say. "I know the truth—I woke up on the side of the road, but my brother and father"—I start to whimper—"they're still here, so I came back." Elias's body goes rigid, but I keep talking. "Then I saw Kenneth and I threatened him. Told him we were leaving. I was so stupid."

"Shh . . . ," Elias soothes me, murmuring that I need to calm down. He holds me until I quiet, my breathing settling into hiccuped gasps. Elias slips his fingers into my hair, cradling me as he rests his cheek on the top of my head. His embrace is comfort. It's misery and grief. "This isn't your fault," he murmurs. "Lourdes lashed out, and now her punishment is to exist how she really is. It's painful, but she's already healing." Elias holds me closer, and I'm trying to comprehend his statement. "You're still going home, Audrey."

I furrow my brow, wondering what he means by "how she really is." Slowly I pull back and lift my eyes to his. He's been crying, and I can see he's scared. Scared for Lourdes and me, scared of Kenneth. But a new question has formed, one that goes back to the first day we met. "Elias," I ask, stepping out of his arms. "How did you get here?"

He stares at me, the color fading from his complexion. Before he answers, a faint voice whispers my name from inside the room. It's ragged and agonized, and I turn immediately, realizing it belongs to Lourdes.

"She's awake," Elias murmurs, and rushes into the room.

Awake? How is that possible? The burns were too horrific, she couldn't . . . I let the reality fall over me. This is the Ruby. It's all possible. It's all terrifyingly possible.

My skin is tight from dried tears, my eyes ache from crying. Slowly I walk into Lourdes's room and see her lying on the bed. Unmoved. Joshua is close by on a folding chair, and Catherine has taken up space against the wall. Tanya lies across the headboard with a washcloth, dabbing white ointment on the bits of Lourdes's skin that are still intact.

I crouch on the floor, close to her. The acrid smell of burned flesh slips down my throat, and I close my mouth and put my fingers to my nose to try and block it out. Elias sits carefully on the edge of the bed. To my surprise, he picks up Lourdes's charred hand and brings it to his lips, kissing it tenderly. "She'll be okay," he whispers, watching her. "Lourdes always pulls through."

"Always?" I repeat.

"This wasn't about you," Catherine says, tipping off

that she was listening to my conversation in the hallway. "You wanted to know why we obey Kenneth. This"—she motions around with her hands—"is what happens if we don't. Eli's deluding himself. Even when Lourdes recovers, Kenneth's not finished. He'll send her away again. There's no limit to his cruelty."

"Quiet," Elias says simply, not taking his eyes from Lourdes. I follow his gaze, fighting the urge to scream again. Lourdes's pupils slide in my direction, and sickness bubbles up in my stomach. She's awake, and I can't imagine the pain she feels, the absolute agony.

"Don't cry," she rasps. The soft sound of her voice fills me with a mix of relief and sorrow, and I wipe my cheeks where new tears have fallen. Despite her condition, I reach out to take her hand. It's rough and brittle like a twig, and I'm careful not to squeeze too hard.

Elias stands and rights a chair from the floor, signaling for me to sit there. I do, and lean on the edge of the bed to comfort Lourdes. The staffers who were waiting in the hall tell Elias it's time for the party, but he waves them away and shuts the door. He grabs another chair and sits next to me. The room is a funeral, weighted air filled with grief.

Braver, I look over Lourdes's condition: the melted earlobes, the oozing flesh on her shoulder. I still. *How she really is?*

I shift my eyes to Tanya, remembering when I noticed the blood on her shirt that first day. My heart pounds

against my ribs, and I turn to Elias. He's trying to antici-
pate anything Lourdes might need. Attentive. And I'm
starting to understand. I saw the crack in Daniel's skull.
Daniel, with that exact injury as he lay broken and lifeless
on the side of the road. *How he really is.*

Oh, God. I know how Elias got here. Lourdes said that
their group had been together for a long time, and Joshua
said the party was in Elias's honor. I couldn't see it then.
Wake the Dead at the fountain, the details of the fire, and
the endless nights of parties he's required to attend. Elias
was in that ballroom fire in 1937. He's dead. They're all
dead.

I carefully set Lourdes's hand on the bed, overcome
with the truth. These are the ghosts of the Hotel Ruby.
They've been the ghosts all along, and I'm just a passerby
who happened to get in an accident outside their gates,
mine and my family's souls coexisting with theirs.

"You're dead," I murmur, looking at Elias. "You died in
the fire." Elias shifts his gaze to mine. His expression bleeds
sadness and regret. The ultimate loneliness. He nods and
lowers his eyes to the bedsheets.

"The Ruby is a gorgeous and terrifying place, Audrey,"
Joshua speaks up, his voice loud and cutting. "Normally,
the people on the thirteenth floor get out thinking this was
some wonderful dream. You've turned it into a nightmare."

"It's not her fault," Elias responds quietly. "I brought
her to the basement in the first place."

Catherine laughs, rolling her perfectly lined eyes at him. "You're such a sap," she says. "Always on some romantic adventure. It was her error for following you like a puppy. I would have had more sense."

"Yes, Cathy," Joshua responds sarcastically. "Because you are the epitome of self-control."

She smiles coldly. "No, darling," she says. "I'm a bad decision waiting to happen. Now Eli, on the other hand . . ." She looks over at him, eyebrows up, willing him to play along. But he doesn't even lift his head, lost in a wound I've reopened. Catherine sighs. "He's good," she tells me, although she's still watching him. "Eli has always been good."

I sit back in the chair; the idea of the Ruby being haunted is easier to accept when you're intimately acquainted with its ghosts. "How can you stand it?" I ask. "Being here, day in and day out, the same every night? All of the tourists and ghost stories?"

"I've always hated that word," Catherine responds. "'Ghost'—it implies that I float around in a white sheet, saying 'Boo!' I can't interact with people, touch them. Hurt them." She waves away the possibility. "What fun would it be, anyway? They can't see me. Half the time I can't even see them."

"People," I say. "You mean the others? Who are they?"

"They're alive," she says. "The others are the guests staying at the real Hotel Ruby, walking over our graves with hideous disregard. Talking loudly of encountering ghosts, when, believe me, they wouldn't know a ghost if she walked up and asked them to dance." She smiles. "They're not always here, though. Sometimes they just fade out. Different realities, I suppose. Personally, I like when they're gone. It's quieter. And they occasionally leave things behind that become part of the hotel. The Ruby is where lost things end up—like you. It's not awful. I get my best jewelry this way."

Elias moves to loosen his tie from around his neck, and I feel a surge of sympathy for him. Affection. He told me that he understood grief, and I assumed someone he loved had died. In truth, he died, left to mourn the entire world.

From the bed Lourdes coughs, a painful sound. Joshua jumps up and comes to kneel next to her, murmuring that she's fine. That she shouldn't try to talk. Her eyes watch him lovingly, and I can see already that some of her skin is healing. Translucent and pale pink. Joshua kisses her forehead and sits on the floor, resting his temple on the edge of the bed close to hers. They're all so connected. I envy their closeness, grateful they have each other. I can't imagine how awful it would be to suffer through this alone.

"What happened the night of the fire?" I ask. "Why didn't anyone get out?"

Catherine's icy features thaw slightly, and she tilts her head as if asking permission to go on. Elias nods. "We have to start at the beginning, then," she says, sitting back and crossing her legs. "It was 1937 and my fiancé was being honored. Well"—she smiles—"Elias's *family* was being honored, but they were too busy to attend so they sent us in their place."

Fiancé? Whether it matters now or not, my muscles tense. I have to fight the urge to look at Elias, even though I feel him watching my reaction. I'm a little angry that he didn't tell me sooner. Then again, he didn't tell me a lot of things. This is probably the least important.

"No need for jealousy, Audrey," Catherine calls out, confirming that I'm easy to read. "Elias never loved me, and I grew restless and bored of him. I slipped away for a drink and a distraction."

"That would be me," Joshua explains. "The distraction."

Catherine groans, and snaps that it was only one time. Besides, her mother wouldn't have allowed her to ride in the same car as him, let alone marry him. He tells her that if she had been engaged to him, they wouldn't have been at such a miserable party to begin with. While they argue, I steal a glance at Elias. He's emotionless, like he's listened to this play out a million times. His eyes lift to mine, apologetic. Catherine and Joshua go on fighting, but for a moment it's just me and Elias.

"Enough," Catherine says to Joshua, holding up her hand. "Now"—she turns back to me—"where was I?"

"Our one time," Joshua replies drily.

"Anyway," she continues. "After my indiscretion I

245

returned to the party and made my way over to Eli. If I had known for even a second that Kenneth was a tyrant, capable of monstrosities beyond understanding, I would have left that very second. Instead Eli and I posed for a photograph for the local paper. An article about our wedding would be featured. And then . . ." Her voice quivers, and she stops, pressing her lips together. Joshua turns to her, a pained expression crossing his face. Obviously, he forgives her for being a constant bitch.

"When I arrived in the ballroom," Joshua says, picking up the story, "I closed the doors behind me and joined Lourdes at the bar. She was crying, dark purple bruises imprinted in the shape of a hand on her forearm. I knew who had done it, of course. But I wasn't in the position to stop Kenneth from abusing her. We would both be out of a job. We'd starve.

"I helped Lourdes with the drinks, making sure she didn't mess up, especially when I saw Kenneth watching us, waiting for an opportunity. Understand, Audrey," Joshua says, "the Ruby didn't make Kenneth a terrible man—he already was. We were scared of him then, and we're terrified of him now."

Kenneth has been torturing them for years, making rules and punishing them at his discretion. Of all the horrible people to have power over you in death, for it to be the one who abused you in life must be unbearable. My sympathy for Lourdes is tremendous; I'm devastated on her behalf. She watches them talk, distraught, like she's reliving the tragedy.

"It was a candle," Catherine says. "There was the smash of a bottle breaking, and Eli and I both looked over to the bar. The housekeeper had dropped the scotch," she says bitterly, and glares at Lourdes's burned body. Catherine's expression weakens, as if she thinks Lourdes has suffered enough.

"The bottle slipped from Lourdes's hand and smashed on the tiles," Joshua continues, "startling the nearby guests. I didn't have to check to know Kenneth would be on his way over. Lourdes fell to her knees and began sweeping up the glass with her hands, shredding her skin on the broken shards. Smearing blood in an attempt to clean before he arrived.

"That was when I saw Catherine and Eli standing together. Only now they weren't so cozy. Eli was questioning her whereabouts, and Catherine lifted her chin, defiant, beautiful and ugly at the same time.

"The colors in the room," Joshua says with a twisted sort of nostalgia, "they were so beautiful, so vibrant. I looked from face to face, people speaking and laughing, and then my eyes fell on Kenneth. His expression was tense with controlled anger; his fingers curled in impending punches as he stomped his way toward the bar. I could see the hint of satisfaction in his stride—he liked to hit women, especially Lourdes."

247

He lifts his head. "Poor Lourdes," he whispers sadly, "was cleaning frantically, thinking there was still a chance she could avoid the beating. I grabbed a rag to help her."

He stops, working his jaw like he doesn't want to continue. Lourdes lifts her hand to touch him, to forgive him. The emotions in the room are palpable, and when I look at Elias, he's watching me with the saddest eyes I've ever seen. My own tears well up in response, and I want the story to end a different way. I want them to survive.

"None of us meant to be here, Audrey," Elias says solemnly. "None of us thought this was a possibility. When Joshua knocked over the candle, there was no slow motion; there were simply not flames and then flames. The alcohol blazed up in an instant. Before the first screams even reached our ears, the tapestries surrounding the doorway caught fire.

"Lourdes never made it off the floor," he says. "Her suffering ended nearly as soon as it began. Joshua tried to put himself out, slapping his blackening hands on his clothes. But he only succeeded in spreading the flames. He threw himself against the closest person, screaming, his hair singed off. Soon the room was ablaze in bright orange fire. Around me, guests shrieked and ran for the door, but their clothing wasn't optimum for escape. An older woman was the first to fall, and she began a chain reaction. People crawled over each other, but the wooden doors were completely lost behind the flames."

I cover my mouth, overcome. I can picture it all; smell

the fire, the burned flesh. I can imagine all the horror of that night.

"I grabbed Catherine and searched for another way out," Elias continues. "I looked up and down that grand room, but there were no windows, no other doors. Catherine gripped my arm tightly, but she didn't cry." Elias's expression softens, and Catherine's lips spread into a watery smile. "She was more determined to live than anyone else in there. Even in that chaos her eyes reflected fire, but it was all her own."

"The walls around us burned," she says mournfully, "surrounding us like an embrace. I squeezed him tighter as the realization settled in—there would be no saving us. Not any of us."

Elias puts his fist to his lips, quiet for a moment before going on. "The room became unbearably hot," he says. "I coughed on the last of the air, knowing we'd be dead soon. I took my arm from Catherine and started toward a table. I pulled off the white linen, sending the plates and silverware crashing to the floor. I grabbed Catherine and wrapped the tablecloth around us, hoping to save our skin from the bite of the fire. It wouldn't, of course. In just a moment we had both fallen to our knees, and when I looked over, Catherine's skin was smeared with ash. Blisters formed on one of her perfect cheeks."

"Please, Eli," Catherine says, starting to cry. "No more. I can't hear any more."

249

Elias turns from her, settling his gaze on me. "It had been less than five minutes since the fire started," he says, ignoring Catherine's plea. "The screams were dying out. In the distance was the crackling of burning wood, the whoosh of fabric catching fire, the burst of bottles exploding. The banging—if it was ever there—had stopped. We didn't know then, but they locked the doors in order to keep the fire from spreading through the entire hotel. I fell forward when the air was too thin to breathe, and I saw Catherine, her cheek pressed to the tile as she lay staring at me, motionless. Dead."

He swallows hard, and when he levels his stare at me again, my heart breaks. "The heat licked at my shoes," he says, "but I didn't feel the fire take my skin. I didn't feel anything until I woke up in the ballroom after it was rebuilt in all its glory. Trapped with everyone else. Forever."

# CHAPTER 19

We all sit silently for a moment, Catherine crying quietly, exposed. I can hear Lourdes's ragged breaths getting stronger and more measured. The entirety of their story is catastrophic, devastating.

"I'm sorry for what happened to you," I say, knowing it's not enough. "I can't imagine . . . I . . . ." My voice startles Catherine, and she wipes away the tears on her cheeks, embarrassed by her emotional vulnerability. She takes out her compact and checks her reflection, sniffling hard. She snaps it shut, the click echoing in the room.

"Eli," she says coolly. "We have to get to the ballroom. We can't risk it now. Kenneth will be on a rampage."

Elias isn't convinced. "Go without me," he tells her. "First I have to convince Audrey what a terrible idea it is to attend the party. Even if she does look smashing in that dress." His compliment is tinged with the tone of an impending argument.

"Get to the party, Elias," Lourdes says in a low voice. She groans, shifting on the bed. Joshua climbs to his feet to check on her, and Tanya sets the washcloth aside, but Lourdes shakes her head, letting them know she doesn't need their help. I notice her fingers have grown back. "You too, Joshua," she adds. "You're bartending tonight."

"Thank you," Catherine announces, as if the command was made on her behalf. She walks to the door and pulls it open, then turns to me. "Don't take this the wrong way, Audrey," she says, smiling softly. "But I really hope I never see you again."

I cough out a laugh, and nod. "I hope I never see you again either." Catherine reaches her hand to Joshua, and after a concerned look in Lourdes's direction, he takes it and they walk out together.

Elias waits near the end of the bed, his hands in his pockets, his jaw set hard. "Lourdes," Elias starts, "she has to—"

"Yes, Eli," she says. "I understand the stakes just as well as you do. If not more."

"Oh, good," I say, crossing my arms over my chest. "Maybe someone can fill me in." I hate being talked about as if I'm not here. Neither of them reacts to me, caught instead in a stare-down. Finally Elias relents.

"Audrey," Elias says, slow to look at me. When he does, color blooms on his cheeks, a sad smile deepens his dimples. "Damn." He shakes his head. "I told you I wouldn't want you to leave if we kept at it."

"You were too charming," I respond, making him laugh. I'll miss the sound of it. It occurs to me that I love him—even if it's still new. Still soon. This is the start of love, and not the circumstantial kind that fades, like with

Ryan. In this there is acceptance and understanding. Lust and admiration. I've always hated good-byes, and this is no exception.

"I'll see you around," I say casually, even though my voice quivers. Elias puts his hand over his heart, like I'm breaking it.

"I look forward to it, Audrey Casella." He flashes me one more dimpled smile, and then he turns and leaves, off to play his role in a haunting.

I lean back in the chair, doing my best not to cry. Tanya helps prop Lourdes up on a pillow, and then she crosses to the other side of the room and pours herself a glass of water. I'm running out of time. I need to get Daniel and my father from the party—but now that I've seen what Kenneth can do, I'm not sure how I can get past him.

"Before you try to talk me out of going to the party," I say, "there's still a lot I don't understand. How am I here? I wasn't in that fire."

"The Ruby is filled with ghosts," Tanya answers. "Not all from the fire. Heart attacks, suicides—most died right here. And some were killed off-site." She motions to where I saw the blood on her shirt. "Hiking."

Tanya sips from her water, rattled by the mention of her own death. "From what we can tell," she continues after a moment, "only the really lost souls find their way here. The ones who are already dead but don't realize it."

Lourdes groans gently from the bed, trying to adjust

her position on the pillow. Tanya sets her glass down on the dresser and walks over, sitting on the edge and grabbing the washcloth and ointment.

"It helps with the pain," she whispers when Lourdes tries to brush her hand away.

"I don't care about the pain," Lourdes snaps. The two exchange a long glance, and then Tanya flops down in the chair next to me, putting her feet up on the bed. She shrugs one shoulder, telling Lourdes to do what she wants. Their tension isn't hostile, more like sisters fighting.

"This isn't just about the party, Audrey," Lourdes says, slowly sounding more like herself. "You have to leave tonight, now. I promised your brother."

"My brother? What does . . . what do you mean?" I ask, starting to feel frantic. "How much of this does Daniel know?"

"All of it. He came to see me earlier, before this." She gestures to her body. "He was afraid you'd stay once you realized what was really going on."

I'm taken aback, furious that Daniel knew about the Ruby and didn't tell me. Heartbroken that he tried to deal with it on his own. "Neither of us is staying," I say. "I would never leave him here. That's why I came back, to take him with me. Him and my father." Lourdes exhales, forlorn.

"What?" I ask. "They won't kick me out of the party this time. I have an invitation."

"Shit," Tanya mutters. My stomach sinks, slow dread creeping up my arms.

"What does it mean?" I ask nervously. "Why did I get an invitation? Why now?"

They're both quiet until Lourdes turns to face me. "Because you're dying, Audrey," she says simply. "Your body is dying, and if you die here, you stay here forever. You'll be trapped in the Ruby with us. The invitation is symbolic. It's letting go."

I'm horrorstruck. Even though I already knew my condition was perilous on the side of the road, did I really think I was going to die? Would I have come back if I did? Wait. That means . . .

"No," I say, shaking my head. "Oh my God. My brother, my father—they've gone to the party. They've used . . ." I jump up from the chair, sending it sideways to the floor. My heart shatters, and a tidal wave of grief crashes over my head and drowns me. "They can't leave," I whisper. "That's what Daniel didn't want me to know. He knew I wouldn't abandon him."

It's hard to breathe. I can't breathe. Trampling past the overturned chair, I rush out the door into the hallway. I double over, gagging on my tears. With my hand on the wall, heavy sobs wrack my body and I fall to my knees on the carpet.

My brother's dead and I can't save him. They're all gone, but I can still live. But how will I survive surviving this? How will Daniel cope when I'm gone? He's dead on the side of that road.

"I'm sorry you ended up here," Tanya says. I lift my head

and find her squatting down next to me. Her dark eyes are full of compassion, sympathy. "But you haven't gone to the party," she says. She motions to where I dropped the envelope when I first saw Lourdes's burned body. "You haven't used your invitation, Audrey. There's still time for you to go home." She must understand what I'm feeling—she's not from the hotel either.

"I can just go back to the thirteenth floor and wake up?" I ask her. She nods. "But I'll be leaving my brother, my father, Elias, and all of my friends behind to suffer in the Ruby under Kenneth's charge. How could I live knowing that?"

Tanya drops to sit on the carpet and shakes her head. "I was like you," she says thoughtfully. "When I first came to the Ruby, I was on the thirteenth floor for a time, both me and my sister."

I sniffle back the rest of my tears and turn to her. "Your sister is here?"

"Not anymore." She looks at the floor, tracing her finger over a pattern in the carpet. "Corey left, hated it here. Lourdes told us what was happening, and Corey—she came unhinged, broke things. Scared a bunch of the others, so much so a news van showed up a few weeks later to do a story. Lourdes got sent away for that—burned first, just like today. She was gone until you came. She's part of the hotel, and the Ruby expects her to welcome new guests. Even Kenneth can't control that."

"What about you?" I ask, starting to regain my focus. "Why are you here, then, if you knew?"

"Because it was too late for me," she says. "I'd already gone to the party, wanted to wear a beautiful dress. Be somebody. I thought, life's a bitch and then you don't die. You stay forever in a hotel with a bunch of other ghosts, passing time, going to parties, kissing in hallways." She smirks at me. "But my sister left me here. And once Lourdes was sent away, I became part of the staff in her place. Just as well. The party really wasn't worth it."

"Do you hate your sister?" I ask. "Do you hate her for leaving you?"

Tanya tilts her head, thinking it over. "At first. But I wanted her to go, to live her life. It wouldn't be fair to want otherwise." Tanya surprises me when she reaches over to brush my hair behind my ear, a movement so motherly it nearly sends me crying again. "Daniel will understand if you leave," she says. "He'll also understand if you don't."

Tanya exhales, leaning her head against the wall. "Your brother's going to be just fine here," she says. "It's Elias I feel sorry for. All the years I've watched him hate those parties. Always so sad and alone. The staffers say he's been involved with girls other than Catherine, especially the few who've passed through the thirteenth floor." She shrugs. "But from what I've heard, he never wanted any of them to stay. Who knows—maybe he only picks the girls who are going to leave. Or maybe"—she smiles—"he didn't care because they weren't you. All this time, Elias was waiting for you. He doesn't want you to go, Audrey. He told us so."

"I can't stay," I tell her. "He knows that."

"Which is why he would never let you," she says sympathetically. "I just wanted you to know you had a choice. The Ruby's giving you a choice." She touches my shoulder and then stands up. She holds out her hand, and as I get up, I'm reminded that I'm still in a gown and heels. Still dressed for a party, the black invitation on the floor in front of me.

It's impossible to digest all I've learned. All that's happened. But I have to see Daniel and my father again—I have to say good-bye. When I imagine it, my heart breaks. How can I not try to save them? I have to at least try.

"Good luck, Audrey," Tanya says, walking back to Lourdes's door. "I'm really rooting for you."

I thank her and watch her go. I don't have a plan, but either way, nothing will ever be the same. So I pick up the black envelope and head toward the elevator.

The lobby is alive and full of people. Many are dressed in gowns and tuxedos, but there are a few in casual clothes. *The other ones*, I think. The people here for a show. For a haunting, even though Catherine says she can't touch them.

I stop suddenly, thinking back to something Tanya said.

Her sister threw a tantrum, scared the guests—the real ones. How? I mean, if anyone were going to be vicious, I'd put my money on Catherine. So how did Tanya's sister have any effect at all?

A guy stops near me, wearing a backward cap, basketball shorts, and a smug smile. He smells of too much Axe and leers at the female guests. Suddenly I have an idea, and my heart starts to race. Slowly I reach to touch his shoulder.

He yelps and spins around, looking in every direction. Looking through me. A chill comes over my body, and I step closer to him. "Can you see me?" I ask in a shaky voice.

The guy doesn't respond, not until I run the backs of my fingers over his cheek. He slaps himself in the face, like he's swatting a fly, but he's scared. He's terrified as he backs away, too embarrassed to ask for help, but too frightened to ignore me. He knows I'm here.

He knows I'm not.

The thrill of it fills me with courage, and I start toward the ballroom. I push the guy in the hat to the side, making contact with his body. He swats around himself manically before running off. The weight of his body on my palms fills me with possibility. I'm going to face Kenneth—even if he burns me to ashes, I'm not leaving without a fight. I won't leave my family under his oppressive watch.

There is a small group gathered at the entrance of the ballroom, and I walk purposefully toward the throng, ready to demand I speak with the concierge. But then I see the blond head of my brother, Elias at his arm, rushing out the doorway in my direction.

# CHAPTER 20

Daniel's eyes blaze as he takes in my dress, the invitation in my hand. He uses other guests as leverage, pushing past them to get to me faster. Just as he clears the crowd, his eyes meet mine. Any brotherly rage he might have felt dissipates into grief; his shoulders hunch forward, the truth of his condition hanging between us.

Elias walks behind him, nervous as he nods to the other guests, making apologies for bursting through. He fidgets with his tie, and once he's past the crowd, he shakes his head at me and hurries forward. "We need to get out of the lobby," he says curtly, taking my arm. I yank it away and watch my brother instead.

Daniel doesn't talk at first. His lips turn white as he tries to hold back his emotion, reminding me of my mother's funeral. I see now why it broke so many hearts, the pain and vulnerability he can't hide. He opens his mouth to talk, but then blinks quickly and rolls his eyes toward the ceiling as if he's doesn't want his voice to betray him.

It's funny how seeing another person hurt can break you down faster than your own emotions. Right now I have to fight hard to keep from throwing my arms around my brother and crying for him. Begging him to wake up.

"I'm not even going to ask why you're in that dress," Daniel says in a controlled tone, "because it doesn't matter. You're going to turn around and leave before the concierge shows up. We can argue about it on the way."

"Yes, I second that," Elias says quickly, motioning down the hall toward the elevators. Although I appreciate the sentiment, neither of them intends to have a heart-to-heart with me away from prying eyes. They plan to take me to the thirteenth floor with a pat on the head and a kiss on the cheek, and then they'll return to face the wrath of Kenneth like a couple of heroes. Like a couple of idiots.

"No," I say, crossing my arms over my chest. I'm fully aware of how my tantrum looks, but if anything, I hope it drives the point home. He's my older brother, but he picked a really shitty time to act like it. "You should have told me what was going on," I say. "I know about the Ruby, about the party and the invitation. We could have figured something out."

Around us a few of the guests have taken notice of our argument. Elias moves another step, trying to usher me forward, but I brush his hand away.

"Don't you think I tried to change things?" Daniel snaps. "Don't you think I *begged*?" His face contorts in misery. "I went to Dad, Kenneth, even Catherine—nobody can change this, Aud. That's why I told you not to trust them. They belong to the Ruby. *I*"—he taps his chest—"belong to the Ruby."

"No," I say, and grab his arm. "Daniel, we can get Dad and go to my floor," I whisper, feeling frantic. "It's a way out, a way back to the road."

Daniel takes my wrist, squeezing tightly to secure my attention. "I can't even get to your floor anymore," he says miserably. "There's no button for the thirteenth floor, Audrey. It doesn't exist. The entire floor doesn't exist. Even if you brought me there, I suspect I'd walk off the elevator and right back in the lobby door." He looks at Elias, who nods, confirming his statement.

My hope drains away, filled instead with mourning. The staff told me it was too late, but I held on to the small chance they were wrong. I thought they had to be wrong. Daniel and I are special—we're survivors. I take a shaky breath; my arms fall listlessly to my sides.

"The only thing that mattered anymore," Daniel goes on, his voice softened, "was to get you home. I asked Lourdes for help because I knew you'd get it inside your head that I needed you. But you've got to leave me here."

"Mom wouldn't abandon you."

Daniel falls back a step, looking betrayed that I brought her up. "No, she wouldn't," he agrees. "But you're not her, Audrey. You don't have to fix this. You can't."

He's right, of course. From the ballroom I hear the faint sounds of the song—the same damn song, calling me back. I let the invitation slip from my hands, watching as it flutters to the floor.

263

"You suck," I say, and lift my eyes to my brother's. Elias turns to me, surprised, but Daniel starts to smile. Boyish and charismatic—that part of him will never change.

"I know," he allows, "but I'm getting better." Despite the moment, the words are filled with heartbreak. "And I'm taking your advice," he says.

"It's about time," I say automatically, my fight drained away.

"I'm going to do awesome things just for myself," he says. "Turns out I'm pretty amazing."

Elias sniffs a laugh next to us, and then he tells me again that I have to go. I look despairingly toward the elevators, toward my escape. I hear Daniel swallow loudly, and then I jump forward and hug him, strangling him around the neck.

"I'm going to remember you like this," I say into his shirt. "In this suit with your hair brushed." He laughs, hugging me tighter. "Because when I wake up," I continue, my voice cracking, "you're going to be on the side of the road, and Daniel, it's so horrible. I can't face it. I can't."

"You have to," he murmurs, pushing me back. The crowd around us has gotten louder, growing restless with the scene.

"Daniel," Elias warns under his breath. My brother looks up, noticing something over my shoulder. He straightens, his expression hardening.

"You have to go, Audrey," he states, his eyes trained behind me. "Right now. You're almost out of time."

"I'm afraid he's right, Miss Casella."

A hush falls over the crowd, my fear ratcheting up until it's got a grip on my throat. I turn and find Kenneth standing in the center of the lobby with a sickening smile and a rosy glow of victory on his cheeks. He's wearing a black tuxedo, and he folds his tiny hands over the breast of his jacket.

Elias puts out his arm, resting his hand on my hip as he steps in front of me. I appreciate his attempt, but I doubt he'll make much of a shield. Daniel closes ranks at my side. Kenneth scoffs at the display of protection, laughing at us.

"You are free to go, Miss Casella. No sense in making such a fuss. Honestly, with all these childish outbursts, one must really question your upbringing."

"Son of a bitch," Daniel says, his anger getting the best of him. He starts forward but gets only two steps before he whines out a terrible sound and grabs his head with both hands. I scream his name, but he's staggering, blood racing down the side of his neck. Seeping from the wound in his head. Elias holds me back as I fight to get to him, but when Daniel collapses, nothing can stop me. I move past Elias and kneel at my brother's side, putting my hands over the crack in his skull, blood rushing through my fingers.

My brother tries to say my name but chokes on the blood filling his mouth and turns to the side to cough it up.

265

His injuries are the most horrific thing I've ever seen, and my hands can't begin to stop the flow of warm blood pulsing over my fingers. I gather Daniel up, resting his head on my lap, telling him it'll be okay. His body jolts. I'm watching him die, just as he did on the side of the road.

"Shh . . . ," I whisper, letting the lobby fall away and disappear. My body trembles, emotionally broken. In my mind we're no longer here. I'm kneeling next to him in the ditch, cold air around us, and wet dew on our skin. The only light shining from the headlights of an overturned car.

"I'm here," I say. "I won't leave you." Daniel continues to struggle for breath, his skin turning gray. He knots his fingers in the hem of my dress, shuddering and in pain. He turns his eyes toward me, and tears leak from the corners. I smile down at him sadly, trying to give him comfort so he knows he's not alone. "I'm here," I whisper, brushing his blond hair away from the blood.

"Audrey, what . . ." My father appears behind me, and I look over my shoulder at him. He's in the lobby with the others, wearing a white tux, smoothed hair. When he sees Daniel, he gasps and covers his mouth. He falls to his knees in the dirt next to me, the lights of the car shining on the side of his face. He takes up Daniel's hand, gripping it tightly to his chest and smearing himself in bright red blood. "Dan," he calls. "Daniel, we're here."

My brother's teeth chatter, his eyes wide, and I can see how scared he is, how scared he must have been to die. He did it all alone once, but now we're here, and he'll never have to die alone again.

His eyelids grow heavy, his grip loosens. I don't cry—can't cry anymore. I've lost everything I've ever cared about and I have nothing left. All I can do now is be strong, stronger for both of us. Strong like I should have been after Mom died. "I love you, Dan," I whisper, leaning in to kiss his forehead. His skin has chilled from the night air. "I love you."

I close my eyes, and when I reopen them, we're in the lobby of the Ruby. I set my brother's head gently on the shiny floor in a pool of bright red blood. A crowd has gathered around the three of us, and Daniel is dead. My father is crying next to me, my brother's fist to his lips.

"Come back," he whispers, eyes squeezed shut. Still out there on that road. "Come back, Dan."

Elias kneels, touching my arm. "He'll be okay," he whispers kindly to me. "Soon Daniel will wake up again."

"No," I say numbly, looking up at him. "Not really. Not in real life. Only here." Elias leans in to rest his head on my shoulder, sorry for me. Sorry for everything.

"As you can see," Kenneth's voice cuts sharply through the room, addressing the crowd, "we are done here. Everyone back to the party. Miss Casella is just leaving."

My father looks up, reminded of where he is. He turns to me, his face gone white. "Oh, kid," he says, shaking his head. "You can't be here. No, you . . ." He swings around, confirming we're still in the Ruby. "I shouldn't have let you stay so long," he says. "Oh, God. I'm sorry." He sets down Daniel's arm and reaches for me. "I'm so sorry for everything."

He pulls me to him, his body wracked with sobs. He realizes now that his son is actually dead. I lay my head on his shoulder, feeling like a little girl again. Forgiving my dad for leaving us after Mom died . . . because he's *my dad*. The one I always knew but forgot about. He apologizes over and over, not just for the last few days in the Ruby, or for the accident on the dark highway. He's sorry for every minute he's wasted since my mother died. For every minute we've ever wasted.

"I'm sorry too, Dad," I murmur, digging my fingers into the lapel of his jacket. I squeeze my eyes shut, inhaling the scent of my mother's detergent. A smell of home. Wishing we could be there again.

"Yes, now, this is all very touching," Kenneth says cruelly. "But we are on a schedule. And unless you plan on using your invitation, Miss Casella," he continues, "I must ask you to return to your floor."

My father and I pull apart, and he brushes back my hair, gazing at me. "I'll miss you, kid," he whispers. "More than I can bear." He sniffles, wiping his cheeks and climbing to his feet. He straightens his jacket, smeared in blood, and nods like a gentleman at Elias.

Elias nods back and holds out his hand to me. I stare at his outstretched palm and then around the lobby. All its beauty and grandeur. The chandelier, the fireplace, the sparkling frames and rich tapestries. It's a beautiful, terrible place. Or maybe that's just because of Kenneth.

Most of the crowd has dissipated, returning to their roles in the party now that Kenneth has commanded it. The others have disappeared altogether, back in their own reality.

I let Elias help me up. Then I stand, looking down at my brother, at my blood-soaked dress. I should be afraid, but I'm not. Not anymore. Not of death. Not of Kenneth. The concierge narrows his eyes, as if my countenance confuses him.

"Miss Casella," he hisses, losing his composure. "Your time is up. Return to your floor."

From the ballroom the music gets louder. It's my song — playing on the side of the road, on a loop. Here it's slow, hard to recognize. It fills me with a sense of longing, but at the same time it reminds me of what I'll be returning to. My body begins to feel heavy, to ache. I look back down at Daniel.

Across the lobby the staff door opens. Catherine and Joshua walk out, her hand on his arm. She's a vision in a white dress, but that's not the startling part; it's Joshua, in a suit, tidied up like a guest. Kenneth's eyes widen, and he takes a step toward them.

"What is the meaning of this?" he asks incredulously, his bald head growing pink. "Joshua, get back in uniform! Miss Masters, this is not appropriate."

Catherine smiles, charming and lovely. She leaves Joshua's side and saunters over to Kenneth, tilting her head slightly as she looks at him. "Yes, darling, I know," she says arrogantly. She glances down at Daniel but quickly averts her eyes. "But you've killed my date. I had to improvise."

Kenneth furrows his brow, trying to guess her intentions. He turns to Elias, about to command him to take her into the party instead, when there's a flash of silver. Before any of us can react, Catherine grabs Kenneth's head and swipes a knife across his throat, splitting it wide open, sending out a fan of blood.

Kenneth gurgles, sliding his eyes up in her direction, his fingers trying to close the wound. She sneers and lets him fall to his knees, choking on blood before he collapses to the floor.

"I'm tired of appropriate," Catherine murmurs to his twitching body, and drops the knife with a clatter. She exhales, long and hard, and then smiles at Elias. "I see why the housekeeper does this so often," she tells him. "Such satisfaction in it."

Joshua comes to stand next to Catherine, pulling a handkerchief from his breast pocket and handing it to her. As she cleans the blood off her hands, they both stare down at Kenneth's body with no emotion. Catherine looks over at me and smiles. "Thought you could use my distraction," she says, indicating Joshua.

"Now you'd better hurry," Joshua tells me. "It only takes

him a few minutes to recover, and he's going to be pissed."

Although part of this was revenge against the concierge's tyranny, Catherine and Joshua tried to help me. I'm grateful, but at the same time I know they'll be punished for it. In the span of eternity it might only be a blip—but it's still pain. And I hate that he'll have that power over them.

"You have to go," Elias whispers. His hand slides over my arm, drawing me closer. "Please, Audrey." He buries his face in my hair, his breath warm on my neck as he pleads for me to leave him. "Before it becomes real."

*Real.* I straighten, my mind working to put together the pieces. "I'm real," I say to myself, considering the words. Elias is still begging me to go, but I'm thinking about the night we went to the fountain. Lourdes gave me a muscle relaxer, a pill that didn't work for the staff. But I felt its effects. I hear the music from the side of the road in this hotel, a song Elias couldn't hear. I can touch people— something Catherine said she couldn't do.

I have a moment of clarity, my body calming, if only for a moment. I realize what it means—at least, what it means in the Ruby: *I'm real.* I'm connected to both realities. I'm still alive, my heart beating, my brain sending electricity through my body. Is that why Kenneth wants the guests from the thirteenth floor to stay away from his staff? If I could touch the guy in the lobby, make him shiver—what exactly can I do to Kenneth?

I'm about to find out.

271

I put my hand on Elias's shoulders to push him back, and he looks me over with such sorrow, such loneliness, as he expects me to walk to the elevators and out of his afterlife. I lean in and kiss him, put my hand on his cheek. He lets me, closing his eyes as he holds back his tears. But the thing is, I'm not going to the elevators.

Without a word I turn and walk directly toward the front desk. I hear Catherine gasp, the shuffle of feet as if someone is about to come after me. The little door behind the desk opens, and Kenneth appears—his face red with rage. Before any of my friends can interrupt, he waves his hand angrily and they groan and fall silent behind me. I don't turn back, imagining they'll all be dead. Burned up and punished for helping me. My hands ball into fists at my sides.

Kenneth steps up to the counter, his chin lower, his eyes blazing. "I see you're still here," he says in a low growl. "Perhaps you don't truly understand your situation."

"Or maybe I do," I say. There is a flicker of worry in his expression, but he's quick to try and cover it, laughing.

"I think not," he says dismissively. "You see, Miss Casella, your body—"

"Yes, Kenneth," I interrupt. "I know. The Ruby already showed me. I'm dying on the side of the road just two miles from here. But I wouldn't accept what happened. I came back for my family."

"What?" His sinister expression falters. "That's—why would you do that?" he demands.

"At first," I say, courage growing by the second, "I thought I could get them out." Kenneth chuckles, but I keep talking. "And when I realized I couldn't, I thought maybe I'd just kill you."

He stops laughing. The words fall around him, and he tries to comprehend the meaning, doubt settling in his expression. The first inkling of fear. "You . . . can't," he says, sounding confused. "You can't," he repeats, trying to convince himself.

I understand now how he controls the people in the Ruby. *Fear.* Lourdes, Elias, my brother, all of them—they're not really here; their bodies can't feel pain. Kenneth has no power over them. Not if they don't let him. In death he can hurt them only because they think he can. They make it real. And in the Ruby it's only real if you make it real.

But I'm not part of them—I'm still connected, even if it's only a little longer. In the background I still hear the song, but it's fading away. I'm dying. I've been dying since I got here. I close my eyes, and when I open them, there are people all around. Checking their bags at the front desk, the bustle and chatter of a lively hotel. They speak with the desk attendant I saw on that first day. The others, walking over the grave of the Hotel Ruby.

Kenneth shoots a frightened gaze around and then reaches to grab my arm, half pulling me onto the desk. "I run this place," he shouts, spittle dribbling over his lips. "I'm in charge."

I think back to when he told me my head was bleeding, only to find there was no injury at all. He's trying to do it again, but I'm no longer under his spell. When he understands this, I see the slow realization slide over his fat little face.

"You can't hurt me, Kenneth," I say calmly "You can't do shit."

"What?" He shakes his head in disbelief, baring his teeth. They're sharp and pointy, but he doesn't intimidate me. Not anymore.

Behind me the song gets louder, calling me back. Time is up—I have to get in the elevator or risk being stuck here forever. I look down at Kenneth's hand clamped on my wrist. He makes his guests suffer by making them as they really are—burned or broken. What would happen to Kenneth if I put him in the real world? How is *he* really?

I reach out suddenly to grab the collar of his tux, holding him fast. He begins to struggle, frightened, and lets go of my wrist, trying to pry my fingers loose. I close my eyes, listening to the song, letting the melody make sense. Feeling the cold air on the side of the road as it climbs over my skin. The aches in my broken bones. The tears in my flesh. "As you really are, Kenneth," I whisper harshly, willing it. "As you really are."

Kenneth howls in pain, but slowly his fight starts to lessen. I open my eyes, inches from his terrible face. He roars, but then his skin starts to wither. Burns appear, dotting the edges of his cheeks with blisters, bursting and then

274

reopening as he screams in pain. His flesh is eaten away, blackening and falling off. His body becomes lighter in his tuxedo, but I hold on, disgusted and horrified, but emboldened and stronger. My pain is fading, the music is quieting. My connection to the outside is evaporating.

I feel myself slipping away, the presence of death stealing my warmth, slowing my heart. I continue to push Kenneth into a realm where he doesn't belong. Affecting him in a way that terrifies him. Destroys him.

The only thing Kenneth is scared of is me. I came back, and he will never understand why. He'll never understand how I love my family, and what I'll give up to protect them. I choose this ending. I choose to live forever with my family, unable to imagine any other way. I control my fear with love, and that makes Kenneth completely powerless.

I let out a breath, one last rattle in my chest. "As you really are," I say again, tears streaming down my cheeks. Kenneth's eyeballs start to dissolve, and his muscles decay until he's just a skeleton. Only then do I let go of his collar. He smashes to the floor and explodes into dust behind the counter.

The Hotel Ruby is hazy, and the desk attendant looks over, surprised. I stare as he gets up, his shoes scraping the shiny floor until he comes to pause at the pile of dust. He furrows his brow. My mouth has gone dry, my entire body trembling. It's my last moment in the outside world.

"Can you see me?" I ask weakly.

For a second the desk attendant pauses, and I hold

my breath. Then he shrugs and reaches inside the small doorway—a closet—and pulls out a broom and dustpan. He sweeps Kenneth away and dumps him into a tiny trash can. Leaving him as he really is: dust.

"Audrey?"

There's a vacuum of air, and I turn. The crisp, color-filled world of the Ruby comes into focus. I see Elias staring at me, wide-eyed. The others are gone now, and like Catherine said, the quiet is nice. Daniel sits up, holding his head while still in a pool of his own blood. His suit is ruined. Catherine clutches Joshua's arm as they both watch me in complete shock.

Guests are gathered at the entry of the ballroom, everyone quiet. I look down at my bloody dress and realize that all my pain is gone. There is no ache, there is no cold. There is no music. I suck in a breath, the sound loud in the silent room.

Elias puts his hand on his heart, tears drip over his cheeks.

I'm dead.

# CHAPTER 21

My mother's name was Helen—a name that took on a saintly ring once she was gone. She died from a stroke at forty-three and never had a chance to say good-bye. It was a tragedy, worse than anything Shakespeare could have written. It broke my family. It broke me.

But now, standing in the lobby of the Hotel Ruby, covered in my dead brother's blood, I wonder what my death means. My immediate family is already gone from the world, but what about my grandmother? She lost her daughter, and now all of us. Could one family be so cursed? Maybe this is Shakespeare after all.

There's a sharp pain in my heart when I think about Ryan, the fact that I've died while he still loves me. He'll have to carry that forever, the calamity coloring his future relationships, hurting him. Or he can find peace. Find happiness.

My life, which I hadn't wanted, was barely starting. But now I'm dead, and I'm never coming back. I'm *dead*. With that thought, I sink down on my heels, covering my face with the shock of it all.

A moment passes, and then I feel Elias's warm touch. He kneels on the floor next to me and gathers me into a hug, crying that he should have fought harder to save me. I rest my chin on his shoulder, listening, wondering if Tanya was right about the way he cares about me — that it's different, that he's been waiting for me all along.

When Elias pulls back, hands on my face as he checks me over, I see how light his amber eyes are, like he's cried the color out of them. "I'm so sorry, Audrey," he says, barely a whisper.

"Stop," I tell him. I lean in and kiss his lips, his cheeks. "No more," I say, tired of the angst. Ready to let it rest with my body on the road. Elias nods, although clearly still not over my new condition, and helps me to stand.

My father waits with Daniel, both looking heartbroken. Despite that, seeing them together overwhelms me with a sense of hope. Hope for us. Now that Kenneth is gone, there is no fear. I have my family. Those words are everything: *I have my family.*

On the other side of the lobby the elevator dings, and the doors slide open. I smile automatically as Lourdes rushes out, Tanya jogging to keep up. The first thing Lourdes notices is the blood around where Daniel is standing, the state of his suit. She goes to him immediately, turning his head to make sure he's not injured. He rolls his eyes, telling her to stop worrying, but I can tell he likes the attention. Across from him Catherine lowers her eyes and holds tighter to Joshua. I think maybe they're a good match — and Joshua was probably right: if she had been engaged to him, she might not have ended up here.

Tanya notices me first and laughs—both horrified and relieved to see me. She nudges Lourdes, who then looks over her shoulder at me. She freezes and then hitches up her eyebrow in an exaggerated *What the hell are you doing here?* stare. I shrug, but bite down on my lip to keep from crying. They said she'd be all right, but I'm so relieved to see it's true. She exhales dramatically and then comes over to hug me, making me fall back a step in my heels.

"Goddamn, your brother was right," she says, squeezing me tightly. "You really wouldn't leave him here."

"I didn't want to leave any of you with Kenneth."

Lourdes pulls back, still rattled by the name. "The Ruby does seem happier, doesn't she?" she says. "I felt it the minute he was gone. I'm not sure how you did it, but you scared him to death." She laughs softly. "You scared him to life. You gave him yours—your escape." Her dark eyes glisten, thankful, but knowing she doesn't have to say it. She knows what I've lost, what we've all lost by being here. She clears her throat and looks over my ruined dress. "Luckily, I know how to get out bloodstains," she says, making me smile.

"Audrey," Joshua calls. I glance behind Lourdes as Joshua bends down to pick up my invitation from the floor. "I guess you don't need this anymore?" he asks.

It's true. I'm part of the Ruby now, using up my chance to leave. Even if I got onto the elevator, there would be no thirteenth floor. It was never really there to begin with. So technically, I don't need the invitation to attend the party. But maybe I just want to make it official.

I turn to Elias, and he looks down at me—his hair disheveled, his tie askew. He holds out his arm and stares straight ahead toward the doors of the ballroom. I slip my palm into the crook of his elbow, and we start forward. I take the invitation from Joshua as we pass, and he smiles, nodding politely now that I'm a guest.

The attendant at the ballroom doors smiles as I pause in front of him. "Miss Casella," he says cordially. He holds out his hand for the invitation. I stare down at the black envelope, my name scrawled across it. I'm suddenly a little scared, nervous. I look back at my brother, our father and Lourdes at his side. He nods that it's okay. No matter what, we're all okay.

I gaze over the stalled party beyond the doorway. The other guests have stopped to stare, waiting for me to join them. Elias's hand slides over mine, comforting me. I close my eyes, searching for any last moments in the world, but there is nothing beyond this. With a steadying breath I outstretch my hand and give the attendant my invitation to the Hotel Ruby First Anniversary Party.

The minute the paper leaves my hand, the singer at the piano smiles and starts a new song. We step inside, and around the room there's a sense of kinship. An affection for the Ruby herself. The other guests watch me, smiling and happy that I've joined them. Heads turn, and I think that maybe the red really does suit me.

"Dance?" Elias asks, glancing over. I narrow my eyes, resting my hands on his chest and leaning in.

"I thought you didn't dance," I say, swaying slightly with the music. He takes my hand and kisses my fingers, twirling me around once to prove that he could have danced if he had wanted to.

The ballroom begins to fill out, the others flickering back into our existence. Daniel and Lourdes come inside, along with my father and everyone else. The sparkle of the chandelier sets everything ablaze with magic, timeless and alive. A never-ending party at the Ruby—where you can stay tonight, or stay forever.

Elias and I dance. I'm part of it now. I belong to the Ruby. The other ones, the guests who aren't like us, mill about, commenting on how cold the ballroom has gotten. Talking excitedly about ghosts. They're on a different plane, existing only in one dimension.

But the lot of us can see it all. We're here together, forever, but it's not so bad. I turn to Eli, draping my arms over his shoulders and coming in close. I see now that the sadness in his eyes will never go away, just like my grief and guilt can never truly fade. It's part of who we were, who we still are. We were lost, all of us, but now we've found a place where we can belong.

Here in the Ruby we can all start our lives again, now that we're dead.

Turn the page for a peek
at a powerful new novel
from Suzanne Young.

MY LIFE IS none of their business.

I don't want to be up here, don't want to explain my reasons, but I can't afford to miss another assignment.

I smooth my crumpled piece of notebook paper on the top of the podium. There's a cough in the back of the quiet classroom, and even my teacher looks bored as he sits in the faux leather chair he brought over from his last school—a school that could afford fake leather chairs, apparently. Mr. Jimenez is definitely slumming with us.

"My brother has an intellectual disability," I read, pausing once the words are out. I feel judged, exposed, and I look up at the class, anticipating a reaction. "He's not stupid," I add defensively. "He just learns differently." One guy curls his lip like he has no idea why I'm talking about this. A girl in the back pops her gum. The gravity of my confession is lost on them and it pisses me off. Pricks of anger crawl up my arms; anger at whom, I'm not sure. All of them, I guess.

I grow flustered and lose my place on my page, the already smudged ink going blurry. I look up accusingly. "And if any of you even think of making a joke about him, I swear I'll—"

"What are you gonna do, Savvy?" Gris calls from the front row. He's leaned back in his seat with his long legs stretched under the desk, his immaculate Timberlands begging to be stomped on. "You gonna stab me like you did your boyfriend?"

I put my elbows on the top of the podium and lean forward, narrowing my eyes. "Give me your pencil, and we'll find out," I say.

Gris smiles, and the scar on his cheek is shiny under the fluorescent lights of the room. I sneer and rest back on my heels. Aaron Griswold is an alcoholic loser, and I'll tell him so the minute I'm finished. Just because we're both stuck in Brooks Academy doesn't mean we're friends. He isn't shit to me. But still, when he blows me a kiss a moment later, I nearly laugh.

"Enough," Mr. Jimenez calls from behind his desk. "Knock it off or I'll see you both after class. Savannah," he says to me, pushing his wire-rimmed glasses up on his nose. "Can you please continue?"

I'm not sure I want to—this is such an incredible waste of time. But I need this class to graduate, so I swipe a tangle of red hair behind my ear and begin again.

"Because of my brother's condition"—I lower my voice—"I picked a special-education teacher for my career project. The pay is terrible but the hours aren't bad. I think I'd be good at it. And I wouldn't be one of those condescending ones either. I'd be cool. I'd help the kids feel cool." I look out at the room of blank faces and sigh. "So, yeah. The end."

There's a halfhearted attempt at applause before Mr. Jimenez comes to stand next to me, barely two inches taller. He smells like copy machine ink and cough drops, and he's generally tolerant of our disinterest in learning.

"Thank you, Savannah," he mumbles, picking up the class roster.

I shrug and walk back to my seat, flipping off Gris before dropping down in my chair. As the heat begins to fade from my cheeks, I chip the clear polish off my fingernails.

"Nice speech, Sutton," Cameron says. He's in the desk next to mine, staring straight ahead and not looking at me. He never looks at me.

"Thanks."

"No problem."

I wish he never talked to me either. Things here at Brooks Academy are usually pretty simple. We show up and listen to the druggies, the criminals, and the anger management cases—like me—give speeches (or whatever pointless project is assigned), then we go home.

This is where the district sends the students they've expelled, keeping their funding by continuing our education. Yep. Glorified GED classes equal an education around here. But it's fine. I came to class and minded my own business.

Then Cameron Ramsey showed up, all sexy and quiet. None of us even know why he's in here. He definitely doesn't fit. I mean, the kid drives a BMW.

He's a distraction. And for some reason, I'm the only one privy to his one-liners. Nice speech? What the hell is that about?

"Cameron?" Mr. Jimenez calls from the front. "Would you like to participate?"

Cameron closes his notebook and shakes his head no. I wonder if he didn't do the assignment or if he just hates people. I understand either way. When the teacher moves on, Cameron takes out his phone and begins playing a game under his desk.

Mr. Jimenez leans on the podium, clearly exhausted. "Well, unless anyone else has something to add, I guess we're done for the day . . ." He leaves his offer open, but if he thinks any one of the twelve of us is going to prolong class, he's obviously having an acid flashback.

"Good-bye," Mr. Jimenez announces loudly and turns away. I feel sort of bad for the guy. He's youngish—young enough to still think he can make a difference in our lives. But he's our third savior this year. I wonder how many times a day he wishes he went into business management instead.

I stand and swipe my notebook into my bag, relieved the day is over. I turn just as Cameron shoves his phone into his pocket. Without looking at me, he smiles.

"I'll see you around, Sutton," he says.

"Uh . . . yeah," I respond. "Tomorrow. Here."

He laughs and starts walking away. "Right," he says. "That's what I meant."

I watch after him, confused, maybe blushing a little. Man. I don't know what it is about him. Okay, not true. I'll admit that part of it is his looks: chin-length blond hair, dark brown eyes, T-shirts that are tight enough to show off his muscles, but not the sort of tight that makes him look like a douchebag. But mostly it's because he talks to me. The fact that it's only me.

"God*damn*," Retha says, sliding up next to me. "Is Cameron getting hotter?" she asks seriously. "I think he is."

"He definitely is." We both stare toward the doorway, even though he's already gone. I glance sideways at Retha. "He talked to me again," I tell her, smiling.

"Of course he did. What did he say?"

"He told me 'nice speech.'"

She's impressed. I can see it in her eyes even through her gobs of black liner. "That's because he wants you," she says. "Now, can you please screw him and find out why he's here? I *need* to know."

"Sure. I'll get right on that for you." I swing my bag over my shoulder and survey the room. Travis is still asleep in the corner, his head down on his folded arms. "Grab your boyfriend," I tell Retha, motioning toward him. "I have to get home. Evan will be there in fifteen."

"Hey!" Retha yells toward Travis, making him jump awake. "Let's take off. Savvy's got her brother today."

Travis stares at us for a second, blinking heavily as if trying to figure out where he is. He straightens and brushes his long, black hair away from his face. "Okay," he says, sounding groggy. "But you drive, Retha. I think I'm still hungover."

"Well," I say as Travis strolls out the door with us, his skinny shoulders sharp under his thin, long-sleeved T-shirt. "That's what happens when you drink in the parking lot of a 7-Eleven until four in the morning."

"Hey." He smiles. "You could have been there too."

"Ah." I raise my finger at him. "But I don't drink. So I would just be tired. Not smelly and hungover."

His expression falters, and he lifts his arm to sniff.

"Gross, Travis," I say, pushing him hard enough to make him stumble. "That is seriously filthy."

Retha agrees and starts cussing at him in Spanish, making me laugh. I'm not bilingual, but thanks to her, I know every swear word. Hell, she even makes a few up as she goes.

"Relax, woman," Travis tells Retha, ready to play at fighting. But suddenly his expression hardens as he catches sight of something behind us in the hall. "Hey, I'll meet you guys at the car. I've got business to take care of." He touches Retha's arm as he moves past her.

I turn and see Gris leaving the classroom, hiking up his low-hanging jeans. Clueless as always.

"Travis," I say as he follows Gris down the hallway. Guess he hadn't been asleep the entire class after all.

"Let it go," Retha tells me, sounding bored. "Gris shouldn't have messed with you. He deserves the ass kicking."

She's probably right. Punches sometimes help—at least they help us. It's not like Travis is going to get in trouble. Gris knows better than to report it.

"Fine," I say, and start toward the parking lot with Retha. "But if I'm late getting home because of Gris, I will come back and stab him."

Hungover or not, Travis would never let anyone else drive his car. His Impala is old, and not in an "I'm restoring it" kind of way. It's rusted and the carpet smells lightly of mildew, but he keeps it clean like he's proud of it. Always swiping dust off the dashboard or sneaking into one of those do-it-yourself car washes when a person leaves before their time is up. So we're proud of it too.

We pull up in front of my house at the same time as my little brother's bus, and I know I'm too late. I grab my bag off the seat, yanking on the door handle. "I'll call you after," I tell Retha.

She raises her hand in a wave and leans over to adjust the radio volume. I slap Travis in the back of the head on my way out. He yells, but I'm already running toward the bus, my heart pounding. Evan is going to lose it.

I toss my bag onto the dirt of my front yard and stop outside the bus doors, panting as I wait for them to open. I can hear Evan crying through the open window. He likes to see me out here before the bus pulls up—he won't get off otherwise. Because if I'm not here, he'll think I left him. But I'm not Mom. And I'm not going to disappear like she did.

The doors screech open, and I climb up the steep stairs, nodding at the driver. She huffs out a hello, looking haggard. Exhausted.

I make my way down the aisle, and another little boy points to a seat across from him. I stop when I find Evan slouched down with his hands over his face. My heart breaks.

"Hey, buddy," I say. My seven-year-old brother hitches in a breath, still crying—but softer now that I'm here.

"You're late," he croaks in a small voice from behind his hands.

I swallow hard. "I know. Sorry."

Evan sniffles, still not showing his face. I hate myself.

"Let's go," I say, grabbing his backpack from the floor. "These other kids have to get home."

He's quiet and then mutters, "No."

"Evan," I warn, not wanting to get into it here. I wish

I could just grab his arm and drag him off; it would be easier. But I don't put my hands on him like that. "Look," I say in a softer voice. "I'm sorry, okay? I fucked up. But if you come with me now, I'll make us dogs 'n' cheese. I promise."

"Really?" he asks quietly.

My lips flinch with a smile. "Yeah. But you'll have to help. You know how much I hate doing the dishes."

Evan finally drops his hands and looks up at me. His pale blond hair is wet where it's grown long near his eyes, and peanut butter from his school-provided lunch has crusted in the corners of his mouth.

He deserves better than me.

"Okay," he says. "I'll help you."

"We can even color," I tell him, taking his hand. I keep my voice light, trying to make it sound like there's something fun waiting for him inside our crappy house. There isn't. But I think he forgets that. It's like every day he starts new.

I wish I could do that.

It's too early for dinner, but I make Evan hot dogs mixed with mac 'n' cheese anyway. I don't ask him to help with the dishes, but he dries the plates. When we're done, we go into the living room and I give him his crayons and the backside of an assignment sheet I got at school.

Evan lies on his stomach across the worn carpet and spreads out his crayons in front of him. He draws a picture, occasionally looking up to make sure I'm still here. For a moment it's peaceful. Normal.

The front door opens, and my heart pounds faster.

My father's heavy boots clop through the hall until I feel his presence in the doorway behind me.

"Is there dinner?" he asks, his raspy voice shattering the contentment in the room.

"Yeah," I respond. "It's on the stove." I don't turn, hoping he'll get it for himself. Evan colors the sky purple.

"Come on, Savannah," my father says. "Can't you go plate it up for me? I just got home from work."

And I've gone to school, cooked dinner, and washed the dishes already, but I don't remind him of that. I lean closer to Evan and tap his paper. "Hey, buddy," I whisper. "Paint the house pink."

He looks up at me wide-eyed, as if a pink house is the most absurd thing he's ever heard. He laughs.

"No," he says. "The house is white."

"Yeah, but I want mine pink." I ruffle his hair and stand up. Evan reaches for the pink crayon.

My father stomps into the kitchen and pulls out his chair, scraping it along the scuffed linoleum floor. He exhales loudly, sounding tired. I understand the feeling.

I go to the stove and use the wooden spoon with the broken handle to stir the now-stiff macaroni before slapping a glob of it on a freshly washed plate. I set it on the table in front of my father.

He stares at the mac 'n' cheese with bits of hot dogs in it for a long moment before poking through it with his fork, looking disgusted. "Again?" he asks me.

I lean my hip against the sink and meet his eyes. "It's his favorite."

"Not mine."

I'd tell him that he's an adult and perfectly capable of fixing his own dinner, but I don't want to argue tonight. Not when Evan will be leaving soon. I look away, biting my lip.

We weren't always like this. When my mother was around, my dad would help her in the kitchen—hell, he'd even cook sometimes. He was never father of the year, but at least he wasn't useless. Now he can't make his own, let alone hold down a job.

There's a loud clank as he drops the fork on his plate. I turn and see him rub roughly at his face. "Grab me a beer, will you?" he asks.

"No. It's barely five."

He glances at me, looking sorry for a second. But he gets up and walks across the room to snatch a beer from the nearly empty fridge. He pops the top on his Bud Light the moment he sits back down at the table.

"Daddy," Evan yells, running into the kitchen. "Look what I made!"

Our father eyes him, taking a loud sip of his beer before answering. "Let's see what you've got there," he says quietly, holding out his hand.

Evan's jumping up and down, his energy out of place in this small, miserable kitchen.

"A pink house," our father says. I appreciate his attempt to sound interested.

"Uh-huh." Evan turns around to show it to me. "Savvy wanted hers pink."

I press my lips together and reach out to push his shoulder. "And see how good it looks?"

"Yeah." Evan laughs.

I look at our father and find him watching Evan with the same expression he always has when he's around him lately. A face of guilt, regret, resentment maybe—I'm not sure. But at least he knows enough to try to keep it to himself. He takes a long drink like he wishes he could drown himself in it.

"What color house do you want, Daddy?" Evan asks, stepping toward him.

"Doesn't matter," our father says. There's a pain in my gut when I see Evan's lower lip jut out.

"Make it a blue one," I answer quickly. "Daddy's favorite color is blue." I have no idea what my father's favorite color is, and I honestly don't give a shit. But I know Evan likes blue.

"Mine too!" my brother yells, flailing out his arms. He accidentally knocks into the can of beer and topples it over.

"Damn it!" our father snaps, pushing back in his seat as beer trickles off the table and onto his jeans. "What the hell, Savannah?" he screams at me, making Evan jump. "You're supposed to watch him!"

I ball my hands into fists.

"Come here, Evan," I say quickly, pulling my brother toward me. But it's too late. He's already begun to cry. Hard. He hates loud noises, especially when they come from our dad.

"Oh great," our father says, raising his hands in the air, his lips pulled into a sneer. "Another fantastic night."

"Shut up," I say, hugging Evan to me. But my brother starts struggling, crumpling his picture into a ball and throwing it to the floor. "Stop," I whisper. But Evan digs his fingernails into my skin, and when I wince, he yanks free and runs toward the living room.

I swear and lift up the edge of my shirt to see the deep scratches along my side. They hurt, but I guess they'll go nicely with the bruise on my back from last week's tantrum.

The kitchen is quiet except for the sound of beer running off the table in a steady stream. I look over at my father and find him red-faced with anger.

"We can't keep doing this," he says.

"*You're* not doing anything," I answer. "I am."

"If your mother was here—"

"She's not. She left, remember?"

He narrows his eyes. "I remember, Savannah. I remember pretty goddamn clearly."

Does he? Does he remember what it was like the morning she left? Because I do. I was the one who called around looking for her. I was the one who had to miss school to babysit Evan. And I was the one who had to tell him that she wasn't coming back.

Evan was destroyed. I sure as hell remember that.

"This isn't working," my father says, motioning the way my brother had gone. "And it's not going to work."

SUZANNE YOUNG is the *New York Times* bestselling author of the Program duology. Originally from Utica, New York, Suzanne moved to Arizona to pursue her dream of not freezing to death. She is a novelist and an English teacher, but not always in that order. Suzanne is the author of *The Program, The Treatment, The Remedy, The Epidemic, All in Pieces,* and *A Need So Beautiful.* Visit her online at www.suzanne-young.blogspot.com.